J

Da leggere in aereo.

Ciao,

J. Wh

HARD RESET

BY

JOHN EDWARD WHITE

TEAMGRUDEN PUBLISHING

PUBLISHER'S NOTE

This is a work of fiction. Names, characters, places and incidents either are the product of the author's imagination or are used fictitiously, and any resemblance to actual persons, living or dead, business establishments, events, or locales is entirely coincidental.

Cover art and design by ©Angela Carole Brown

ISBN-13: 978-0615773964
ISBN-10: 0615773966

During the writing of this book, many friends and family members provided advice and encouragement for which I am very grateful. I am especially indebted to Jaryl Lane for her comments, Alex Bacon for technical expertise and Angela Carole Brown for her cover design. Finally, I would like to thank Barbara Freeman for her unconditional support.

Commit a crime and the world is made of glass. Commit a crime, and it seems as if a coat of snow fell on the ground, such as reveals in the woods the track of every partridge and fox and squirrel.

Ralph Waldo Emerson

Chapter One

You have to go back to start over. Back as far as you can, back as far as possible within world and time, and then back a little farther. You have to start at that place that is both familiar and unknown. A place populated by hazy, half-formed memories that float unresolved just below the murky surface of mind's reach. The place where the downfall began: A backroom of repressed memory festooned with guilt, regret and remorse.

I put my suit jacket across the passenger seat and climbed into my MG. An old car, an old acquaintance, really, the only constant in three decades of false starts, minor triumphs, and a lot of self-abuse. Just a machine made of metal, glass, and rubber, but most people have a special car in their personal history, and this one was mine. It was the first car that I owned, the first place in which I experienced sex, the first refuge available during the turbulent years of high school. A car with so many embedded memories it was like a family member and, like a family member, not without foibles, eccentricities and shortcomings. It carried my best friend Tom and me for an ill-prepared Easter break's journey 200 kilometers south into Mexico's Baja Peninsula with two beat up surfboards strapped to the roof and the blissful ignorance of teenage optimism packed in the boot. We were on a quest, two mavericks of the Senior class, tipping our toes into the sea water of independence, searching for adventure and maybe a chance to get laid, writing our final adolescent chapter in bold strokes: It is a rite of passage for every teenager on the cusp of maturity to embrace recklessness, and we were not to be denied.

Ever since, my legacy of ownership has required that I prop open the hood or crawl beneath the chassis at the most inopportune occasion to effect repair. As a result, I have a collection of scars on my knuckles, wrists and forearms from third degree burns and abrasions, a split thumbnail that refuses to knit after thirty years, and compromised hearing from gasoline that dripped into my right ear while I was under the gas tank replacing a ruptured fuel hose.

Each time that the car fails, I find a way to get it running. Even with all the unreliability and trouble, I can never bring myself to sell it. The lessons learned at the price of inconvenience and indignity serve to demonstrate one fundamental truth: the most defining personal characteristic is not integrity, not virtue, not even honor. The most defining personal characteristic is tenacity.

I rolled down the entry drive, released the clutch and the engine fired. I checked the instruments, flipped on the lights and glanced at Stray. He'd be in the same place when I returned, at whatever time, standing guard and patiently waiting. I turned onto the street and a mile later entered freeway traffic. Cars sped past at terrifying speed. Semi-tractors with double trailers that dwarfed my diminutive British GT; contractor's pickup trucks laden with hand tools, building materials, and ladders weaving from lane to lane; a charge of motorists sipping coffee drinks in one hand and talking on cell phones with the other. Nobody drives freeways as fast as drivers in Southern California: And nobody drives as well. Considering the number of vehicles and the speed at which people drive, the freeways should be a nonstop demolition derby of gene pool attrition.

Half an hour later I exited, crossed the boulevard that bifurcates residential real estate values, and turned into the suburban neighborhood where I'd grown up. The same gnarly oaks and peeling eucalyptus trees lined the block. A bare lot cul-de sac where I used to ride my bicycle with the neighborhood truants was ringed with two-story, stucco homes. The horse pasture at the end of the street had been enclosed with a cinder block wall and the remaining acreage filled with town houses tightly clustered side by side. I stopped in front of my old house. Outside of a minor change to the landscaping, it looked the same. I turned around in the driveway and retraced my daily route to the high school. For four years I'd walked and then driven those few blocks yet I couldn't recall a single detail. Another chunk of memory submerged below the murky surface. One mile beyond the high school campus, I pulled into the Westland Hills Country Club. It occupied a broad arroyo at the base of the foothills and comprised an 18-hole golf course, tennis courts, Olympic-sized pool, pro shop, and Mediterranean style clubhouse facing the links. Terraced lots of the gated Westland Hills Estates overlooked the country club. During the time of my high school incarceration, these were the exclusive aeries of the well heeled, the doctors, lawyers and successful executives. In order to provide cultural diversity, the school district was drawn in a north-south swatch incorporating Westland Hills Estates, a narrow buffer zone of middle-class residents straddling the boulevard, and the blue-collar neighborhoods residing below. Those high school students who lived in the affluent Westland Hills

Estates embodied an elite minority dominating student government, social clubs, college prep courses, and the tennis team. The majority of the students came from families south of the boulevard and made up the better part of the football, basketball and baseball teams. The economic division extended beyond athletics. In a state well known for its car culture, class demarcation was obvious when appraising the high school parking lot. In the first row, unofficially designated Seniors Only, was a string of Westland Hills' BMWs, Mercedes, and one Italian, blood red Ferrari that always parked across two spaces. The driver was a bench warmer on the varsity basketball team, a position rumored to have more to do with his parent's social prominence than his athleticism. Rick Fellows was his name. Not quite six feet (I'm a six footer so the comparison is easy), indolent and flaccid as if he'd never worked a physical job, he was a supercilious rich kid with a jowly face and weak chin who affected a preppy, East coast accent, turned up his nose at anyone outside his social clique, and went sockless year round in leather loafers with metal heel wedges that clicked on the polished hallways. You can't fault a guy whose father is willing to lease him a Ferrari for his senior year, but that doesn't mean he has to be an asshole about it.

Tonight, the Westland Hills Country Club parking lot contained the luxury sedans and SUVs of baby-boomer prosperity. I parked at the end of one row next to a faded Fiat convertible that looked almost as bad as my mottled MG, grabbed my suit jacket from the passenger seat, and walked across the parking lot. A fully dressed Harley Davidson laden with far too many chrome accessories screamed mid-life crisis near the clubhouse entrance. Ahead of me, backlit by the entry's diffused lighting, a woman stumbled and dropped to the pavement. She sat on the sidewalk with a very short red skirt riding high up her waist. Her white, fringed panties had clusters of red cherries on them. She wore shoulder length, light brown hair with those Bride of Frankenstein blond streaks that women favor, an off white, scoop neck blouse and an intricate, Native American silver necklace. She had square shoulders and over one breast was a washed out tattoo. The edges were blurred and the skin lighter in tone as if after some reflective consideration an ill-chosen adornment had been bleached into submission. I offered my hand and she grabbed hold, stood up and stabbed her foot into a red pump. On one ankle was a plain silver chain and on her ring finger she wore an aquamarine gemstone set in a patterned silver band.

"Are you all right?"

"Goddamn it," she hissed and squinted sideways.

I nodded as she dropped my hand and straightened her skirt. She brushed off bare legs, studied my face and then took my hand and poked a two-tone fingernail at the palm. The cloying odor of patchouli caught in my nose and nerve endings fired at the top of my spine and rippled downward toward my crotch.

"Thought so…I could tell right off."

I turned my good ear toward her and angled my head to keep her lips visible in the diffused lighting.

"You work with these, don't you?"

"I do, now."

She rotated my hand and studied my fingers.

"Mechanic," she said as she released my hand. "I'd guess airplane. My dad worked at Hughes."

She flipped back her hair and then fluffed the Bride of Frankenstein streaks around her ears. She had a slender nose, razor thin lips drawn in glistening red lipstick, and green eyes, not hard and not soft, but with the steady, unblinking focus of a woman who has seen the worst in men and still hoped for the best. Her cheeks were rouged in some earth tone hue and long, complicated silver earrings dangled from each lobe. She stared at me, rocking unsteadily as she adjusted her foot in the pump and clutched my arm as if support, either to stay vertical or to face the evening, were what she needed.

"Am I right?"

Lip reading is mostly context and guesswork. I'm pretty good at it as long as the vocabulary is simple and the lighting adequate. During my corporate career, only a handful of people realized that I had any hearing limitation, and when they discovered my impairment, inevitably they would exaggerate their pronunciation and speak in slow, measured rhythm as if I were mentally retarded rather than hard of hearing. In normal conversation, or with someone I know, no change of volume is necessary. If someone speaks softly or stands in shadow, comprehension is problematic. When unsure, I cant my good ear their direction, nod my head affirmatively and respond with *'Is that so?'* Usually more information follows and I can deduce what was said. Occasionally I guess wrong, especially in dim light, if the speaker is on my right side, or if the voice is in a low register. Women's voices are easier to hear than men's voices. The higher pitch makes the difference.

"Well?"

I cocked my head, bent closer and watched her lips from the corner of my eye.

"CORRECTOMUNDO?"

"Is that so?"

She studied my face, confusion filling her eyes, took my hand again and held my fingers. I heard a car enter the parking lot and lost it as the noise transitioned from one ear to the other. She leaned forward out of the shadow and said something into my right ear. Then she held her face close to mine, hesitated, and quickly kissed my cheek. I hadn't been kissed, or even touched by a woman for that matter, since Susan. The patchouli hung between us and a blurry image of a teenage girl struggled toward the murky surface.

A polished, refrigerator white Cadillac with dealer plates skidded to a stop near the entrance. The driver's door opened and a tall, skinny man with a long neck stepped out. The interior bell chimed repeatedly as he stretched his arms across the roof and looked up at the night sky.

"You're welcome?"

The woman tilted her head, squinted at me, and the look on her face made it clear that I had guessed wrong. The passenger door of the Cadillac opened and a short, portly man stomped past us trailing a musky cloud of Old English cologne.

"Fine," the tall man called. "I'll just park the car. Bitch."

The tall man got back in the car. It lurched forward, tires squealing, and skidded into a handicap parking spot. He stopped with a violent yank on the shifter and sat inside with the engine ticking as it cooled.

"Got a cigarette?"

I shook my head.

"You sure?"

"Yes."

The tall man slammed closed the door of the Cadillac, walked past us staring straight ahead, and entered the clubhouse without turning around.

"You don't remember me, do you?"

I took a deep breath. Odors are powerful stimulants, closely tied to memory, and my sense of smell, even before the damage to my hearing, is highly acute. The patchouli triggered a blurry image but it floated unresolved in my mind. That is one of the things about alcoholism. It drops pieces of your life into deep water where they are almost irretrievable. Events, experiences, and people become fragmented sections of a past rendered inaccessible. There's no rhyme or reason to it. It's called alcoholic dementia. Tom told me most memories eventually emerge, even for a blackout drunk: Take it one day at a time; keep moving forward. He claimed that he was still remembering things after twenty years of sobriety.

"Say something else."

The woman settled into her pumps and reached underneath her blouse to tug at her bra. She smoothed her skirt, patted her stomach, and then raised her eyes to stare into my face. One eyebrow racked upward. I shut my eyes and stopped breathing in order to concentrate.

"Go ahead," I said and turned my good ear her direction. "Say something."

There was a pause. A fetid bouquet of steer manure drifted past on the fall air but the patchouli had taken residence in my nose. In the blurry image the teenage girl was wearing a uniform. I opened my eyes to the manicured landscapes of hybrid roses and dichondra lawns of the Westland Hills Estates. When I looked down, she was staring at me but the teenage girl was gone.

"I've lost a lot," I said. "Also, I can't hear too well in my right ear."

We entered the clubhouse along a corridor lined with framed photographs of country club members playing tennis and golf. Just past an adjoining hallway was a staircase. Balloons tethered to the handrail led down the stairs. A freestanding signboard stated "Welcome Graduate." Apparently our collective presence already doubled expectations. The woman shook her head with a derisive snort and then looked me in the eye.

"I'll-see-you-lat-er, O-K? We-can-catch-up," she said. "If-you-can-re-mem-ber."

"Sure," I called as she turned down the hallway. "I'll remember."

I'm a little claustrophobic and stay out of cellars, basements, and even elevators if I can help it. Being underground or beneath multiple stories puts me on edge. I've no rational reason for it, outside of the high probability of earthquakes in a geologically unstable region with more than 100 active faults, but since I was young I'd always felt anxious beneath grade. As an adult, I'd learned to manage my anxiety with the perfect antidote: It was called liquor.

Downstairs, a woman named Nancy with a clip-on badge and a blurry, senior year photograph manned a card table. She checked my name off a list and held out my badge.

"Good turnout?"

She pointed to the array of unclaimed badges spread across the top of the table and shrugged.

"Looks like some people changed their minds."

Among the rows of badges were one or two names I recognized, but the name I was looking for wasn't one of them.

"It's still early," she said.

The reunion was held in the multi-use room, equipped with a bar at one end and sliding partitions for expansion along one wall. I'd attended dozens of corporate mixers in rooms just like this, tossed down weak Scotches and thin Manhattans, suffered the tired jokes of overworked colleagues and the small talk of stressed out managers, all of us convinced that in some way participation would advance our careers but none of us certain as to just how. Each event was different but they all held the same stale odor of desperation in the highly patterned carpeting and neutral-colored walls. Round, linen-draped tables were arranged adjacent a temporary dance floor, and a row of trestle tables in the center held chafing trays, a salad bar, stacks of plates and flatware.

Around me stood classmates I didn't recognize. Men lingered near the bar, mostly wearing dark suits, a few in sport shirts, one bearded guy dressed in leather pants, a black tee-shirt, and a skull and crossbones bandana that covered his head and tied at the base of a sunburned neck. The portly man and his tall partner were seated at a table in a corner. Two women walked past me without comment to join a group of others. Then a petite woman in a button down, shiny blue blouse and conservative black skirt stepped out of the group and wrapped her arms around my neck. She smelled of lavender soap and three decades disappeared in a single whiff. Marce was the ADD girl, sassy and energetic, a member of the track team, someone in constant motion never without Chapstick. For some reason, crystal clear memories of her came to mind. I always liked Marce and she knew it.

"Hello, Marce. How are you?"

I looked past her to the group of disinterested women who watched as Marce rose on her toes and whispered in my ear.

"What?"

She looked confused so I reversed position and pointed to my good ear. The group of women all smiled at once, as if by virtue of Marce's attention, I'd been granted social clearance. Marce was a very popular girl in high school. Our junior year she had a boyfriend named Edward, a tall, slump-shouldered and moody guy with a mass of tangled, black hair and few friends. I remember he was so smart that he rarely attended class and probably didn't need to. He was one of those guys who should have gone right to college after middle school. Marce said he was a genius. He struck me as being pretty dark at times, but what I remembered most were his eyes; they were amber, and he'd look past you without speaking as if his focus were on something in the middle distance. After they broke up, she disappeared at the end of spring semester, and when she returned in the fall for senior year you could tell that something about her was different. I saw Edward around school a few times. He fell in with a crowd that congregated at lunch under a huge magnolia tree and generally seemed pissed-off and contemptuous of the entire school body. They dressed in black, talked about the 5th dimension and a parallel universe, and made weekend trips to the Mojave Desert. I don't remember if Edward attended our graduation ceremony, but about the time I left home for college I heard he was living nearby with a girlfriend.

Edward had a twin sister, Carolyn, who was slender like him but his opposite in almost every other way: average height, perfect posture, bright and outgoing with a constant smile on her oval face, involved in almost every school activity, and universally well liked. I had a schoolboy crush on her then and she wanted nothing to do with me. As a result, I'd behaved badly toward her, authoring a mean spirited declaration that thankfully was lost among the hundreds of self-serving prevarications in the final edition of the school paper. I doubt that she ever read it, but still she deserved an apology. That was one of the twelve steps. It was not the only thing for which I needed to make amends. Marce took my arm and pulled me toward the bar.

"I knew you'd come," she said. "Even though you never came before."

The bartender poured Chardonnay and I asked for water. Marce ran an index finger along the rim of her wine glass and pushed the sleeve of her shiny blue blouse up her forearm.

"You knew?"

She nodded her head and looked up at me from beneath thick, natural eyebrows. I looked around the room at the sparse turnout. Women sat at the round tables in the back as if they'd staked out their turf. Men huddled near the bar, holding mixed drinks in one hand while they exchanged business cards with the other.

"She's not here," she said.

"I can see that."

Marce dug a business card, pen and tiny address book from her purse. She handed me her glass and scribbled on the back of the card.

"She sent me a postcard, once. Edward is still around. He's homeless, living on the streets, but she lives in New York."

"That's not the only reason I came."

"Yes it is. Because you still love her."

"I owe her, Marce. I owe her an apology."

"Of course you do."

By the end of the evening, I'd made two trips outside for fresh air when I felt the room begin to close in, spoken with classmates I couldn't remember, and managed to winnow my personal history down to three terse statements: living half-a-year sober in a carriage house apartment with a brindle-coat Boxer with a mangled, right ear; between careers and unsure of which direction to go;

no kids, never married but once engaged. That was enough. No reason to fill in the empty places. People mostly wanted to talk about themselves. Mixed recollections of high school experiences, a predictable succession of events during the intervening decades leading to middle age: the people we were then were the people we are now. No one had really changed. Those well-adjusted teens expected to follow traditional paths had done just that and built successful careers in business, education, public service, medicine or law. Others, not so well adjusted, had traveled rougher roads, endured harder times, survived by sheer perseverance and grit. Most fell somewhere in the middle, settling for a life far from youthful ambitions but affording relative comfort and security. The rest, the truly unfortunate, are under-represented at high school reunions. A reunion attracts only those people with experiences worth recounting. Those whose histories are laced with guilt and pain have long since found ways to nullify their past.

At the end of the night I walked Marce out of the building. Faux gas lamps lit the parking lot. Marce leaned one hip against her car, a gigantic SUV that dwarfed her petite frame, and searched her purse. She reached up, put her arms around my neck, and hugged me so tightly that her feet lifted off the ground. Even in platform heels, she was barely more than five feet tall, but she managed to fold herself into my body as if she were snuggling into a comfortable sofa. Then she sighed, released her grip and hoisted herself into the driver's seat.

"It's good to see you," she said as I closed her door. She lowered the window and looked down at me.

"Do you need a ride?"

"No, I drove," I said and pointed.

She looked across the parking lot. The mottled MG and the faded Fiat were parked beneath the only nonworking lamp.

"Still have that old car, huh. Some things never change."

"It's a family member, now."

She smiled and started her engine.

"We used to be friends, right? So call me."

"I will."

"You look good, Martin. You've grown up," she said.

"Thanks. You look good, too."

"I know."

The gigantic vehicle backed and turned. It pulled forward, and backed again before Marce could square it down the lane. They ponderous way in which she maneuvered it was like watching a cargo ship leaving port. All that jogging this way and that before the vehicle could depart. Marce piloted down the lane, turned and exited the parking lot with a squeal of tire rubber as I walked toward my car. The driver's door of the Fiat was open. The woman in the short, red skirt sat motionless with one red pump in the parking lot and the other in her car. She watched as I approached, appraising me with each step, staring through flat green eyes as cigarette smoke drifted from her nose. Then she turned back to the windshield, gone away in thought, as if I weren't there.

"You found a cigarette."

She cast a slow assessment head to foot, eyes drawn down to slits, and then dropped her hand between her legs and fingered the hem of her short skirt. Smoke hung across her face. On the passenger seat was a package of cigarettes, small purse and an empty wine glass. She took a long, slow draw on the cigarette. Her eyes bore into me as if she could see through my charade, as if every inadequacy, character flaw, and undetected felony were scrolled like a headline across my face.

"We were going to catch up."

"Catching up is good," I said. "But I want to *Remember* you."

She held out the cigarette, examined the ember, and then tilted her head. She looked at me with a carnal lift of eyebrow that prompted nerve endings rippling down my spine to my crotch.

"Yes, you do," she said and tipped the ash from her cigarette. "You want to *Remember*."

I waited for her to say something else but she only stared through the windshield with the cigarette held close to her face.

"Well, OK," I said and walked to my car. She sat, eyes locked forward, with that one red pump in the parking lot like she was unsure if she were coming or going. I climbed into my car and twisted the ignition key. Nothing happened. I twisted it again. Still nothing. I lowered the driver's window and got out. With some effort I pushed the car out of the parking space, turned and saw the woman approaching. She nodded her head at me, put her hands on the rear fender and smiled.

"Let's go," she mouthed.

I looked at her, in bare feet, and the blurry image of a teenage girl in a uniform came back. She was bent at the waist, loose hair drifting across her face and she definitely was familiar. I did remember something but still couldn't place her in my past.

"Ready? I've done this before."

"I think I remember you," I said.

We pushed until the car gained some speed and I jumped in. The woman continued pushing as I released the clutch. The engine coughed and caught, stumbled and then settled into a fast idle. I backed to where the woman was standing beneath a working lamp.

"Thanks, I owe you."

She shrugged her square shoulders and peered at me through the flat, green eyes.

"I'll take it out in trade," I think she said.

She held up her hand beckoning me to wait and retrieved her purse. Two fingers reached into the passenger window and dropped a business card into my lap.

'Salon Bellezza. Hair and Nails by Tamara Greene.' The address was local. She leaned into the window before she spoke.

"It's not far away," she said. "Follow me."

She crossed the parking lot and climbed into her car. I don't think that I'd really looked at her until then and I hadn't seen her anywhere since we entered the clubhouse together: not at one of the round tables, the food serving line, or mingling among people clutching weak drinks as they stared over the heads of alumni. I took a deep breath and caught the faint odor of patchouli. Another blurry image of the teenage girl, this time in a cheerleader's uniform, and this time her face almost clear. I did know her.

The Fiat started and blew a black cloud out the exhaust pipe. Most likely bad valve seals. Like everything else, time and mileage do the damage. She pulled alongside, mouthed something, and nodded her head as if I should understand. Maybe all that either of us needed was some company, more than anything else, just the close comfort of human contact with someone who shared your experience even if only one of you could remember it. I followed her car as she exited the parking lot and together we headed across town. One day at a time.

Chapter Two

During the week, Marce and I made plans to meet for lunch, but in the end she left me a message and cancelled. The memory of lavender soap had peaked my interest, but the patchouli had haunted my dreams. Twice I picked up the phone to call Tamara. The first time I listened to the salon's recorded greeting but didn't leave a message; the second time I stopped in the middle of dialing with a stark realization: I must be kidding myself. Here I was, living paycheck to paycheck in a rented apartment, no career or any real prospects for one. Any relationship with me was a non-starter. Just another recovering alcoholic in a mid-life crisis with nothing to offer. One of the many things your sponsor tells you is to stay out of any romantic relationship the first year of your sobriety. The truth is that no woman in her right mind would have anything to do with me. Why should she? I might as well toss Tamara's business card into the trash. I needed to forget about her. It would be the last time I had my hands on that lithe and fragrant body. But the night played back in my mind like exquisite torture. Tamara sitting on the pavement in front of the entrance to the clubhouse; smoking a cigarette while she fingered the hem of her short, red skirt; barefoot at the rear fender of the MG; naked in her bedroom.

As soon as we entered the rooms above her salon, she kicked off her pumps, stripped in front of me without hesitation and helped me undress. We embraced before a freestanding, full-length mirror. A streetlight outside the bedroom window held us captive, a merged image of two consenting adults staring back. She had aged but her body was fit and firm. Whatever awkwardness she may have possessed as a teenager had morphed into the compound curves of a mature woman. Her skin was evenly tan without tan lines, and the toned, smooth expanse of arms and legs was sculpted and well defined. Small, matching tattoos of burgundy chrysanthemums were located on her back, just beneath the collar line, so as to be invisible when wearing a blouse. Beneath her left hip was an ornate image of a green parrot with its vibrant red and yellow tail feathers and blue-tipped wings trailing between her legs to terminate at the inside of upper thigh. The psittacine adornment was too carefully executed, too artistically rendered to be a mere expression of rebellious youth. I envied the intimate proximity the tattoo artist must have shared. Burgundy chrysanthemums, green parrot, and that one elided tattoo above her breast spoke to an unconventional consciousness. This was not the spontaneous embellishment of impulsive youth; these were well considered choices. Regardless of the reasons behind the tattoos, or the person she was when they were inked, there was much more to Tamara than met the eye.

By comparison my body was unadorned, growing flabby with age, exhibiting a career spent sitting behind a desk augmented by a decade of alcohol abuse. In full dress I could pass for almost handsome, but six months of abstinence and moderate activity had yet to reform my physique. We were a study of two types; one closely in touch with her body's needs and the discipline required to meet them, and the other only now becoming aware of any personal health responsibility. It seemed in the cruel comparison captured in slanting light that she had embraced her senescence while I had done everything I could to deny mine.

In bed, Tamara was sexy as hell and a ferocious lover. She knew what she wanted and she wasn't shy about asking for it. In the post-coital quiescence, not a word was said. She simply kissed me goodnight, rolled over and let me find my way to the front door. No spooning, no pillow talk. A one-night stand conceived in high school reverie, aided by alcohol, and rationalized by the guilt-free choices that come with maturity. And then my early morning drive navigating the nearly empty streets, on and off the freeway, across town with the cloying odor of patchouli in my nose and a raw, sad, almost desperate feeling of loneliness in my heart as a familiar tune, "*Reeling in the Years*," the theme song from the Baja trip, drifted through my head.

At the apartment, I looked up Tamara in my senior class yearbook. The blurry image that I remembered wasn't entirely correct. She did wear a uniform, but as a flagster and not a cheerleader. Flagsters were considered second-rate cheerleaders, not popular or attractive enough to make the first team. They carried decorative flags that flanked the marching band during half-time performances at football games. Flagsters performed gymnastic routines, tossing their flags to each other or into the air, adding twists, spins or back rolls before catching them. Technically, a far more difficult execution than the cheerleader's pointless karate chops and jazz hands that accompanied sophomoric, repetitive chants, but at the time, flagsters were overshadowed by the short shirts and tight sweaters of the cheerleaders. Now, it was easy to appreciate the greater degree of difficulty in their routines and as far as their level of attractiveness, from a distance of three decades, even wearing knee-length tartan jumpers, they were all cute.

I was working part time for Tom at Big Magic Foreign Auto. A decent job, relatively free of stress and much different from my former occupation, but I felt certain that my career was not in automobile repair. Tom had built a strong following using a business model that specialized in the collectible, vintage vehicles owned by a niche of wealthy, hyper-critical, type-A individuals. Working on the vehicles was complicated; fault diagnosis was challenging. It required calm ratiocination to separate the symptom from the underlying cause, and deductive reasoning to chase down false leads and red herrings as if you were solving a mechanical mystery. But it wasn't my calling. For the time being, it was an honest way to make a living and, quite frankly, I felt obligated to Tom. He was the only friend I had after my professional life imploded and my colleagues, in personal acts of self-preservation, put as much distance as they could between themselves and me. It's one thing to be the rising department star picking up tabs for drinks after work, and quite another to be the doomed co-worker sinking fast in company waters. Following my fiancée's departure, an event that was just another in a series of self-destructive acts including totaling my BMW in a single car accident and incineration of almost everything I owned, pulling into Big Magic Foreign Auto Repair was the first good thing to happen. Tom was my AA sponsor and at the moment I needed the income and the routine of steady employment. With his support I'd managed to locate a place to live, hang on to sobriety and recover a little self-esteem. At least I had that much.

Stray and I were in the kitchen. I fed him a few dog biscuits, put him on a sit command, and then balanced a rawhide bone on his blunt nose. We had been cohabitants for a short time, but already he'd learned this trick. I snapped my fingers and he snatched the bone off his nose, wagged his stubby tail and paraded the kitchen with his prize held high. I don't know if he did it just to please me or if he really enjoyed his performance, but every time we enacted this ritual, I came to realize the lengths animals go in order to earn approval. I was unloading the dish rack when the phone rang. I didn't get many calls at the apartment line, and when I did, it was usually a telemarketer or Tom wearing his sponsor cap and calling to check on me. The ring sounded the same as always, but this time it felt ominous. I slung the dishtowel over my shoulder and answered.

"Hello?"

The line was quiet. I could feel my stomach tighten as I strained to listen.

"Hello?"

I pressed the receiver close to my good ear and held my breath. On the other end of the line was the rhythmic patter of rainfall and slow breathing.

"Who is this?"

There was nothing but the sound of rain, more breathing and then some muted voices in the background. I took a leap of faith.

"You got my letter."

A definite, forceful exhalation and then finally, in a voice that hadn't changed with time, she spoke.

"Carolyn wants you to find Edward."

"Carolyn?"

"Find him."

"Why?"

She cleared her throat.

"A plastic hangar for a plastic smile?"

The rain grew louder and then went away. A few seconds passed.

"Guilty," I said. More rain, breathing, and a raspy cough. "I regret writing that. I do."

People in the background were speaking but I couldn't make out what they were saying.

"Find him," she repeated.

"I apologized, already. I wrote you that I was sorry."

Another pause, this time with no breathing, no rain, no background voices, but a definite personal presence that I could feel through the phone line.

"*You owe Carolyn.*"

Then the line went dead. Stray pressed against my leg, stubby tail wagging, loose lips stretched around his bone as if he were smiling. I hung up the phone and reached down to scratch his back.

"You'll never believe who that was."

Stray stared at me as if waiting for an explanation. I returned to the dish rack and put the last few plates in the cupboard. Stray went to the front door and sat as I leaned against the counter, dishtowel in my hands, mind back in the high school parking lot where Carolyn stood, textbooks in her arms, long dark hair framing her oval face. I sat watching from my car, hands squeezing the steering wheel, stomach clenched with an ache that made my eyes water. Stray dropped his bone as I ran a hand through my hair and probed my gut. All these years later and I still nursed the duodenal ulcer that began in high school. Stray crouched on the floor watching my every move.

"Well, what do you think?"

Stray stood and his good ear ramped upward. He tilted his head and watched me walk to the bookcase that held the only books I owned after I burned down the rental house; the four feet of red-bound Harvard Classics I'd received as a graduation gift from my grandmother, and my yearbook. Edward's photograph was on the second page. Everyone knew that he was destined to do something extraordinary. The guarded smile, disinterested eyes leveled at the photographer but looking past him, the high forehead that hinted at intelligence. Every academic honor you could possibly accumulate was listed beneath his name: All the necessary ingredients for success and fame. But behind that guarded smile and those disinterested eyes was a gifted man with a troubled soul, as if along with his genius intelligence came an equal amount of personal anguish in some unjust equation of aptitude and burden. I grabbed my car keys and cell phone.

"Go for a ride?"

Stray picked up his bone, confirmed in his suspicion, and focused on the front door.

"Okay, then."

We loaded up and Stray settled into his place. He fit perfectly on the rear seat and even had enough room to stretch out and sleep. It turned out that the MG was a perfect fit to accommodate a medium-sized dog, like a Boxer, as if Stray were destined to select an owner with this particular car. We rolled down the entry drive, another fortuitous coincidence seemingly destined. At the bottom, I released the clutch. The engine fired and I turned toward the freeway, dialing as I drove.

"Hey," Marce yelled.

In the background there was laughter, shouting and the sound of a television.

"Sounds like you're in a good mood."

"Big football game. Bill's barbequing for his frat buddies," she said. "They all brought their boys. It's a testosterone cook out. He doesn't even know I'm here."

"Carolyn called."

There were shouts and clapping as Marce talked to someone.

"I can't hear you."

"I'm driving."

"What?"

I turned onto the freeway onramp.

"Okay, start over," she said.

"Carolyn called."

The reception was probably poor, here. I merged into traffic unsure if Marce had heard me.

"Carol called? What did she say?"

"She told me to find Edward."

"What?"

"She told me to find Edward."

"Wait."

Stray posted himself between the front seats. He liked to plant his front paws on the center console and brace his shoulder against the passenger headrest: That way he had a clear view through the windshield and ample access to my bad ear if he felt it required a healing lick.

"Okay. I had to come inside. Say it again."

"You said that Edward was living on the streets, right?" I could hear Marce breathing into the phone. "Somewhere around here?"

Stray dropped his bone on the passenger seat and stared at it.

"Take me with you," she said.

"What?"

"Take me with you, *Please*?"

"What about the barbeque and big game?"

"Get me away from these pig iron idiots!"

I merged into the next lane beside an enormous semi-tractor and trailer. My eyes met the trailer at axle height as the rumbling ensemble rushed past and the trailing vortex sucked us along in its wake. Quite often, in this small car, I thought I'd be better served wearing a helmet than a seatbelt.

"It's pig skin," I said.

"Pig skin?"

"Not 'Pig iron.' Pig skin."

"Whatever."

"Do you know where he is?"

"I know."

"Where?"

"I'll tell you only if you take me. Meet me at the Vons. It's on Colima. Remember?"

"Do I have a choice?"

"No."

"I've got Stray with me."

"Oh, right. The lonely bachelor and his roommate."

"He's more than a roommate. He's my partner."

Marce sighed into the phone and clicked her tongue. Another semi-tractor and trailer rolled past with a hollow, sucking roar. I involuntarily ducked my head.

"We've got to get you a girlfriend."

"Anyone you know available…?"

"Hah! Don't you wish."

"Thanks, Marce. I can feel the love."

"I'm not kidding."

Stray leaned toward the driver's seat, swiped my bad ear with his rough tongue and returned to staring at his rawhide bone.

"See you soon."

He licked his lips and yawned. I checked the instruments; 65 MPH, engine temperature normal, oil pressure normal, plenty of fuel. Stray shifted his weight to the passenger side and belched. The small interior filled with the odor of dog biscuits. I laughed and cracked the wind wing. Stray may be man's best friend, but Marce was right.

Chapter Three

In casual clothes, Marce looked young for her age. She still wore the same long brown hair she wore all through high school, had the same tom-boy figure she'd probably always have, and moved with the same coquettish prance like the popular girl I remembered. She dressed in fashionable, low-rise jeans and chunky, platform shoes, green striped neck scarf and black wool jacket buttoned against the fall weather. Her eyes locked on mine and smiled first, and then her lips, cheeks, and entire face colluded in joyous mutiny. Her eyes sparkled as her cheeks spread. Fine lines radiated from her temples and the skin stretched tight across her forehead as her eyebrows arched. Even her ears moved when she smiled. A woman who smiles when she sees you can change your whole attitude. And Marce had an infectious smile. She dropped on the passenger seat with a rattling bundle of keys in her lap and Stray shoved his nose against her head to sniff. She giggled, pulled his rawhide bone from beneath her butt and then reached back to let him take it. His stubby tail wagged in response.

"Hello Marvin Gardens."

I smiled, but after all these years, it still wasn't funny.

"So this is your partner? What happened to his ear?"

"Battle scars. It's sensitive. He doesn't like it touched."

"Looks like he lost the battle."

"But he lived to fight another day."

She said something and I leaned across the seat. "What?"

"Battle scars?"

"I've collected my share."

"But still fighting?"

"You could say that."

"Is finding Edward part of your battle?"

"More like starting over, you know? Finishing unfinished business and putting the past behind. A fresh beginning. Completely fresh. A hard reset."

Marce dug into her front pocket and withdrew a small squeeze tube.

"I'd like a hard reset," she said, unscrewed the top of the squeeze tube and ran it across her lips.

I nodded in agreement. "Still using the Chapstick."

"Better. This has aloe. You want some?"

As I idled through the parking lot, she reached over and squeezed a gelatinous ribbon along my lower lip.

"Purse your lips."

I rubbed my lips together, drove down the exit ramp and stopped.

"Here, like this," she said, smeared the gel with a finger, and then pointed. "Go right."

She rubbed the remainder across her own lips and arched her hips off the seat to put the tube in her front pocket. We came to a red traffic light. Marce sat up, leaned across the center console and kissed me on the cheek. Then she sat back, thighs jiggling in place, and latched her seat belt.

"Thank you," she said. "I needed this."

I could feel heat rise from my throat to my forehead.

"You keep that up, I'm going to think that you're hot for me."

"Just go!" she said, kicked the floorboard in protest and flicked her fingers with impatience at the green light. "You should be so lucky."

We drove a few miles along the boulevard. Block after city block the same worn-down businesses from my adolescence flanked each side of the road. Some of the names had changed but not much else. A collection of flyers plastered to a plywood-covered doorway rippled in the wind. Scraps of paper scooted along the empty sidewalk, lodging against doorways, or collecting beneath deserted storefronts. Windows lettered in bright, hopeful pastels with "Going Out of Business Sale!" and "Forced to Close our Doors - Everything Must Go!" and "Quitting after Thirty Years - Thanks to Our Customers for Their Patronage" lined the block. The history of various economic downturns from past to present was evident in the delirious optimism of the fonts. Some script was dull and sun faded, while others in comparison seemed newly fresh with bold exclamation points punctuating the exaggerated serifs. A solitary man wearing worn out athletic shoes and a dark overcoat lingered near a breezeway between two empty buildings. Stray stood on the back seat and pressed his nose to the side glass. Marce pointed at the next intersection.

"Turn there and go down to the alley behind the Police station. That's where they congregate."

"What makes you think he'll be there?"

"He's either there or his other place."

"I figured he'd be hiding from the cops if he's doing drugs."

"He's a drunk, not a drug addict."

"Not shooting up?"

"Afraid of needles."

"So he hides behind the Police station and drinks?"

"He doesn't need to hide; the druggies hide because they're breaking the law. The alkies hang around here, near the cops, so they won't get jumped by the druggies. Killing yourself with alcohol is legal."

Marce stared at me, holding my eyes with intense focus as if she knew all about my alcoholism, the years of abuse, my battle with myself; then she looked back to the road before speaking.

"I saw him the last time we were here."

"What were you doing here?"

"Bill's kid's an aspiring juvenile delinquent."

"Bill's kid?"

"Alan. Comes with the territory."

"Not yours?"

She shook her head. Her face went quiet and she dropped her gaze to the floorboard.

"Weren't you married after high school, and pregnant…."

Marce took a deep breath, shrugged her shoulders, and crossed her arms. Her eyes gleamed with tears and she sniffed, pulled a wadded tissue from her jacket pocket and blew her nose. I stopped in the turning lane and waited for traffic to clear.

"God took the second one. Punishment for the first."

She pushed the tissue at her nose. Her entire face clenched as she squeezed her eyes and her shoulders folded toward her chest as if she were revisiting a past horror too painful to acknowledge with words. She took several deep breaths and cleared her throat before she spoke.

"My battle scars."

I turned onto a side street. We were below the boulevard now, only a few miles from the high school we'd both attended, but we were a world away from the gated community of Westland Hills Estates. I turned into an alley. On one side residential garages bordered the crumbling asphalt road. Chain link fences exposed bare dirt back yards filled with discarded children's toys, exercise equipment, rusted patio furniture, stacks of old tires, and pacing dogs. Stray stood up and wedged his blunt nose into the open corner of the side glass. A pair of Pit Bulls raced along the fence and stopped, nipped at each other, and began to bark. Ahead, the alley widened for parking directly behind the defunct businesses, and at the end of the alley, two Police cruisers were parked behind the station. Vague lines on the asphalt indicated the remains of an ambitious parking grid at the rear of the buildings. Half-a-dozen shopping carts filled with bottles and cans, and girdled with bulging garbage bags tied to their baskets, sat next to the buildings. Low mounds of ragged blankets and elaborate hovels pieced together from cardboard, scrap lumber, and blue and black tarpaulin covered the loading dock. A pair of worn out athletic shoes, apparently the homeless footwear of choice, protruded from one mound. The shoes shifted and a high-pitched laugh followed by a stream of harsh gibberish reverberated in the afternoon quiet. A backyard dog barked at the noise, and the mound rose and then settled as if overcoming gravity were too exhausting a proposition. Two men occupied a cushion-less sofa near the loading dock. One was prone with a green blanket pulled to his neck. His head rested on what remained of the upholstered armrest. He didn't move, but under a matte of dark, greasy hair, his amber eyes were alert and watchful. The other was seated upright in a fetal position, grasping his legs, and wrapped in a filthy, patterned quilt. He shouted something unclear and snapped his head back with a demented smile.

"That's him," Marce said. "On the end."

She was right. Though time had ravaged his features, the high forehead was evident. There was a bare patch of scalp crusted with dried blood above one ear. Marce nudged me in the ribs and I parked and shut off the engine.

"What are you going to do?"

I opened the door and got out. Stray jumped onto the driver's seat to follow but I held him back as a low, warning growl rippled in his throat.

"Talk to him."

"I'm going with."

Marce held my arm and we walked together toward the sofa. From ten feet away, the stench was noticeable. From five feet, it was overpowering. The fetor was part urine and body odor, sweet and acrid at the same time; I had to breath through my mouth. Marce stopped short, pressed herself against my hip, and covered her nose with her tissue. The man in the fetal position straightened and shook off the filthy quilt. His clothes were a collection of ragged cast-offs, indistinct from each other, as if he'd been dipped in a vat of road tar and set out to dry. He must have been wearing three or four layers, and each layer had holes in different places revealing beneath it another layer equally ragged. His forehead was sunburned and smudged with trails of dirt from temple to temple like he'd been consecrated with muddy fingers.

"The other one," Marce said.

At the sound of her voice, the prone figure tilted his head our direction. The amber eyes walked over us, side to side, and then the man shucked the green blanket and slowly sat upright.

"Your sister sent me," I said. "Carolyn."

He looked at me, Marce, Stray at the window of the MG. Then very, very slowly, he rose from the cushion-less sofa. It was a shock to see him upright. He stood hunched over with a pronounced hump across his shoulders and his head canted sideways to look upward. His clothes were dusty, but not dirty, and appeared fairly new. He wore heavy, lace up boots, blue jeans without any holes, and a dark brown corduroy coat with thick, plaid lining and high collar. Along with the bare patch of scalp above his ear and some dried blood on his forehead, one eye was swollen as if he'd been in a recent fistfight. Spidering blood vessels spread from the base of his nostrils into a carmine bloom on his cheeks and disappeared beneath beard stubble that covered his face. He turned toward the loading dock as I reached into my back pocket.

"She wanted me to give you some money," I said and pulled all the bills that I had from my wallet. The man on the sofa locked his eyes on the money in my hand. Edward looked at him, turned and stretched out fingers laced with abrasions. Dried blood filled the folds around the knuckles; the nails were caked with dirt, and on the back of his wrist was a tattoo of mathematical symbols that disappeared up his coat sleeve. His reach was steady as he took the bills and crumbled them into a wad. Marce tugged on my arm and he looked at her, turned and shuffled toward the loading dock.

"He'll just use it to get drunk."

"Probably."

"It's a waste of money."

"Maybe he'll buy some food, too."

Marce's dark eyes teared and she pushed at them with the tissue, shook her head, looked at Edward, and then me.

"It's still a waste," she muttered.

"A 23 dollar investment."

"I'll come again," Marce called.

Edward turned his head.

"And bring some food. I promise, Eddie. I promise."

Edward stopped and craned his neck to stare. Amber eyes flashed in the sunlight as he looked us up and down. Over the years, my appearance had changed, but Marce still looked the same as she did in high school.

"Maria Flores Alvarado Sanchez Estrada."

The man on the sofa looked up, stared at Marce, and silently mouthed her name. Edward turned and shuffled past the loading dock toward the breezeway between the two buildings. Almost there, he stopped, called out 'John' and waved the wad of bills. John sprang to his feet and followed with surprising agility.

"Who's that other guy?" Marce said.

"His partner."

"You mean his enabler."

"Everyone needs a partner," I said.

We walked back to the car and I opened Marce's door. Stray was in the passenger seat.

"In the back."

Stray looked at Marce and hunkered down on the seat cushion.

"Go on, Stray. Get!" He slinked over the center console to the back seat. Marce sat down and I closed her door, went around the car and climbed in.

"You named your dog Stray?"

I closed my door and twisted the ignition key. There was a metallic click.

"Seemed appropriate," I said.

I twisted the ignition key again. Another click.

"It's stupid," Marce said, her dark eyes filling with tears as she pressed the tissue at them. "So stupid, stupid, stupid!"

Once more I twisted the ignition key and this time it worked. Around us, nothing had changed. The mounds hadn't moved; no one had emerged from their hovel; no one had reacted to our presence. The dogs paced their bare dirt back yards behind chain link fences and watched us with wary concentration. In the car the mood was somber. Neither of us spoke as I pulled forward, past the Police cruisers, to the end of the alley. Marce was lost in her reverie, conflicted, I imagined, over the degree of obligation she held to a former boyfriend, what role if any she should have, what role if any she was responsible to play. For me, it seemed as if some greater power had foreshadowed a grim simulacrum of where I would be if I returned to the bottle.

When we got to the boulevard, I turned east to drive back to Vons. Marce stared out the side window, one petite hand under her chin, the tissue clutched in the other, her thighs jiggling on the seat. As we neared the Vons, she reached over and grabbed my wrist.

"Not yet," she said.

I continued past the parking lot. Ahead was a Coco's restaurant most of the kids would go to when we were in high school. I pulled in and parked.

"Remember this place?"

Marce nodded.

"I took my first and only high school date here. Kristine Carlson."

"Trying to impress her, huh?"

"Needless to say, I didn't get lucky."

Marce laughed, covered her mouth and shook her head.

"How about a cup of coffee?"

Stray shoved his head forward between the seats and sniffed Marce's hair. She reached back to scratch his head and remembered to avoid his sensitive ear.

"All right," she said. "But this doesn't count as a date."

Chapter Four

It was almost 10:00 by the time I got home. Marce and I had talked for more than three hours, eaten dinner and shared cheesecake dessert. Our first server, a middle-aged redhead like you rarely see waitressing tables anymore, called me 'Honey' when she took our order and clicked her tongue each time she refilled my coffee. Sometime during our protracted conversation, she punched out and was replaced by a second server, a teenage girl who couldn't stop texting on her phone long enough to visit our table. It didn't matter, anyway; I'd already drunk enough coffee to keep me awake most of the night.

At first Edward had been the topic of discussion, then dissatisfaction with her career, some regrettable life choices, followed by a punch list of every one of Marce's relationships, beginning with a childless marriage that ended in divorce, to a series of shack-ups with broken men that she wanted to repair, concluding with her current union that was slowly going nowhere. The words were only one element in the telling; her body was the rest of the story. With each chapter, her history was punctuated by rapid head nods, expansive sighs, dramatic shoulder shrugs and relentless squirming. She'd rise up and lean forward across the table to emphasize a point, and then throw herself back on the booth cushion and cross her arms in righteous frustration. One time, fork in hand, she poked at me and flung bits of cheesecake into my coffee. When she got to her current relationship, she let out a grunt, and slumped across the table on one elbow. It was either a display of pure despair or latent sugar crash.

Then it was my turn for a quick synopsis. I stuck to my three terse sentences, left out the part about termination, alcoholism, separation from my fiancée, the house fire, and the ongoing effort to reinvent myself. The whole thing stank of self-indulgence masquerading as a mid-life crisis, anyway. That was then and this is now. One day at a time, learn from your mistakes and keep moving forward. No benefits in rehashing the past.

Stray followed me into the apartment, went directly to his dog bed and flopped on his side. The answering machine was blinking with two messages. The first was from Carolyn and consisted of a guarded *'Hello?'* She must have called right after I left. The second message was Marce. All she whispered was *'Good Night,'* but it was a pregnant utterance with implied, romantic familiarity that troubled me. She was an attractive woman and a merciless flirt, but what you do without hesitation in your twenties you give due consideration in your forties. As much as I liked Marce, and I always did like her, she had her own problems. It's not one of the twelve steps to sobriety, but the old adage, *'Never sleep with a woman whose troubles are worse than your own,'* endures for a reason.

I don't remember falling asleep but I woke at the first ring to sunshine leaking past the bedroom curtains.

"Hello?"

"Pick Carolyn up."

"What?"

"LAX, 2:20 PM."

"Carolyn?"

"American 1018."

There was a click and the line went dead. I rubbed the sleep from my eyes and looked around the bedroom. The interior was dim but everything looked normal; outside, a flock of feral parrots squawked as they did almost every morning from the Monterey pine in the back yard of the main house. Stray was watching my every move.

"Good morning."

He sprang forward, ran to the bed and flopped his front legs on the mattress.

"Is it time to get up?"

He stepped back, circled in place and then returned to the side of the bed. I slumped down at the edge of the mattress. Stray pushed at the side of my face with his nose and posited a wet lick on my bad ear. In his canine way, he seemed to know it was deficient and always chose it over the other ear. Each lick was his effort to mend what was ailing but so far my hearing had not improved.

"Okay, okay, I'm awake."

I sat up and Stray butted his head against my thigh. This had become our ritual. Every morning, as I sat on the the bed, Stray would wedge himself against my thigh while I rubbed his side. Then, he'd back out, turn and wedge himself the opposite direction so that I could rub his other side. He was a physical dog and demonstrated his affection through contact. He signaled the end of his morning greeting by stepping back and shaking like he was wet while his full ear slapped the side of his head. I stood, stretched, and wandered into the kitchen where Stray was standing over his empty food bowl. He looked at me and then back to the empty bowl, again and again, refusing to leave his spot.

I started a pot of coffee and filled Stray's bowl. He was a determined eater, pushing his bowl with his nose across the kitchen floor as he rooted out every last crumb, and stopping only after the bowl was licked clean. I let him out the front door and he descended the stairway to the side yard. The side yard was separate from the main grounds, blocked by a low hedge between parking court and main house, the only hacienda left of the original Herrera rancho land grant. The owner, who lived year round in Miami, was an actual descendant, and during the mid 20th century the rancho had been subdivided into parcels and sold off to developers. The hacienda occupied half the residential block, enclosed by a wrought iron fence on all sides, bordered in back by a subdivision of low-cost townhouses built in the development boom of the early 80s. The main house was vacant, attended by a weekly yard service that cut the lawn, trimmed shrubbery, blew dust into the air with whining blowers, and generally ignored my presence. At the top of the entry drive was a parking court and two-car, carriage house garage with a second story apartment. Tom knew the owner from work he'd done on his Hispano-Suiza parked in the garage. He contacted him and recommended me as a tenant. Less than a week later a door key and gate control arrived in the mail at Big Magic. I moved out of my month-to-month bachelor studio and in to the fully furnished apartment the following weekend. Everything was included; electricity, gas, water, trash service and rotary dial telephones linked to the main house. My responsibilities were minor: keep an eye on the property and empty the junk mail from the mailbox. Stray had found his favorite post at the bottom of the entry drive to fulfill the first request. The second required a daily exertion of less than a minute's time. Each month I mailed a rent check to a property management agency in Torrance. In the five months I'd lived there, never once had I talked to the agent.

Two hours later, the apartment was dusted, mopped and organized. Picture windows were cleaned, furniture was wiped down and curtains were opened to let in the sun. Spartan would describe the furnishings: wood rocking chair with the Baja adventure Mexican blanket across the back, matching side table and library copy of '*Trouble is My Business*,' floor lamp, picture windows bordered by bookcases containing the four feet of Harvard Classics and senior class yearbook, brown leather sofa, heavy wood buffet with a pair of old brass lamps and clock radio, small dining table and chairs, and two stools at the high, peninsula kitchen counter. In the bedroom, a suite of matched furniture included a double bed, bedside table, chest of drawers and armoire. All of the pieces in dark, stained wood and none of them mine. Behind the basic kitchen was a small and very exotic bathroom. It had wainscoting in light, bleached hardwood. Above the wainscoting tiny ceramic tiles a mixture of earth tones in a geometric pattern swept to the ceiling and ended in a collage of white constellations against a ribbon of dark blue. It was a work of art.

The shop was closed on Sundays, but I'd planned to bring in the MG to service the starter, so I called and left Tom a message. If I didn't show, he'd come here riding his AA sponsor horse with white hat in hand, assuming I was drunk, drinking or about to begin. Stray waited by the front door. We always took a morning walk and on Sundays stopped by the Mercado for a newspaper and breakfast burrito before going to Herrera Park. Outside of the hacienda, Herrera Park was the only remaining vestige of that family's vast rancho, gifted to the city when it incorporated in 1930. The park was dog friendly and had a pathway that looped through mature laurels and juniper shrubs at the perimeter, two baseball fields, and picnic tables with barbecues beneath a stand of great oaks. It was the only green space in a hardscape of apartment buildings and single story storefronts. Commerce had intruded from every direction and my small residential neighborhood contained the remaining single-family homes that hadn't been razed for commercial development. The park was where Stray had appeared out of nowhere and followed me home.

The clock radio announced the day's weather. Highs in the mid 60s, sunshine and Santa Ana winds: gusts to 50 MPH in the canyons, and red flag warnings for increased wind velocity at sundown. The latest poll numbers on the upcoming Presidential election, more bad economic news, an officer shot in south central Los Angeles that authorities insisted was not gang related. Just another day in paradise. I grabbed Stray's leash.

By the time we got back it was past noon and my body had begun to stink. Not the stink of alcohol leeching from your pores that you get after a bout of heavy drinking, I'd been through that when I went cold sober, but this was more of a gamy funk like a week of shower free camping in the middle of the summer. For the past three months, the odor had persisted for a period of one day to more than a week with no apparent pattern, sometimes interrupted by a two or three day omission, followed by consecutive days of a noticeable stench. I'd tried several deodorants, bath powders, even an old wife's tale mixture of vinegar and distilled water. During the worst periods, I showered in the morning, after work and sometimes before I went to bed. The odor always returned, triggered by body chemistry beyond my control. There was a window of two to three hours after I'd showered before it started and then it would rise from my chest, seep past my shirt collar, and fill my nostrils. At Big Magic, I stayed in the garage area away from customers, letting the mixed aromas of grease, oil and cleaning solvents mask my gamy funk. Tom had not said anything about it, but I was certain he had noticed.

I gave Stray a bone, stripped down and showered. I was using a tea tree, oil based cleanser that I found at a health food store, and so far it had been the most effective. I dried in front of the mirror and examined my face. Tilting toward 50 and the years were becoming evident. Lines around my eyes, bags, some sagging of the lids, and a growing coarseness to my gray-streaked hair. I wondered how Carolyn would look after three decades.

I put on my suit pants, button down shirt, and only pair of nice shoes. My wardrobe was not intentionally limited. Almost every article of clothing had been lost in the fire that destroyed the rental house I shared with my fiancée. Furniture I purchased with Susan's insistence (we had met at Restoration Hardware), an oil painting that I didn't like but bought at an art fair to impress Susan on our first date, entertainment center, video library, DVDs and CDs and television and stereo and books and photographs; all gone. The entire summation of my life represented in conspicuous consumption had been reduced to ashes. I remember sitting on the curb in tee shirt, briefs and for some inexplicable reason my dress shoes, fireman's blanket draped around my shoulders, wide eyed and sobered by adrenaline. The investigation indicated the fire spread from the stove, but was inconclusive as to how it started. It could have been an electrical short; it could have been a forgotten pan on a gas burner. That was during a post-termination period punctuated with lethal levels of liquor, depression and self-pity in which I drifted from moment to moment in a purple haze of intoxication. Of course then I managed to deny what I knew. Everything was gone and that was what I'd wanted: Possessions, career, the soul crushing weight of the world on my back, and Susan. Ten thousand pounds worth of one bad decision after another suddenly erased. The entire, ill-considered, mind numbing, scribbled slate of corporeal existence wiped clean with a bottle of Scotch and elemental conflagration. All that I owned was a tote bag of gym clothes, a suit destined for the cleaners, the cardboard box of Harvard Classics in the back of the MG, and ironically, my high school yearbook. Freedom really is nothing left to lose. Be careful what you wish for.

Stray followed me out to the veranda. Halloween decorations filled the windows of the house across the street. A loose-limbed skeleton hung from the front door and pumpkins lined the porch steps. I went inside and called the airline: American 1018 was on schedule. The apartment looked orderly and neat. The dishes were washed, the bed was made, the kitchen counter wiped clean.

Stray barked from the veranda. I let him in and he found his favorite place to curl up against the front door. I went to the bookcase and took down my yearbook. In it was page after page of faces from the past. The notables dominated the clubs and organizations; student government, academic societies, the Girl's League. The same people again and again, and then thumbnail photographs of the entire graduating class. Relatively few had been at the reunion; relatively fewer that I could remember. The floor lamp flickered, went out and came back on. Stray lifted his head and I checked the time. The airport was almost an hour's drive, give or take traffic. I put down the yearbook and grabbed my keys. For a moment I hesitated, thought about taking the yearbook, but changed my mind. I could picture Carolyn as clear as yesterday. The long, straight hair, high forehead she shared with her brother, and her constant smile in that oval face. She was a beauty then and I assumed she'd be a beauty, today. Stray followed me out the door and I left him on the veranda.

I climbed into the MG as Stray watched with a mixture of anxiety and confusion in his eyes. Both his good ear and the mangled one racked forward in anticipation of a command. I calculated the odds. If Carolyn weren't a dog person, he'd be a liability to bring along, and I didn't want to start our reconciliation on a bad note. I looked up and Stray had dropped to a crouch on the landing, his head resting on crossed paws. He stared through the iron railing, eyes locked on me, and tilted his nose into the air as if he could smell what was coming. He knew the difference between the workweek and the weekend routine, and he was accustomed to going places with me on the weekends. I stuck my head out of the car and whistled. Stray raced down the stairway, sprang from the bottom step and skidded to a stop. I opened the passenger door and he jumped in and took his place between the seats. He wagged his stubby tail, wedged himself against the headrest and gave me a quick lick on my bad ear. I don't know what I was thinking. Leaving behind my partner because I was worried about offending a woman I hadn't seen in three decades: Ridiculous. The lengths that creatures go to when seeking approval did not exclude me.

Chapter Five

You hear the expression 'You haven't changed' and most of the time it speaks more to limited powers of observation than to reality. When Carolyn exited the boarding ramp, it was an accurate assessment. She hadn't changed and she was stunning. She held her head high and walked with that perfect, high school posture that made her seem taller than her average height. She carried a black leather bag over one shoulder and pulled a wheeled suitcase behind her as she navigated the line of passengers. Her hair was long, dark brown, parted at the center of her head and fell forward to cover her face. Make up was subtle, elegant in restraint with glossy ochre lips, pale mascara and those plucked eyebrows that taper gradually to thin lines and give women a perpetually startled look. She wore black, spike-heeled leather boots, a knee length, olive skirt, beige, button-down blouse, and carried a drab green, trench coat draped over her free arm. The entire ensemble presented a businesslike persona, professional and confident, composed and powerful, yet altogether feminine. She was the type of woman that drew people's attention and she knew it.

When she walked, she thrust her pelvis forward, rolling off each foot and reaching with a spike-heeled boot as she stepped. The reach lowered the leading hip, and at the full extent of her stride, she paused, almost imperceptibly, before planting her foot across the centerline causing her hips to rock. It was a model's catwalk strut, deliberate and affected in earth tones from her beige nail polish to the drab green, trench coat. From homecoming queen to classic American Beauty, the transition was complete.

She hadn't seen me yet, or maybe she didn't recognize me, so I let her pass before I called her name. She slowed, not so much stopping her forward progression but for a split second abbreviating the catwalk strut.

"Martin?"

Her voice was low and raspy with a breathy quality that trailed away as if she'd run out of air.

"Guilty," I said.

She looked me up and down. There was nothing to read in her expression. Her cold, brown eyes and the set of her glossy, ochre lips never changed. I felt as if I were being evaluated for potential employment without the usual obstruction of the interviewer's desk.

"I suppose that *is* you."

The sharp sweetness of expensive perfume hung between us. She twisted her head forward and resumed the catwalk strut.

"Come…," she said without looking back. "Carolyn is dying for a cigarette."

I became aware of the people flowing past, their conversations, the repeated thump as rolling suitcases bumped from the carpeted waiting areas to the tiled concourse. Overhead, speakers blared. A few recognizable words stood out but most of what was being said was an unintelligible riddle. I was in a riddle myself: I had imagined a greeting involving some level of affection that hinted at intimacy to come. A greeting based on thirty years of a fantasy built around my high school crush. Carolyn was ten feet ahead of me, strutting down the corridor, boot heels snicking on the concourse floor. I took a deep breath and jogged to catch up. She was searching in the leather bag, the trench coat slipping free and dragging on the floor. I scooped it from her arm and took hold of the suitcase handle. Without slowing, turning around or the slightest acknowledgement, she let loose the suitcase handle, dug deep into the leather bag and withdrew a silver lighter and foreign package of cigarettes. We descended an escalator stairway. Standing behind her, I could see strands of gray mixed into her long hair as if a hairdresser had calculated the proper ratio of gray to brown to confer a semblance of maturity without disturbing the overall presentation of ageless perfection. She stepped off the escalator and headed directly for the exit. The cigarette was in her mouth and the lighter positioned in her hand as she slowed, looked at me with impertinent annoyance, and waited. I reached past her to push open the door. The expensive perfume was noticeable but so was the stale odor of tobacco smoke. She lit the cigarette, stepped past me to the sidewalk and stood with one hand cradling her elbow. It was the first time she'd stopped moving since deboarding.

"Carolyn has been needing that for five hours and three G and Ts."

She exhaled with her head back and eyes closed, took a second drag on the cigarette and then glanced toward the curb.

"Where is the car?"

It was a simple question and it provided immediate insight to her character. From how she dressed to the way that she had surrendered her coat and suitcase without pause, the world was parsed into two groups; those who served and those who were served. She was someone people served. Someone carried her bags, transported her from place to place, and no doubt deferred to her authority without question. I'd experienced it before in my former corporate role and I knew what to do. I took her arm to keep her on my good side, stood up straighter and dropped my voice an octave.

"My car's parked near by."

She fell in step beside me, somewhat startled by my actions, but I'd had plenty of practice. You don't log thousands of hours in an executive environment without picking up some of the alpha dog behavior.

"Across the street."

She watched me with eyes aslant and I could tell a re-evaluation was going through her mind. At the crosswalk, she narrowed her eyes, looked me over and took another long drag on her cigarette. The ash fell to her skirt and beige painted nails flicked it onto the ground. Cars sped past, followed by the hotel jitneys and parking lot shuttle buses that circulate the airport day and night. The noise drowned out conversation and I couldn't so much hear her words as read her lips.

"Who are you?"

The traffic signal changed and we crossed to the garage. It was quiet inside the parking structure. Normally I don't park in the airport garage. Claustrophobia mixed with the persistent fear of earthquakes is my immediate reason, but it goes deeper. It probably had something to do with a childhood experience in which my friend Ken and I dug a cave in the sand bank beside his house only to have it collapse on us. We dug ourselves out as much surprised as scared. At my only post termination therapy session, the psychologist had encouraged me to retrace all my experiences, from childhood to present, as if any one of them might be a clue to my self-destructive behavior. I didn't need a psychologist to tell me that. Enough sleepless nights had passed in reflection. Facing what I already knew was the challenge.

I kept a decisive grip on Carolyn's arm and continued walking. The confidence I exhibited served merely to mask the anxiety that churned in my gut. Beneath the low ceiling my forehead grew moist. My breathing became shallow and difficult. My palms began to sweat. I focused on the rows of cars until I located the MG halfway up the parking ramp.

"You don't remember me?"

Carolyn took another drag on her cigarette and let it fall from her hand to the pavement as we walked. It rolled, still smoking, up against the rear tire of a pickup truck. She didn't seem to notice.

"Carolyn remembers someone, but that someone is not you."

I smiled, considering that statement could almost be a compliment, as we stopped at the car. Inside, Stray was in the passenger seat, panting at the window and wagging his stubby tail. Carolyn looked at him, the car, and then me.

"What is that?"

I opened the hatchback and put in her suitcase. I folded her trench coat, first down the center so that the lapels were to the inside, then over itself in thirds with the collar to the interior. Focusing on simple tasks kept me from thinking about the thousands of tons of concrete positioned above my head.

"He's still a little thin but he looks better than when he found me."

I walked around and opened the passenger door.

"In the back. Go on."

Stray hopped over the seat, turned and assumed his position with front paws on the center console. Carolyn sat down and swept her skirt into the car.

"Carolyn did not know you had a dog."

I cranked her window down part way and closed the door.

"How could you? Carolyn doesn't remember me."

I walked around, got in the car and twisted the ignition key. Nothing happened. I took a deep breath and looked out the windshield at the low ceiling. All that concrete just waiting for the next temblor. Seven levels poised to crush us like a fly swatter crushes a fly. I felt the air draining from my lungs as my chest sucked inwards beneath the weight looming overhead. The gamy funk was rising from my chest and leaking past my collar.

"I remember you," she said and for the first time the third person reference was missing. "But you have changed."

"I'm trying."

I twisted the ignition key again. Nothing. Stray flopped against my shoulder and I reached up to scratch his chin. Man's best friend sensing my rising anxiety. Another turn of the ignition key and still nothing. I opened the door and using my left foot, pushed the car out of the parking spot, turned the wheel down the parking ramp and coasted. The motor stumbled, coughed and finally fired when I dropped the clutch.

"You had this car in high school."

"You remember that?"

"I *said* I remembered you, Martin."

We exited into sunshine and almost immediately I felt better. Air rushed in to fill the void in my lungs. My breathing became deeper and less constrained. Carolyn rolled her window down the rest of the way and cupped her chin in one hand. We waited in line to exit, both lost in our thoughts. I was staring through the windshield and thinking about what was to come. Carolyn was staring through the side glass, no doubt thinking about all the weeks and months and years gone past, ticking off the events that had led her to this moment, with me, in this old car, from the plus side of 30 years ago. Carolyn audibly sighed and let her shoulders sink.

"I have not been home since graduation. Did you know that?"

"I didn't know that you'd left."

Ahead of us a station wagon rocked as children wrestled with one another and climbed back and forth over the seats. A man laughed in the rear view mirror and shouldered one of the boys to the back seat. In front of him, the car had paid and driven off. I tapped the horn twice and a hand waved from the driver's window. The station wagon pulled up to the parking booth and stopped. Carolyn dug into her leather bag and withdrew the package of foreign cigarettes. She cleared her throat, sat up straight, squared her shoulders, and spoke in a flat, officious monotone.

"Carolyn smokes a pack of these a day and has only brought three. There is no time to waste. Find Edward."

I pulled up to the parking booth and Carolyn lit her cigarette with the silver lighter while I paid. I hadn't noticed before, but she held it between ring and middle fingers.

"All right, we can drive by his camp but there's no guarantee he'll be there. I only saw him once."

She exhaled and the smoke drifted into the small interior. Stray sneezed and leaned back. I could see his contorted face in the rear-view mirror.

"You'll have to blow the smoke out the window, Carolyn. Stray doesn't like it."

Carolyn looked back at Stray, then at me, and then at the cigarette. She dropped it out the window and put the lighter into her bag.

"Fuck it," she said. "Carolyn smokes too much anyway."

I turned on Sepulveda toward the freeway. Traffic was light, as you'd expect for Sunday afternoon, but cars still rushed to get ahead of me as if it were a race to the onramp. I merged into traffic and Carolyn clamped her hands between her knees. Santa Ana winds had cleared the basin of smog and the mountains leaped into focus. Downtown buildings stood out in sharp relief against a piercing blue sky. We passed the light-rail terminus for the Metro Green Line. The Green Line originally intended to connect light-rail service to the airport, but the tracks ended four miles short. Though editorials stated the obvious benefits, the politically craven mayor folded to the demands of taxi companies, airport jitney services, parking lot owners, and anyone else who felt that light-rail service posed a threat to their personal commerce. As a result, the country's third busiest international airport in a city perpetually congested with bumper-to-bumper traffic did not have light-rail service. The greater good of the public was sacrificed on the altar of capitalism.

"I suppose that Carolyn owes you an explanation."

"Carolyn doesn't owe me anything."

She nodded, rubbed at her thigh with one hand while twisting strands of hair in the other. Up close, she was still beautiful but the years were visible. Crow's feet at the temples, fine wrinkles beneath her ears and around the corners of her mouth, vertical cracks at her lips; and the high, arrogant forehead that she shared with her brother was etched with wisdom lines extending above each eyebrow. On one side of her face, pancake makeup covered a thin scar starting at her upper lip and ending at the hollow of her cheek.

"Carolyn is not who you think she is."

Stray stretched out on the rear seat and sighed.

"Who is Carolyn? Who is?"

Chapter Six

There was little activity in the alley behind the police station. Gusting winds kept the residents secluded in their hovels, hunkered down beneath mounds of blankets along the loading dock, or tucked into recesses in the buildings. Edward's sofa was empty so we circled the block. Newspaper and plastic bags skidded ahead of the car and floated down the street, tattered awnings flapped above vacant storefronts, street signage suspended above the boulevard swung and rattled. We drove through the alley once more but nothing had changed.

"If he isn't here, I don't know where he'd be. We'll have to come back."

"Where is his car?"

"His car? He owns a car?"

"Father gave him his car when he retired."

"What kind of car?"

"The one all the VPs drove. Dark blue."

I pulled onto the main street and drove past the vacant shops once more. A blast of wind rocked the car and Stray jumped to his feet with his nose pressed against the side glass. Carolyn fidgeted in her leather bag until she found cigarettes. She looked at me and then at Stray.

"Carolyn just needs to hold it."

Something moved in my peripheral vision and Stray barked. As I turned, a lean figure beneath layers of holed clothing darted into a breezeway and watched us from the shadow. The face was obscured in the dimness but the eyes burned clear and bright.

"I think that's…."

Stray barked again and pranced in place as if preparing to make chase. Carolyn closed her eyes, raised a hand to her face and pinched the bridge of her nose.

"Just go."

"...John."

"Go!"

"Okay."

As we drove off, the figure leaned out and then disappeared. I shifted through the gears to keep up with the flow of traffic. At Colima Road, I pulled into the left turn lane.

"I could drive past the high school...."

Carolyn snapped her head my direction and her eyes flared.

"No. Don't-You-Do-That."

"I thought you'd want to see it."

She exhaled with a smoker's rasping stridor deep in her throat, her shoulders went rigid, and her eyes stared straight ahead. The unlit cigarette, held between trembling fingers, went in and out of her mouth.

"Carolyn, where I should take you?"

She pinched her nose again, closed her eyes, and then she raised the hand with the cigarette and indecisively waved her wrist as if I should know what that meant.

"Carolyn needs to rest," she whispered.

We drove across town to the freeway and then toward the apartment. Carolyn sat with eyes closed and let her head slump toward the corner. The unlit cigarette dangled between her fingers. She grew smaller and slid lower into the seat until her knees were propped against the dashboard. The farther we drove the more of the composed and powerful persona leaked from her shrinking frame. Her blouse hung open at the neck and over one breast was a washed out, pale scar like Tamara's. After twenty minutes of silence, I exited the freeway. Carolyn was curled in her seat, head on her knees, arms clutching her legs, a pint-size protective ball of shrinking woman slumped against the passenger door. I stopped at a signal and she slowly uncurled herself, stretched her legs and clasped her hands between the folds of her skirt. The cigarette fell unnoticed to the floor. She yawned, opened and closed her eyes, rubbed at her forehead with the heel of one hand and shook out her long hair. There was something childlike and charming in her waking as if the impenetrable shell she affected had slipped away.

"My place is around the corner."

She nodded her head, eyes still closed, arms hanging loose from her shoulders. This was no longer the professional and confident woman who had exited the plane. Now, she seemed vulnerable and fragile. Beyond the fine lines at her eyes and the rigid weariness around her mouth, I could see the girl from high school revealed in all its adolescent insecurity. As I drove up the entry drive to the parking court, Carolyn sat up, looked at me, the main house, at Stray who was upright on the back seat wagging his stubby tail, and then shook her head with confusion.

"You live here?"

"Yes."

Around us, the neighborhood was still. Not a noise could be heard. No television voices from open windows or children screaming as they played in front yards across the street. Then the wind began to blow, brushing the hair at the back of my neck, building with concerted force like the roar from an oncoming train. You hear it before you feel it. Everything stationary begins to whistle and sing. The trees along the street bowed and the overhead power lines sang. A yard sale sign taped to a telephone post folded over on itself, quivered, and tore lose to sail down the sidewalk. The neighbor's plastic trashcan rolled out a driveway and lodged against the curb. Just as quickly as it had built to a crescendo, the wind stopped. I parked, opened my door and Stray jumped out. He went to the nearest shrub, peed, and then bounced up the stairway.

"Actually, we live, there," I said and pointed to the carriage house apartment. Carolyn looked at me through red, jetlagged eyes. I got out, opened Carolyn's door, took her hand and helped her to her feet. She stood up, straightened her skirt and kissed me quickly on the cheek. Her lips were cold and dry, and she looked away immediately.

"Carolyn needs to rest."

She picked up her leather bag and followed Stray up the stairway. I retrieved the suitcase and trench coat, met them at the front door and the three of us went inside.

"I know it's not much, but it is what it is."

Carolyn looked around the apartment and I felt as if I were seeing it through her eyes: Sunlit and cheery, but definitely masculine in design and definitely not much of a home. Whatever of me that occupied the space was nowhere to be seen in the furnishings. Until that moment, I hadn't realized that outside of my four feet of Harvard Classics and high school yearbook, there was not a single personal item. No framed photographs, no artwork, no significant tchotchkes collecting dust on tabletops; nothing of a past life. All of that had been destroyed in the fire.

"I need to feed Stray and then take him for a walk. You can come with us. There's a Mercado not far from the park. We can sit outside and get something to eat. You must be hungry?"

She walked straight to the bedroom. I heard the sound of her dropping onto the bed, and then the unmistakable clunk of falling boots. When I looked through the door she was lying on her back with her eyes closed.

"Carolyn needs to rest."

I went to the kitchen and filled Stray's bowl. While he was eating, I took off my good shoes and glanced into the bedroom. Sunlight angled through the windows and cut across Carolyn's body on the double bed. I went into the bedroom and as nonchalantly as I could, pulled off my dress pants, and put on a pair of jeans. Carolyn shifted on the bed.

"Here, scoot up."

I lifted her head and helped her onto the pillows, retrieved the Mexican blanket from the rocking chair and covered her.

"We'll be back in a little while," I said.

She never opened her eyes.

Chapter Seven

Stray was waiting at the front door. I grabbed his leash and my gym shoes, and we exited as quietly as we could. I sat at the top of the staircase tying my laces while the wind pushed at the Monterey Pine. October brings the Santa Anas and for a few weeks, paradise is lost. The winds blow, the threat of fire escalates, and people teeter along a tightrope of civil deportment. During a wind event, misdemeanor rates soar. Complaints of domestic violence escalate. Otherwise law-abiding citizens lose their balance and commit acts strange and horrific. The local news is filled with details of gruesome assaults and heinous felonies. Sociologists posit vague theories about positive ions but no one has an answer. People lose their grip and they fall.

We walked toward Herrera Park. Halfway there a burst of light from a power transformer stopped us short. Sparks like rain drops of white lightning fell on the pavement and disappeared in the wind. Men emerged from their houses and stood on front porches with cigarettes in their mouths and hands on their hips. Women and children joined them, looking at the street, into the air, each other. At the intersection, the signal was out. Anything that wasn't tied down flew past. Litter skipped across the street, collected against curbs, bunched and then cascaded along the gutter to lodge beneath car tires. A plastic pumpkin rolled across a front yard and down a driveway. An empty trashcan careened into traffic and bounced off a parked car. Vehicles slowed to avoid the debris as they passed.

Between cars, we ran across the street and into the park. Stray stayed by my side, twisting his head from side to side, anxious and wary as if he were spooked. I considered the park safe during the day, but not after the lights went out at night. Tattooed gang bangers loitered along the pathway, and a couple of times, yelling and screaming followed by gunshots and police sirens could be heard. We walked our usual route, around one side of the park and back on the other, exiting just in time to see service trucks arriving at the power pole. The wind continued to howl, coming in gusts that surged in intensity and just as quickly subsided. Linemen spread orange cones around their trucks and strapped on climbing gear. We stood around and watched for a while as a man ascended the pole, and then we headed home.

Carolyn was sitting at the kitchen counter. In the gray light of the fading day, the high forehead and oval face were the same. Any adolescent fat had long ago disappeared to reveal the skeletal shape of cheek and jaw. We don't so much change in appearance as we age but rather accentuate what was there all along. Her features had become sharper, more pronounced with the passage of time, but glimpses of the high school girl I ached for while I sat in my car and dissolved in unrequited love were visible. I knew that anything she wanted, anything that she asked, I had no defense to resist. The heart is a muscle bereft of delusion, impervious to the slow trickle of years. It knows only what it wants.

I gave Stray a rawhide bone, and then scrounged beneath the kitchen sink, found a votive candle, and put it on a plate. Carolyn removed a cigarette from her leather bag as I lit it and then looked at me. I nodded and she bent to the flame and inhaled. With the first drag her shoulders relaxed and face softened. She leaned on her forearms at the kitchen counter and smoked. Starting near the corner of her mouth the thin scar was visible. It swept about an inch from the edge of upper lip in the direction of her left ear. The plastic surgeon had done the best work possible, reducing the incision to a hairline striation that was easily covered with makeup. Stray leaned against my shin, all the time watching Carolyn, and I scratched him behind his good ear.

"How long have you had him?"

Wind pounded the picture windows, shook the front door, penetrated the room. The candle flame flickered.

"I got him right after I moved in."

Carolyn held out her cigarette and I pointed to the plate.

"He adopted me, although I consider myself the lucky one."

She drew on her cigarette with eyes closed and then yawned. Stray looked at Carolyn, sneezed and went to his dog bed.

"You must be tired from the flight. Did you get any sleep on the plane?"

She shook her head. Smoke drifted from her nostrils, past her eyes and vanished upward. A howl rose outside and the candle flame flickered again.

"The wind, what do they call it?"

"Santa Anas," I said and pointed to the library book. "Raymond Chandler called them *'The Red Wind.'*"

She nodded as she drew on the cigarette and the orange ember surged.

"'When the Santa Anas blow, wives finger the edge of the carving knife and study the back of their husband's neck.' Or something like that."

Carolyn nodded again.

"Linemen were working down the block when we came in. Power should be on soon."

Stray got up from his dog bed, stretched, and came over to stand beside Carolyn. She switched hands with the cigarette and reached down. Stray sniffed her fingers before stepping away.

"We had a dog."

The sun was setting and the apartment was growing dim. Carolyn's face was in shadow where she perched on the stool, the cigarette going in and out of the candlelight. Each time she bent to flick the ash, her silhouette shifted against the wall like some ghostly apparition, an impenetrable larger than life image of mysterious intent. She took another deep drag and balanced the cigarette on the edge of the plate.

"We got him one birthday. We must have been twelve or thirteen."

"What was his name?"

"Edward named him Buddy."

Stray came to me and put his head into the back of my knee. His stubby tail wagged and I rubbed his side as he leaned against the stool.

"He was for both of us."

Carolyn searched the interior of her leather bag and withdrew a hairbrush. Stray settled on his stomach next to my stool.

"He slept on my bed." She held out the hairbrush and turned her back to me. "Edward had a water bed. When we rolled, it was like riding the waves on the ocean."

Wind blasted the front door. Carolyn reached for the cigarette and with her hand halfway to it she paused, seemed to forget what she was doing, and touched the pale scar above her breast.

"I suppose I was to blame. Like most children, we grew up playing doctor."

She sat still, lost in the reverie of her past, as I brushed her hair. The only sound was the wind, rising and falling, and the front door when it rattled. Carolyn picked up the cigarette and held it motionless between her fingers.

"Girls mature so much faster than boys. It was curiosity, at first, more than anything else."

A long ash dropped to the floor. The cigarette didn't move. Stray lifted his head, sighed and then rested it on his crossed paws.

"Doctor Kennedy did all that he could," she said. "It wasn't his fault."

The front door rattled again, a low howl from outside caught Stray's attention and his good ear peaked. Carolyn looked at the cigarette as if she'd only then realized it was in her fingers, and brought it to her mouth. She took a long drag, shook her head, and sat up as ashes rained to her thigh. She stared straight ahead with her hands on her knees.

"Curiosity killed the cat," she said with a sardonic sneer. "After that … everything was different. And then Buddy."

She reached an index finger to her mouth and traced the thin scar. Her posture became upright and rigid, and her shoulders tensed.

"Well, I …," she hesitated, took a deep breath and cleared her throat. "Carolyn could not stop him. He had a razor." She brushed ash from her thigh. "The gardener found him. Father never said a word." She chuckled, low in her throat, and shook her head. "That bastard."

Daylight was almost gone. Downstairs something thumped against the garage. Stray lifted his head with eyes focused on the front door. I stopped brushing and kneaded Carolyn's shoulders. They relaxed slightly but her rigid posture didn't change.

"I'm sorry," I said.

"Yes …Yes. So am I."

Stray looked at Carolyn, then me, settled his head on the floor and then popped to his feet at the chiming ring of my cell phone. Carolyn opened her eyes wide as if she were startled. I answered on the second ring.

"Hey!"

"Hello Marce. How are you?"

"What are you doing?"

"I'm sitting in the dark talking with Carolyn."

"Alan's taking John to a counseling dinner, so do you want …Carol's there?"

"She is."

"Put her on the phone!"

I handed the phone to Carolyn. She stared at me, eyes narrowed with suspicion, and then pressed the phone to her ear.

"Yes?"

Stray stood up and leaned against my leg. I reached down and scratched him beneath his chest. That was his sensitive spot and it always made one leg paddle off the ground like he was running in place.

"This is she … this afternoon."

Marce kept talking as Carolyn gave me the phone and stubbed her cigarette into the plate. She looked around the dim room, and then stood behind me and wrapped her arms around my neck. Almost immediately she jerked her head back

"I know," I said. "It started after I got sober."

Carolyn wrinkled her nose and let lose of my head. Marce was saying something about eating.

"Sometimes I shower two or three times a day, but it keeps coming back. I need to shower now, obviously."

Carolyn nodded her head and walked toward the bathroom.

"… now where, where, where? Let me see… how about someplace in between, halfway? Is that all right?"

Even flatfooted she had the catwalk strut. In the dim light, she could have been 18 years old crossing the commons' court in high school. My gut clenched with the familiar duodenal knot as she entered the bathroom.

"Is it?"

"Huh?"

"To eat…."

"You lost me Marce."

"For dinner. What do you think? CPK? Or maybe somewhere else, like the Olive Garden?"

"I'll have to ask Carolyn."

Carolyn dipped in and out of shadows in the bathroom. An olive skirt dropped to the floor, then a slip, and then a pair of black, lace trimmed panties. One hand reached down and her bare shoulder and naked thigh caught in the candlelight.

"If you leave now there shouldn't be any traffic. I can hardly wait to see her!"

"Uh…."

"Right now, OK? OK?"

Carolyn emerged wearing a bath towel and holding her clothes. She put them in the bedroom, stood at the bathroom door and looked at me with a blank expression on her face. Her eyes held no lusty glint, no wanton desire, no seductive intrigue or mystery, but somewhere, in the depths of her stare was the undeniable entreat of a sad and despondent woman. Somewhere, beneath all the pretense, the professional pomp and affected demeanor, she shared a troubled soul with her twin. Maybe genetic, maybe the result of childhood trauma or parental neglect; I couldn't know which but here, in my apartment, removed from the obligations of her profession and the expectations of those around her, a crack in her thin armor of pretense was evident. One hand rested against the pale scar above her breast and her hair was coiled and knotted on top of her head. She turned, went into the bathroom and left the door standing wide open. I watched as she dropped the bath towel on the vanity. The shower taps began to flow and I lifted the receiver to my ear.

"I have to go."

"All right, CPK then, at the new mall?"

"I have to go."

"At the new mall."

"What new mall?"

"You know, the *new* Santa Fe one."

"Huh?"

"Honestly, you have to get out more."

Chapter Eight

From the moment that I joined Carolyn in the shower, she exerted control. First she soaped the back of my neck, shoulders and arms. When I tried to kiss her, she only brushed my lips before turning her head. She washed my back, chest and legs, and then she washed herself and we stood in the shower spray. Outside the bathroom window, the wind howled. Through the open bathroom door, dusk slipped to darkness and the apartment disappeared beyond the darting purlieus of candle flame. As part of my effort to reinvent my life, I had written a letter to apologize to a woman I wronged, a woman for whom I'd harbored a teenager's unrequited love, and now that woman stood with me in my shower. I put my hands on Carolyn's shoulders to study her face, and she closed her eyes and pulled in close. Her small breasts spread against my chest, and she pressed tight to me. I bent to kiss her and she pushed away, turned around and presented herself with her hands on her knees. Water rained over us, splashing off our bodies; the candlelight bounced along the bathroom walls and the ceramic constellations. Carolyn guided me, catching her breath with a wince, and held rigid with arms braced against the wall. When I finished, she stood up panting, raised her face to mine and pecked my lips. I held her to my chest where she rested her head for no more than a few seconds and then slid out the shower door. All at once I was alone. Moisture collected on the bathroom window. Steam filled the shower. I buried my head in the spray and tried to focus. What seemed like my fantasy fulfilled felt like a brewing storm. Everything happens for a reason, and the reason in this instance was beyond me. I shut off the water and watched Carolyn drying herself. First she balanced on one leg like a ballerina, pointing her toes and drying one foot, then, with a quick hop to the other leg, she dryed the other foot. She was still breathtaking, an ageless performance artist in dancing candlelight, and as I watched her, it was clear that the power of her beauty could drive a man to do things he'd regret.

Carolyn patted her loose hair and flipped the bath towel onto the vanity. I stepped out of the shower just as she exited. Not one word had been spoken.

I finished drying myself, applying deodorant and skin lotion, brushing my hair by the dim image in the bathroom mirror. Even in the meager light I could not pass for much. I was not the successful professional I had tricked myself into believing was my destiny. I was approaching middle age, just another baby boomer, not unattractive but a little weathered, unsure of my future and living in a rental apartment with a stray dog. The clearest realities arrive at unexpected times. Maybe it was the post-fornication repose, but unprepared and unguarded, the subconscious truth surfaced from where I'd held it submerged beneath a murky surface of liquor. The house fire was not accidental. It was deliberate. It was arson. I suppose with a few more therapy sessions I could have gotten to the reason behind it, but therapy was expensive. I was on my own.

Carolyn was sitting at the kitchen counter, smoking, dressed in a pair of black designer jeans, beige polo shirt and oxblood leather loafers. She looked transformed from corporate executive to college co-ed. Her hair hung loose and framed her oval face. With her makeup washed away, she had the colorless pallor of someone who spent her days indoor and rarely saw the sun. I dressed and joined her at the adjacent stool. She tipped her cigarette ash into the plate and handed me the hairbrush while staring into space.

"Carolyn likes her hair brushed."

I sat close so that my knees captured her stool, and she bent to let hair strands drape down her back. I gathered a wad in my fist and dragged the brush through them with inept strokes.

"That was unexpected," I said.

She swept her hair to one side and leaned backwards against me.

"Gentle. Let the brush do the work."

"Not that I'm complaining."

I worked the brush through the long strands for a few minutes. She gathered her hair, put the bright, gold barrette in place and stood up. Almost simultaneously, there was a rush of light and a click as the refrigerator started. I looked around at the apartment, now well lit and considerably less romantic than before, as my eyes adjusted to the brightness.

"Maybe we should go now?"

Carolyn took a final drag on her cigarette and mashed it into the plate.

"Yes."

I blew out the candle and grabbed my keys and phone. Stray followed close on my heels.

"I am here to find Edward."

We exited and Carolyn waited as I locked the front door. Stray ran down the stairway and stopped at the MG.

"He is coming with us?"

"He is," I said.

We loaded into the car and rolled down the entry drive. The engine caught when I released the clutch. Stray took his place with front legs firmly planted on the center console.

"That's his sentry position. Commands a sweeping view of the road ahead."

Carolyn opened her leather bag and removed lipstick, compact and a pack of the imported cigarettes.

"He'll settle down in a few miles."

She paused, lipstick and compact in her lap, polished fingernails rotating the cigarette package like a card sharp fingering a fresh deck.

"Do you know what it is like to be ruined, to have one person destroy your entire life?"

I shook my head. Stray watched the package of cigarettes in Carolyn's hand.

"Carolyn knows what it is like."

She tapped the top of the cigarette package with an index finger and then put it away.

"Carolyn is here to find Edward."

Chapter Nine

Marce was on her feet as soon as we entered. She bolted from the booth and ran, squeezing past a family of four standing by their table, past the hostess folding napkins at the waitress station, past a busboy carrying a tub of dinnerware, and slid to a stop in front of us. I held the inner door of the vestibule and Carolyn stepped past me without acknowledgement. Music blared from an elaborate collection of wooden panels and billowing fabrics suspended from the ceiling. A muscle-bound bartender glanced our direction and took an extra long look before flashing Carolyn blinding white teeth in a cocksure grin as he wiped the counter with a towel. At a distance or by candlelight, Carolyn could pass for a co-ed with her long straight hair and youthful figure, but up close under the harsh illumination of restaurant lighting, it was clear that her collegiate days were well behind her. She extended her hand toward Marce.

"Hello Maria," she said in her flat, officious monotone.

Marce rushed past her hand and hugged her. Carolyn stiffened, her right hand held rigid in mid air, and brushed her other hand across Marce's back. Marce pushed away and grabbed Carolyn's hands, bouncing on her toes and grinning like a giddy schoolgirl.

"You look wonderful, you really do. It's so great to see you!"

She hugged her again and turned to me.

"Hey you!" she said.

"Hey you, back," I said with my own cocksure grin.

"Come," Marce said and led Carolyn by the hand. "Over here."

She led us, skipping with teenage glee at each step, to a booth near a large window that overlooked the parking lot. Marce plopped into the booth and studied Carolyn. I sat opposite Marce and kept Carolyn on my good side so that I could hear. Marce smiled with a suspicious smirk as if something were going through her mind and her eyes went from me to Carolyn and then back to me. She leaned across the table about to say something, and then sat back on the seat cushion with a thump and crossed her arms over her chest. Her brows scrunched together and she clenched her lips as she stared. It seemed like she was studying my face for clues, evaluating my cocksure grin, comparing against her female gauge of romantic interaction the intimacy level between Carolyn and me. No doubt she wondered how far it had gone and if our reunion were actually an assignation.

From our vantage point the entire restaurant was in view. The muscle-bound bartender had a folded newspaper in one hand and a towel in the other. He put the newspaper down as a waitress stepped to the bar to load drinks on a tray, and then nodded my direction with a confident smirk in his eyes. He was average in appearance, a little short in stature, pushing forty but bulked up and cut like a competitive body builder in a tight, button-down shirt that hugged the curve of bulging biceps and trapezius muscles on each side of a thick neck. His brown hair was close cropped and brushed upward across his forehead into a line of spiky, blond stalagmites. He smiled with that characteristic gap-tooth of the long-term anabolic steroid user, and nodded to me again as if we shared some sort of gender-based bond. This was no casual gym rat; this was a guy who loved the needle and spent his free time injecting HGH and pumping iron. The waitress collected her drinks and the bartender returned to whatever Ponzi scheme of financial security remained hidden in the pages of his newspaper. He jabbed at the paper with a pen, scrunched his brow in concentration, and furiously scratched notes into the margin. He turned the paper over, found something in the print, slapped at the page, and then looked across the room to our table with blinding white teeth and cocksure grin filling his mouth. Another dreamer, deluding himself while one day unfolds into another until the temporary bartending job has become his career and whatever chance he has left to make something happen rests on grasping after any opportunity that might come his way. Almost a stereotype in this entertainment town, they are wannabe celebrities, usually actors or screenwriters, hoping for that break-out role or full-length feature to change their fate while filling time waiting tables and tending bar as they slowly meld into the faceless landscape of the almost famous. There was something predatory about the way he studied Carolyn when we entered, and I could see the wheels spinning behind his eyes as he looked her direction once more. I knew the type; ever watchful, ever calculating, always angling for an opening. It wasn't unique to muscle-bound bartenders or wannabe celebrities. I'd witnessed it countless times in meeting rooms and at corporate socials, but in this case, the goal was not the next promotion within the department. It was something far more basic laced with testosterone and ego and evidently his next victim had been identified. Little did he know Carolyn was with me and the joke was on him.

The waitress arrived with menus while the music reverberated in an aural assault that necessitated yelling to place our orders. Marce wanted Chardonnay, I wanted iced tea and Carolyn ordered a Gibson. The waitress looked up as if unsure of the drink, and before she could speak Carolyn continued. In her flat, officious monotone, she raised her voice above the music and ordered what amounted to enough food to feed the three of us.

"Carol, when did you arrive?"

"Carolyn. This afternoon."

Marce looked up at me with that suspicious smirk on her face and then she clucked her tongue with a head nod.

"You used to be Carol, right? In high school, everyone called you Carol."

"Carolyn."

The busboy stopped at our table with a tray of water glasses and flatware and distributed them as Marce talked. .

"It's been so long since I've seen you. What have you been doing? We never heard hardly anything from you."

Carolyn took a drink from her water and leaned backwards in her seat.

"I am senior vice president for a pharmaceutical reformulation company with corporate headquarters in Manhattan."

She reached for her water glass, drank, and then clasped her hands together and smiled as if there were nothing more to say. Hidden speakers blared a country western song and Marce shot me an exasperated look.

"And what else?" she asked.

Carolyn took another drink.

"That is all," Carolyn said and smiled with practiced disingenuousness.

Under the table Marce kicked my shin and crossed her arms in frustration. I drank from my water glass and Marce kicked me, again. Carolyn stared out the window, eyes half-closed like she was falling asleep, hands loosely folded in her lap. The country western music boomed on with a soaring chorus of voices that rang off the windows. Even for someone with compromised hearing, it was painfully loud.

"Carolyn's here to find Edward," I said.

"I bet you didn't find him, did you?"

Carolyn sat up, eyes widened with interest, her hands on the edge of the table.

"We looked behind the police station on the way from the airport but he wasn't there," I said.

"Martin owes Carolyn."

Marce nodded and leaned forward to drink from her water glass. She sat back with a tight-lipped smile and licked her lips. The country western music ended and diners at other tables looked up from their plates, mouths frozen mid bite, unsure of what to do in the thunderous silence. Even the bartender stopped mixing drinks and stared at the ceiling as if he expected to find the missing music buried within the elaborate décor.

"Do you know where Edward is?" Carolyn said.

Marce shrugged her shoulders. "Maybe."

Carolyn put her hands flat on the table, ringless fingers extended, nails shining with the beige polish that matched her polo shirt. She stared at Marce and spoke without taking her eyes from her face.

"Do you know where Edward is?"

Marce crossed her arms and sat back in her seat.

"He looked really bad. I don't know if you can help him."

Carolyn looked Marce in the eyes, dropped her gaze to her hands as if examining the fingers, and then very slowly raised her head with a changed countenance. Everything about her face was alert, sharpened and focused, her eyes narrowed with a venomous gleam.

"Do you know what it is like to be ruined?" Carolyn whispered in a voice not quite her own. "Carolyn is not here to help him. Carolyn is here to *Remove* him."

Marce sat forward on her elbows. Bewilderment crept from the corners of her eyes to her mouth. She looked at me and then at Carolyn and then back at me. Both hands raised toward her chin and she repeated *'to be ruined.'* Her hands lowered from her chin to the table as some type of private comprehension informed her features. Her forehead tightened, cheeks flattened, lips clenched and a sinister sneer pulled at the corners of her mouth. "Remove him," she whispered. Her eyes were riveted on Carolyn as though she understood the import of her statement, and all at once her mouth opened wide with a screeching *'Yes!'* as if every memory of every thoughtless act of every heartless and manipulative and self-serving man were contained in that affirmation. She stretched her forearms across the table and extended her petite fingers. Her mouth closed and her eyes retreated behind resentful slits of malicious complicity. She nodded her head, repeating *'Yes, Yes.'* Carolyn stared into Marce's face, holding her captive in a hypnotic trance, and then reached across the table and took Marce's hands in hers. Marce stopped nodding her head and stared with a blank expression for almost half-a-minute. Carolyn released Marce's hands and Marce jerked back in the booth, smacking against the seatback, and spit a deprecating invective that seemed to cement the deal. In that brief, transcendent act a righteous agreement was secured. The two women were conspirators in a pact made outside the laws that govern civil behavior, a communion of revenge too heinous to voice yet too obvious to ignore. Music exploded across the silence of the restaurant and I ducked my head. Both women smiled at me as if I were on the outside of something only they understood. Carolyn looked my direction with smug, self-satisfaction in her cold eyes and in that moment I realized that our relationship had changed. The bartender crossed the floor with a body builders waddle, stiff in his thick legs, almost awkward as he balanced a tray of drinks in one hand and swung his other forward and backward in a counterpoint motion.

"Good afternoon," he finally said in an affected baritone. "Someone ordered something very unusual, so I wanted to deliver it myself."

He looked at Carolyn and set the Gibson in front of her.

"A drink I've only made a few times. I gave it *extra* special attention so that it would be perfect for the *extra* special lady."

He wore a nametag embossed with 'ASST. MANAGER' in capital letters and 'Restaurant Guy' hand printed beneath. He flexed his pecs and the nametag rose and fell and you could tell that it wasn't his first performance. He waited by the table with the gap-tooth smirk and bulging biceps for Carolyn to comment.

Carolyn looked at him with contemptuous disdain. I'd seen that look before, in my fiancée's eyes as she recited a laundry list of my shortcomings, as she lectured me on how I should live my life, as she glared at me when I drank. I'd seen it in her eyes more than I wanted to remember, and seeing it again brought back images I'd unsuccessfully submerged with liquor.

"I doubt that."

The bartender blinked his eyes as if he didn't understand and put the other drinks on the table. He took a deep breath and clenched his teeth. His cheeks bulged like he was holding his breath and his face grew red. I leaned back, expecting a full-tilt onslaught of roid rage, but he only exhaled, very slowly, and then snapped his head to one side like he was cracking his neck.

"Enjoy your drinks," I think he mumbled as he waddled away.

Carolyn tipped her drink to her mouth and emptied the glass. The bartender returned to his position behind the bar, picked up his newspaper, looked across the room to our table and almost smiled. He may have been a pumped up, pretentious clown, but I couldn't help myself from feeling some level of sympathy. Every man, at one time or another, has been coldly dismissed by a woman, but no matter how often it happens, it always carves an emasculating slice from your self-esteem.

Country western music rumbled from the mountains to the prairies in what seemed to be even louder than before. People in other booths looked around in dismay and finally, after an interminable pounding, someone lowered the volume. You could hear a collective sigh of relief from the customers.

"Jesus, That was really loud."

Marce nodded in agreement and Carolyn closed her eyes. When they opened, her affected composure had returned. She looked across the room toward the bartender and smiled, the first time that I'd seen her smile since I picked her up at the airport, and she seemed almost relaxed. She brushed a strand of hair from her eyes and raised the empty cocktail glass with another smile that caught the eye of the bartender.

"Carolyn is famished," she said.

Almost on cue, the waitress arrived with plates of food. Before I could get my napkin in my lap, Carolyn attacked. She ate with furious concentration, only slowing between bites to take a drink of water before continuing her ravenous assault. She tore apart a quarter, roasted chicken, shoveling pieces in her mouth with her fingers, inhaled julienned potatoes and scalloped carrots, pushed the unfinished remains aside and started on a bowl of pasta. The bartender arrived with another Gibson but Carolyn didn't look up. Halfway through my sandwich, she abandoned the pasta and began on her Cobb salad. By the time I finished my soup, she had drained the second Gibson and pushed the half-empty plates away. She closed her eyes behind a stifled burp and contemplated the empty cocktail glass. Marce looked at me as if she couldn't believe her eyes. Carolyn raised high her empty cocktail glass and held it without looking toward the bar. For a few minutes Marce and I ate our meals beneath the soundtrack of *'The Good, the Bad and the Ugly.'* Carolyn burped again, covered her mouth and then motioned for me to let her out of the booth. With leather bag on her shoulder, she excused herself from the table. Marce squinted and lifted her hands to her throat like she was gagging, and made a grotesque face. Carolyn stopped at the bar counter, placed her hand over the bartender's hand and said something that made him break into a sheepish smile. Marce slid from the table and exited the booth. The bartender pointed toward a hallway at the rear of the restaurant. Carolyn leaned her head close to him and he penned something on his folded newspaper. He looked up at me with the cocksure grin replacing the sheepish smile, shrugged his shoulders, and watched Carolyn cross the room with Marce on her heels. The women disappeared out of view and he shrugged his muscular shoulders, wiped his hands on the bar towel and then slung it over his shoulder. I guess that in the exchange he'd been absolved of any venial offense or, at the very least, pardoned. He nodded at me as if I were a partner in his game. Yes, we were members of the brotherhood of men. Yes, as men we'd experienced rejection from a woman. Yes, I knew what it was like. Yes, yes, yes. I could tell that he was back on his game. A woman can break a man or a woman can save a man. All it takes is a few kind words. Such important, kind words.

Chapter Ten

Santa Anas continued to blow. Along the street, light standards shimmied and traffic signals swayed. A sparse ring of young trees bent in unison, branches folding back on themselves with each gust, leaves clinging with tenacious resolve before they tore free, followed by scraps of paper, drink cups, water bottles and plastic bags that skidded across the parking lot. A man, reed thin and close to 80, battled the wind to hold steady the passenger door of a late 60s, four door, Ford Thunderbird. His chubby wife clutched a heavy, double-breasted jacket to her chest, dropped on the passenger seat. He pressed against her door with all his skeletal weight, impotently banged at the door with his hip, over and over, and in a momentary slackening of wind, managed to force it closed. He smiled to himself in celebratory accomplishment before another gust whipped his loose clothing and nearly pushed him from his feet. Fighting to stay upright, he eased himself along the trunk and around to the driver's side, where he wrestled the driver's door open against the relentless wind, and the car swallowed him one extremity at a time. He was inside, safe from the wind with the driver's door closed and a pant cuff caught at the sill. The sedan pulled forward billowing blue smoke from the exhaust and then abruptly stopped. The man cracked his door and the pant cuff vanished as the wind pushed it closed. Through the rear window I could see him turn to his wife, shake his head and point his finger. The brake lights flashed as the man smacked the dashboard and the sedan lurched into motion, crossed the parking lot and exited. As they drove past the restaurant, it was clear that the passenger door was ajar. The woman had her thick fingers in a death grip clutching the dashboard while the man, slumped low in the driver's seat, stared straight ahead and rowed the steering wheel from side to side. The Thunderbird continued down the street, hugging the edge of one lane, drifting out of it and into the next one, correcting course only to begin drifting again. It approached a four-way intersection with a red signal and I held my breath. Two cars traveling crossways slowed and one came to a complete stop as the Thunderbird rolled through the intersection against the red light. God watches over children and fools. Tonight you could add septuagenarians to the list.

The window adjacent our booth rattled with a sudden gust. I slid over as Carolyn and Marce approached. When Carolyn sat down, Marce pointed two fingers to her open mouth with revulsion painted across her face. A few seconds later, the waitress appeared, followed by *'Restaurant Guy'*.

"Will there be anything else?" the waitress said and placed the bill on the table. Restaurant Guy reached across and picked up the bill.

"I think I can take care of this," he said and looked at Carolyn. The predatory, gap-tooth smirk was plastered across his face, and as he picked up the bill, he made sure to flex his biceps beneath his shirt. Carolyn nodded her head, reached into her leather bag and withdrew lipstick.

"You will call Carolyn later, *Restaurant Guy*?" she said and then coated her lips in the glossy, ochre hue.

"Actually, it's just 'Guy'. Sort of a joke. I'll call." He looked at the waitress whose eyes were throwing daggers his direction.

"That doesn't mean you don't have to tip," she said.

Guy shook his head and smiled with the cocksure grin. I got the feeling that they'd been through this performance before, probably more than once, as the waitress turned and stomped off.

"It's true," the waitress said over her shoulder.

"Sorry about that," Guy said. Then he turned to Carolyn. "See you later?"

Carolyn put the lipstick away and retrieved a package of cigarettes. She smiled at him and then stood up from the booth.

"Carolyn is ready," she said and walked toward the front door. Marce and I looked at each other, then the bartender, and then back to each other. Marce swooped her purse from the booth and followed Carolyn. I dug some bills from my pocket and dropped them on the table.

"Be careful," I said.

Guy smiled, that smirk of ignorant confidence filling his face, the cocksure grin securely planted on his mouth.

"I know what I'm doing," he said.

"No, you don't."

Carolyn was smoking a cigarette in the protection of the vestibule. Marce took her arm. The outer doors pressed in and then out with the buffeting wind and a screeching, high-pitched whine filled the small space.

"Carol's going to stay with me, tonight," Marce said.

I looked at Carolyn, her face inscrutable behind the cigarette smoke drifting from her nose.

"Carolyn…?"

She tipped the ash off her cigarette and cupped her elbow beneath one hand.

"I think this is better Martin, don't you? Have Carolyn's things sent to Marce's."

Then she stepped through the outer doors and dropped the half-smoked cigarette on the ground. As it struck it flared in an eruption of embers immediately swept away. Marce's SUV chirped as the doors unlocked and Carolyn climbed aboard.

"Talk with you later, OK?" Marce said.

I nodded and watched as the SUV pulled out of the parking lot. Carolyn never once looked my direction.

Stray had been waiting for more than an hour, so I let him out to pee. He found a place he liked alongside one of the young trees, and returned to my side. He jumped back into the car, sat in the passenger seat and wagged his stubby tail while I sat.

"I guess it's just the two of us," I said and twisted the ignition key. Nothing. I tried again. Nothing, again. I lowered the window, climbed out, and got the car rolling across the parking lot. When it was rolling as fast as I could make it roll, I jumped in and dropped it into gear. The engine caught and started. I let the car come to a stop and sat idling while I panted from the effort. If there were any fitness aspect to my re-invented life, this was it. Stray gave my ear a quick lick in commiseration or congratulations; I didn't know which.

"Go on, Stray. Back."

He climbed into the rear seat, turned around and then resumed his usual post on the center console. We made it through the light at the four-way intersection without God's intervention and a mile later I pulled on to the freeway and checked my mirror to merge. Not much traffic filled the northbound lanes; in fact in front of me, as I climbed a low rise to an overpass, not a single vehicle was visible in either direction. This could have been the only car in the world, the only two lonesome souls in the entire universe; at least it felt that way. Stray hopped off the center console and stretched out on the rear seat. He settled into place, sighed and closed his eyes. A gust of wind pushed the car to one side of the lane and then fell off. I shifted into top gear. There really wasn't anything new to consider, but Carolyn had taught me something. I'd learned how she might have felt 30 years ago when, out of mean-spirited, unrequited affection, not so very different from now, I was compelled to author derisive comments for the year's end high school publication. In her fashion, she'd repaid me. I'd learned other things about her, about Edward, the reason for her visit, and had a glimpse into her manipulative behavior. Not good, what I'd learned, and not reassuring, either.

When I picked up Carolyn at the airport, she had made it clear: people served her. Now, in place of me, Guy was her new man. If I were any example, he was the next in a line of men Carolyn seduced to achieve her ends. My gut held that familiar ache, but it was my heart that felt hollow and empty. Tomorrow, after work, I would leave her things at Marce's door. Tonight, on the way home, I had a purchase to make. What was half-a-year, anyway? Just one spirited drop in the tide pool of an ocean of time.

Chapter Eleven

"Marvin Gardens" she said with a grin. It still wasn't funny, but seeing Tamara was enough to improve any Monday. I smiled like a love struck teenager as the memory of her naked body filled my head and the aroma of patchouli sent a familiar ripple down my spine.

"This is a nice surprise."

Tamara climbed out of her Fiat and hugged me. She wore a loose fitting pair of flowered pants, gold colored, long sleeve top that shimmered in the sunshine, and flat, rope sandals with the silver ankle chain. One wrist was swaddled in dozens of stringy, leather bracelets. The aquamarine gemstone was missing from her ring finger. Tom came out of the office and walked over to where we stood in front of a vacant automobile bay. In the bay next to it, a client's rare Alfa Romeo coupe was on the lift.

"You two must be familiar," Tom said.

Tamara smiled and looked at me.

"Tom, this is Tamara. Tamara, the shop owner, Tom."

Tom extended an arm and bowed like a thespian. Closing in on 400 pounds, he was still remarkably agile. That is not uncommon with former athletes; they retain their formidable grace and athleticism even after they've exited their sport. Tom's problem was that after football, he could never step away from the training table, and as a result he still ate like an athlete burning 7000 calories a day.

"Tamara, is this a social call or can we help you with something?"

"Tammy, please. Or just Tam, if you're my friend."

"Well, your friend Tam I am," Tom said with a grin and bowed once more.

"My car's making a noise. A thump. It never thumped before."

Tom scanned the car, no doubt noting the ragged soft top, faded paint, and the fact that the rest of the car appeared surprisingly well kept.

"You have time to check it out?"

"I do."

"Fine then," Tom said. "I'll leave you in Martin's capable hands." He turned and went back to the office, closed the door, and sat down at his desk and computer. From his vantage point, he could see into the garage and through the front door to the lot when he wasn't preoccupied on the computer. From inside the garage, I could see him. In the afternoon, it was his habit to catnap in his chair while I worked.

"Tam?"

"I told you, remember?"

"No."

Tamara shrugged her shoulders with a sideways head dip. People do that and it either means *'I think you're an idiot'* or *'That's OK.'* I believed she had a big heart so took it to be the latter.

"Show me what you're hearing."

The interior of Tamara's car was tidy and clean and, outside of the usual broken switch knobs, in good condition. As everything ages, the switch knobs crack and grow brittle as old bones. They are always the first part wasted. There is nothing you can do to prevent it; time inevitably extracts its toll.

Tamara started the engine, put the car in gear and pulled out of the driveway. As soon as she accelerated, I could feel the driveshaft banging against the tunnel. We circled the block, returned to the shop and I directed her into the empty bay. Tom joined us as I was setting the lift.

"What do you know?" he asked.

"It's the donut. I'm going to take a quick look."

"I can get one pretty quick. They're usually in stock," Tom said. He turned to Tamara.

"Could I offer the pretty lady something to drink while she waits?"

Tamara smiled and shook her head. Tom smiled and cocked one eyebrow like a modern day Lothario; he was still a man who favored the ladies. At one time, in his athletic heyday, he was handsome. He had half-a-dozen girlfriends in high school and rumor was he wasn't without company after every football game. Now, with all the weight, his pleasing features and boyish good looks were overshadowed with bulk. His face had gone broad as a barn, his arms jutted diagonally from his sides, unable to hang vertical because of a barrel chest that continued in an unbroken swell to his gut and massive legs. He was huge everywhere but not particularly fat anywhere: everything was in supersize proportion. Except his feet. He had very small feet. Maybe once just a little undersized but now, at this weight, very undersized. In his eyes, he must have thought himself the lady's man he used to be. Whenever we had a female customer, and we had more than a few, he was attentive and without exception, chivalrous and flirtatious. As a result, a high percentage of regular clients were female. Women viewed a guy like Tom as a big teddy bear. His size made him appear more bodyguard than potential romantic interest, although from his reputation in high school, I doubt he thought of himself that way.

"Well, for insurance reasons, I need you to wait outside the garage. I'd be honored to entertain you in the office."

Tamara followed Tom into the office. I put the Fiat on the lift, grabbed a trouble light and checked the driveshaft. Sure enough, the donut was cracked in two places, resulting in the thump, just as Tamara had described it. I looked along the rest of the chassis, checked for other problems, noticed a minor leak at the main seal, and saw that some steering linkage had been replaced. Outside of the leak, everything looked to be sound. I went to the office and stuck my head inside.

"Donut," I said. "Everything else looks pretty good. A leak around the main seal, but that can be replaced when you change the clutch."

Tom was filling out a repair order and looked up from the form.

"When was the clutch replaced?"

Tamara signed the repair form, and shook her head.

"I don't know. It's probably in my file. I'll have to check when I get home."

"All right. You check and we can get you on a schedule for regular, preventive maintenance," Tom said and beamed with his broad grin. "I will personally guarantee every detail of maintaining your car to my highest standard."

I had to hand it to Tom; he was a good salesman. With almost every job we did, he managed to put the customer on a maintenance program and schedule return visits. It was just smart marketing, and over the years, Tom had taken business away from a number of small repair shops that eventually went under. Customer's seemed to trust his avuncular approach, and more to the point, wanted to be told when to return for service and what to anticipate in terms of cost. As a result, he'd managed to build an appreciative clientele, some of whom sent cards or dropped off gifts at Christmas. The office was filled with them. On a shelf above the front windows were a dozen bottles of liquor and wine and behind his desk a number of framed photographs of clients alongside their vehicles. A few diecast model cars sat on the shelf, and a signed poster from a former B-movie celebrity who had frequented the shop hung above the front door. Unlike most repair shops, there were no personal photographs, trophies or awards, or any paraphernalia that reflected involvement in the usual automotive related pursuits like racing, rallying, or exhibiting. The only personal item, and it was directed not to Tom but to Big Magic Foreign Auto Repair, was a plaque from the Automotive Business Owners Association recognizing 20 years of exemplary business practice, which really meant that he'd been a dues paying supporter of the association for that length of time. Every automotive shop had the same thing, but it impressed the customers. For Tom, automobiles were not a passion but a business, one he enjoyed, but still a business, which may have been the reason why he was so good at running it.

Tamara returned the repair form and Tom picked up the phone. I stepped outside of the garage into the sunshine and Tamara followed.

"I wanted to see you," I said.

She looked at me as if expecting more. Her clear-eyed gaze was unnerving as she held my attention without blinking. I was at a loss. What do you say to a woman you slept with and never called back?

"I'd like that."

Tom stuck his head out from the office. "Can't get the parts until tomorrow morning."

Tamara looked at him and then at me.

"Do you want to leave it here? We can have it ready by noon."

Tamara shielded her eyes with her hand. I looked over to Tom and he pointed to the lift.

"If you're done with the Alfa, maybe you could run the pulchritudinous Tam home?"

Tamara looked at me and mouthed *'pulchritudinous?'* I smiled and shrugged my shoulders.

"That would be fine by me," Tamara said.

"Sure, " I said and turned to Tamara. "Just give me a minute to clean up."

"All right."

Tom watched me walk into the shop. "Go ahead," he said. "I'll close up."

I changed my clothes in the bathroom and washed up at the sink. Tamara was waiting in the office.

"I need to make a stop at my place," I said.

As we exited the office Tom called after us: "See you in the morning, then?"

I waved and led Tamara to the MG. I held the passenger door for her while she got in and then climbed behind the wheel.

"You sure you don't want me to push?" she offered.

I twisted the ignition key and the engine started. Tamara smiled and her eyes sparkled with mirth.

"You're not exactly the tattooed woman I remember from the reunion," I said.

She stared at me, the mirth slipping from her eyes.

"Especially that parrot."

"Zippy was my first bird. I got him when I was 12. He died from cancer."

"I'm sorry. He must have been very special to you."

Tamara looked at me, not annoyed with my inquiry, but a little sad or fatigued as if I'd lifted the lid on some history she preferred to remain covered. She sighed and turned to stare out the side windows.

"They're just tattoos, Martin. They aren't me."

I put the car in gear and pulled into traffic as Tamara latched the seat belt and balanced her purse on her lap.

"Then who are you?"

"I'm complicated," she said, and turned to face me. "Who isn't?"

Chapter Twelve

Dogs have a way of selecting specific people to befriend. Some dog owners like to think that a dog can tell who is a good person and who is not. I've never found that reasoning credible, but when we arrived at the apartment, Stray sidled up to Tamara, stubby tail waggling like he'd found a new friend, and stayed close by her side.

"I realize that it's not much, but we call it home," I said.

Tamara climbed the staircase, stood beside me at the front door and smiled.

"I wasn't expecting Park Place," she said and laughed.

"It isn't even Baltic Avenue."

We went inside and I scooped a cup of kibble into Stray's bowl. It was the only interest that trumped Stray's attachment to Tamara. While Stray inhaled his food, Tamara gazed around the apartment, from one side to the other, and her eyes stopped on the bottle of Old Bushmills. It sat unopened on the counter where I'd left it the night before. She looked at me, smiled, and went into the kitchen. She ran her hand along the beveled frame of the cupboards, opened and closed their doors, and then walked to the bathroom. The door closed behind her as I collected Carolyn's suitcase and trench coat. When Tamara came out, she was smiling.

"That is amazing," she said. "I've never seen anything like it."

"I got lucky, didn't I?"

"We'll see," Tamara said with a giggle.

Stray finished eating and walked to Tamara. He wagged his tail and then belched. Tamara laughed and scratched him behind his good ear.

"You know, Boxers," I said.

I let Stray out the front door while Tamara looked around the rest of the apartment, peered into the bedroom, and then at the suitcase and trench coat in my hands.

"Bringing something to wear?"

I looked down at the suitcase and shook my head.

"A chore," I said.

"Those aren't for you?"

"No."

We descended the stairs and walked toward the MG. Before I could open Tamara's door, Stray was standing beside her.

"He wants to go with us."

"Of course. This is his pack," she said. "I get that."

I put the suitcase and trench coat into the back of the MG. Stray jumped past me, over the low backrest to the rear seat, and then took his post on the center console. Tamara stood motionless by the passenger door. She bowed her head and chuckled under her breath as I held the door for her.

"You started it," she said with a smile.

I closed her door, circled round and climbed in.

"Or should I get out to push?"

I twisted the ignition key and the engine started.

"Seems to work fine when you're in the car."

Tamara laughed, lifted her knees toward her chest and wrapped her arms around them.

"I remember when you drove this car to high school."

We descended the entry drive and turned into the street.

"Really? You remember that?"

"Sure," she said. "I noticed. You were the only senior with this kind of car."

At the end of the street I turned toward the freeway. Stray stretched out on the backseat after a few blocks. We entered the onramp and merged into traffic. Stray sighed one of his deep, loud sighs that either precipitated a pre-digestive belch or post-digestive fart according to the contiguity of his most recent meal.

"You knew your cars," I said.

"My dad did. He always had some foreign car to work on. He liked to tinker."

"Is that why you bought the Fiat?"

"Maybe," she said. "It was a spontaneous decision. I needed a car and, it's Italian, so I liked that. You?"

"Mine was more of a hand me down than a decision. From my Uncle."

"Nice Uncle."

"Yeah, but I think it was really about his wife telling him to get that old car off their property or start looking for a divorce lawyer. It was pretty rough when I got it. I had it towed to our house and spent my whole junior year working on it."

Tamara nodded her head. I changed lanes and settled into the drive time gridlock behind a mammoth camper with national park stickers covering the rear window.

"I had a crush on you in high school and you never once talked to me. Even though our lockers were almost next to each other."

"I was an idiot, back then."

Tamara put her hand over mine and said something.

"Missed that. What?"

She shook her head, turned toward me so that I could see her lips and spoke up.

"Let's leave the past behind, OK."

"Amen to that."

Traffic slowed ahead of us and we crept along, stopping and starting behind the swaying camper. Every time we moved, cars would jump from lane to lane ahead of us. I honked at one and Stray lifted his head with curiosity, and then resumed napping. Tamara seemed content to watch the freeway landscape slip past her side window at a snail's pace. It felt comfortable, not talking, just sharing each other's presence in this time capsule of what could have been. Twenty minutes later we exited the freeway. Stray woke up and took his post on the center console. He peered through the windshield ready to navigate and licked my ear.

"Thank you," I said.

Tamara looked at me and smiled.

"Never discount the healing power of canine saliva," I said.

Stray wagged his stubby tail as if he knew he were the object of conversation.

"He loves you, you know."

I turned at La Soma and parked in front of Tamara's salon. She got out before I had a chance to open her door and stood by the car.

"Do you want to come in?"

"Yes, I do."

Stray watched us from the back seat.

"Stray can come in, too," she said. "It's all right."

The western sky burned orange along the horizon. The Santa Anas had left the air electric with positive ions that raised the hair on the back of my neck.

This was one of those nights when the butcher's knife comes out of the kitchen drawer and men, entering the apartments of women they barely know, fall victim to its steely edge. Tamara stopped at the street-side door to her upstairs apartment. Streetlights lining the block glowed dimly as they warmed.

"I think I'll leave him in the car. He'll just sleep."

I followed Tamara up the stairway and into her apartment.

"Here we are," she said. "Make yourself comfortable."

Tamara switched on a table lamp and walked through the front room into the kitchen. The first time that I was here, I had not looked around. The front room was simple and neat, with sofa, two upholstered armchairs, side tables with lamps, coffee table, and a bookcase. An entertainment center with television and stereo against one wall; a collection of ceramic vases with dried flower stalks framed a gold Buddha on a carved, wooden plinth. There were three small, abstract oil paintings in bright, primary colors arranged in a triangle above the gold Buddha, and framed photographs of a young woman with Tamara on a side table.

"You want something to drink?"

"OK."

"I have sparkling cider?"

"Great."

I sat down and picked up a photograph from the table. Tamara and a girl were standing in front of a passenger train. A conductor stood behind them, one arm raised as if signaling imminent departure. The girl was wearing a backpack, and two suitcases were next to her. She was taller than Tamara, slender, with dark hair, and although she wore a broad straw hat, amber eyes peered into the camera from beneath the brim. Tamara sat beside me on the leather sofa and handed me a glass.

"The day she left for college. Seems like yesterday."

"Your daughter?"

"Uh huh. Brenda. You didn't know?"

"No. I didn't notice the photograph the last time I was here."

Tamara nodded her head. "That was a short visit."

"But sweet," I said.

Tamara smiled and drank from her glass.

"And her father?"

Tamara shook her head. "He wasn't a part of her life."

"You raised her on your own?"

She nodded with a thoughtful smile. "Took a lot of haircuts and dye jobs."

I drank and watched Tamara. She put the photograph back on the table and clasped her glass with both hands.

"And now you own the salon."

"I got a little money from the insurance when my father died and bought the salon. It gave me some flexibility, which was really important raising Brenda."

"And your mother?"

"She developed Alzheimer's when Brenda was a teenager. Couldn't participate much after that. It's sad. I've been saying good bye to her for ten years."

"I'm sorry."

I leaned back and Tamara settled against my shoulder. She sighed, and this woman, strong of will and determined to do what was best for her daughter, snuggled close. My experience isn't foolproof, but I usually know, within a few dates, if I could love someone. Not that I will, necessarily, but if the possibility of love exists. I project the next month, next year, and then ten years into the future. If I see myself beside that person in any location, at a restaurant, sitting down for dinner, on a vacation, then I know. I'd had precious few opportunities to test my foresight. Susan had been the most recent example of its failure to predict. But Susan had never offered so much of herself in so candid a manner. Tamara was something special. As I lifted my arm to put it around her shoulder, she wrinkled her nose and sat upright.

"Are you in a hurry to go?"

"No."

"I could fix some dinner?"

"That would be nice. Thank you."

Tamara stood up and disappeared down a hallway. When she came back, she had a bath towel and washcloth in her hand.

"You can clean up while I cook?"

I put down my glass, dropped my gaze and scratched the back of my neck. It's always best just to confront the elephant in the room.

"Tamara, I know that I have this weird odor. It comes and goes."

"The bathroom's down the hall. I hope you like pasta," she said and went into the kitchen.

"Thanks, Tamara."

"Tam."

"Right. I'll get cleaned up, then."

She said something as she switched on the stereo.

"What'd you say?"

Tamara came back, stopped in front of me and put her hands on my chest while she looked deep into my eyes.

"Sorry. I forget about the hearing. Go on, I'll start dinner."

"All right."

I walked down the hallway to the bathroom. On the right was a spare bedroom; on the left was Tamara's bedroom. The full-length mirror was in the corner. That much I remembered. I went to the bathroom and closed the door. Thinking back to yesterday's encounter with Carolyn, I opened the door a crack, undressed, pulled a curtain around the tub and turned on the shower. After lingering longer than necessary, I discarded any hopes of Tamara joining me, dried off and dressed. When I emerged from the bathroom, Tamara had the table set. In addition to place mats, flatware and glasses, there was a wooden bowl with salad, bread wrapped in a towel, and candles. She stopped stirring a pot at the stove, came over and pressed her nose to my neck.

"Uhmm. Better. Are you hungry?"

"Yes, I am. Anything I can do to help?"

"Light the candles and have a seat. I'll be right there."

She drained pasta at the sink, served two plates and covered the noodles with sauce. Then she put sliced carrots, broccoli, and chunks of cauliflower on top.

"My version of pasta primavera," she said as she put the plates down. She added a ceramic bowl of grated cheese to the table and sat across from me.

"This is great. Thank you."

"You're welcome."

"Really, this is a treat."

"Brenda's favorite. She likes green peppers, but I wasn't sure if you'd like them."

"Brenda still in college?"

"Graduated. Completing her surgical residency, now."

"Smart girl."

"Seems pleased with her choices."

"Where'd she go to med school?"

"Johns Hopkins."

"Really smart girl."

"Almost a genius. Literally."

"Johns Hopkins is impressive."

"All it took was perfect grades, perfect test scores, and one single parent with a very low income."

"You must be proud of her."

Tamara stopped eating, fork in her hand, and looked at me across the table.

"I'm proud that she followed her dream, didn't repeat my mistakes, and mostly that she's happy. That's all we really want, isn't it? To be happy?"

"You make it sound simple."

"It is… the happy part at least."

"Are you happy?"

"I am tonight!" she said and lifted her glass. "Our first dinner together. Aren't you happy?"

"Sometimes. Sometimes I'm happy."

We ate our meal, stopping in unison to drink, lifting our forks in synchronicity. I heard a soft rhythm in the background, maybe jazz or something easy listening on the stereo, as the candle flames flickered against the walls of the room.

"I've made some of those mistakes. It's one day at a time, you know what I mean?"

Tamara set down her fork, got up and came around to my side of the table. She took my face in her hands and cupped my cheeks.

"I do know what you mean. I've had some experience with someone caught in his own nightmare. You move forward at your own pace. All right?" she said and kissed me on the forehead. I held her wrists and pulled her hands down.

"All right," I said and kissed her on the mouth. She kissed me back, then smiled and stood up.

"And I have dessert, too!" she said with a giggle and began to clear the table. "You might think I had this planned!"

We laughed together and I did feel happy: happy to be with Tamara, happy to be treated as if I were important to someone. I hadn't been important to anyone in what seemed a long time. Then my cell phone chimed. I let it go to message and then it chimed again. I ducked in embarrassment. I'd never figured out how to put it on silent. Not much of a tech guy, I prefer the simplicity of old cars. I smiled and let it go to message once more. A few seconds later, it chimed, again.

"I better get this. Hello?"

"Carolyn's bag has not arrived. Did you send it?"

"Hi Carolyn."

"Did you send it?"

I mouthed to Tamara *'It's Carolyn.'*

"I have it with me."

"Carolyn needs it."

"I was going to drop it off."

"Carolyn told you to send it."

I looked up at Tamara. She was rinsing the dishes, stacking plates and putting pots into the sink.

"I'll bring it by."

"Of course you will."

"Give me Marce's address."

The phone went silent. I could hear conversation in the background and Marce came on the line.

"Hey you."

"Hey you, back."

"You coming over?"

"Soon. Give me your address."

Tamara handed me a pen and paper, and I scratched down the address.

"How's it going?" I said.

There was a pause before she answered: "You have no idea." Another pause. "I missed my pole class."

"Your pole class?"

"Forget it. Just hurry, all right."

"OK, see you soon."

I closed the phone. Tamara was at the refrigerator.

"Your chore?"

"Yes, things to drop off. For Carolyn."

"Carolyn… do I know her?"

"Sure. You remember Carolyn, from high school. The Prom Queen? She had a brother, Edward. You remember him?"

Tamara froze, motionless in a puddle of refrigerator light as if she were stuck in place. One hand cupped her throat and the other touched the place above her breast with the excised tattoo.

"Tamara? You OK?"

She nodded her head and closed the refrigerator door. I could see her chest rise and fall.

"Well… maybe you better get going," she said.

I put the phone in my pocket.

"You sure you're OK?"

"Yes."

She came to me, took my arm and walked me toward the door.

"Thank you for the ride home."

"Anytime. Thanks for the dinner. And the shower."

"You're welcome."

"See you tomorrow? When you pick up your car?"

She opened the door for me and stood back.

"Yes, tomorrow."

I leaned forward to kiss her and she intervened, kissing me hastily without lingering. All of a sudden, I didn't feel like the important someone in her life, anymore.

"Good night," she said.

I had to step back quickly as she closed the apartment door. I turned and heard the latch click behind me before I could say anything. I went down the stairs, through the street-side door and to the car. Stray was in the passenger seat waiting for me. I let him out and he peed on a light post.

"Come on, let's go."

Stray jumped back into the car and I climbed behind the wheel. I turned the ignition key and nothing happened. I turned it again, and again, and once again. Nothing. Nothing. Nothing. I got out of the car and looked up at the rooms above the salon. All the lights were out. I rolled the car forward, got it moving at a good speed and jumped in. When I put it in gear and released the clutch, the engine didn't start. I got out, pushed until it was rolling faster this time, jumped in and tried again. Nothing. I sat in the driver's seat, panting from the effort and cursing to myself. This is the way of things: two weeks ago, rolling around with Tamara; yesterday afternoon, my high school fantasy in my shower; a few minutes ago, dinner with Tamara and then abrupt dismissal. Over and done. Nothing is permanent; nothing remains the same. A car that won't start now even though an hour ago it started fine: The yin and yang of personal relationships and capricious machinery. Stray positioned himself with his front feet posted on the center console. I dug the paper with Marce's address out of my pocket. It wasn't far. Just for kicks, I turned the ignition key. The starter spun and the motor caught. I put the car in gear. Personal relationships and capricious machinery. I'd had enough of both.

Chapter Thirteen

As soon as I stopped in front of the townhouse, the front door opened and Marce darted out. Behind her, Carolyn stood in the open doorway. Neither of them looked pleased to see me. Carolyn had her arms crossed over her chest, shoulders pinched to her ears, face squeezed tight with eyes narrowed into icy slits. Marce raced to the car as I unloaded Carolyn's suitcase and trench coat. She whispered something and I looked up.

"What?"

She whispered again and then Carolyn yanked the suitcase from me, zipped open the top compartment and removed a package of cigarettes. She ripped off the cellophane wrapping, withdrew a cigarette, lit it, and leaned back with her eyes closed. Marce drew her thumb across her throat and made a face. Carolyn took another deep drag on the cigarette, her eyelids fluttering like hummingbird wings as she inhaled, and almost immediately she began to change. The relentless craving from nicotine deprivation departed as the smoke curled from her nose. Her face relaxed, brows eased their rigid arch, and even her lips seemed to soften. She opened her eyes, let her free hand fall to her side and then coughed. She took another drag and her shoulders slumped with satiation. Nicotine may be a legal drug but that doesn't make the physical dependence less addicting. She cleared her throat, straightened her back and spoke in the flat, officious monotone.

"When Carolyn tells someone to do something, she expects it to be done."

She stood with elbow cupped in one hand, the other hand holding the cigarette near her face as smoke drifted past eyes that glared at me as if I were an errant employee.

"I don't work for you, Carolyn."

Carolyn took a long, deep drag on her cigarette. The ember flared bright orange. She watched me with those glaring eyes and slowly exhaled.

"Of course not."

Stray climbed over the rear seat and pushed his nose against my hand. I scratched his good ear and he wagged his tail to affirm our partnership. Carolyn turned with the suitcase in tow and walked to the front door of the townhouse. She disappeared inside without looking back.

"Take her with you."

"Huh?"

"I Said Take Her With You!"

"Already overstayed her welcome?"

Marce put her hands on her hips and shook her head.

"All she does is sit and smoke. I came home early and she was still sitting on the patio where I'd left her in the morning with her phone and an ashtray filled with cigarette butts. I don't think she'd even moved."

"Last night it seemed the two of you were best friends."

Marce stared at me with her mouth drawn into a tight sneer.

"You don't know what you're talking about."

"I was there Marce, remember?"

Stray pushed his nose against my hand. Marce turned around and walked back to the townhouse. She said something as the door slammed, but all that I could catch was '*...that dog.*' Stray found the nearest shrub to pee. I stared at the closed door with Carolyn's trench coat in my hand. The yin and yang of personal relationships, again. In the course of 24 hours I'd managed to alienate three women; definitely a personal best.

"Come," I called. Stray jumped into the car and I walked to the front door and hung Carolyn's trench coat on the knob. Back in the car, Stray looked at me as if he knew what was happening.

"We are done with that."

I twisted the ignition key and the engine started. The first positive sign since leaving Tamara's apartment. I drove to the end of the block, made a U-turn and drove back watching the townhouse as I approached. Stray took up his position on the center console, ever vigilant, scanning the dark road ahead. He braced himself against the passenger headrest and sniffed the air. The porch light was out but as I neared the townhouse, the front door opened and Carolyn stepped outside. She stood on the porch, holding her trench coat, the door open behind her. A lighter flared and a surge of orange ember followed. The hall light spotted her head held high in that same, haughty pose and one hand cupped her elbow. Her face was hard and inscrutable, her posture erect and rigid, eyes following the car. She was in Los Angeles for a reason, to find Edward, and any personal interaction with former classmates meant no more to her than a means to her ends. The brief, post-coital time spent at my apartment while brushing her hair was as close as I would ever get to the woman I'd imagined; she wasn't going to change to accommodate my fantasy. She was not the high school girl that I'd remembered, but who really is? Whose memory 30-years past goes untouched, free of the revisionist shaping that comes with time?

She watched me drive past without acknowledgement. I could see the cigarette ember glow in the darkness. I took a deep breath. You can't change other people. It's a full-time commitment trying to change yourself. Learning to see the world without distortion was difficult enough after a decade of alcohol saturated reality. Stray leaned forward across my body to watch Carolyn on the front porch. I leaned forward so that I could see the road and he took a quick swipe at my bad ear. That familiar act brought some balance to my thinking: Man's best friend.

"Let's go home, OK?"

Stray climbed to the back seat, stretched out and sighed. I checked my cell phone for messages and then shut it off. I'd already had a full night; all I wanted was to go home and sleep. What else could happen, anyway? I slowed at the end of the block and stopped. Turning onto La Sombra was an older, black BMW sedan. Behind the wheel, a man with a cocksure grin that I instantly recognized. The car passed and a booming bass line rattled my windows. Guy was searching addresses and didn't look my direction. I watched as brake lights came on in front of Marce's townhouse and the sedan stopped. Carolyn appeared in view, stood by the passenger door and waited. Guy went around to open it. As I turned and entered traffic, a stream of smoke exited the passenger window. That muscle-bound wannabe had no idea what he was getting into. No idea at all.

Chapter Fourteen

Ignorance is bliss but knowledge is complicity. The simplest realization can rest unrecognized, lodged deep in the subconscious until knocked clear of the day's minutia. Those simple realizations erupt, unbidden and unexpected, to populate your dreams, waking you from a sound sleep with their symbolic vagueness, driving you to fret through the nighttime hours with their unsettling implications.

I checked the time: 5:13. Through the window the sky was giving way to the creeping dimness of morning, the transition between night and day at a tipping point. My dream lingered out of focus, hiding in the shadows, resisting the fine scrutiny of illumination. Carolyn was there, and Marce; we were in the restaurant the other night. A conversation ensued. That was all that I could recall.

Stray rose from his dog bed, planted his forepaws in front of him and stretched. His eyes were bright in the dark, his stubby tail wagging. I braced myself on one elbow and he came to the bed, flopped his chest on the mattress and licked my arm. He was a good dog and a good companion. Good dogs are.... I sat upright. First Buddy, then Carolyn. And her scar. Sunday's post-coital conversation became clear: *'Do you know what it is like to be ruined?'* Then the dinner conversation. Marce and Carolyn staring into each other's faces with sadistic consensus, the blaring music that nearly drowned out the exchange. The words resolved like text on a movie screen: *'Carolyn is here to remove him.'* I knew what I needed to do.

I slid from bed directly into my jeans and pulled on my shirt. *'Put your clothes where you can find them in the dark,'* came to mind, a pragmatic admonition gleaned from a favorite science fiction writer of my youth. I padded my way to the kitchen, started a pot of coffee, spilled kibble into Stray's bowl and laced my gym shoes. On the back of the rocking chair was the black field jacket that I bought when I first moved into the apartment. It was a fully functional winter coat, with a flannel liner, hidden hood in the collar and plenty of pockets. It looked just like the US military jackets issued to GI's, except that it wasn't khaki camo, was made in China, and sold by a Spanish speaking immigrant off a wheeled rack next to the Mercado. Buying it had been an extravagance, but I needed a winter coat and for whatever reasons, convenience, serendipity, or a subconscious desire to re-invent myself, I bought this one. Stray barked from the front door. I let him out to do his business while I washed up, filled a tall mug with coffee, grabbed my jacket and stepped onto the veranda. The world was blurred monochrome, an indistinct gray palette of suggested shapes awaiting sunlight to provide color and definition. Lights in the main house were evident in multiple rooms on the lower floor, but the upper floor was dark. As usual, the lights were on but no one was home. I descended the stairway and called for Stray. He responded without hesitation and jumped in the car when I opened the door. This was something out of the ordinary for him and he wasn't going to be excluded. We rolled down the entry drive and I dropped the clutch. The engine started and I turned into the empty street, the only car in the neighborhood out this early in the morning. By the time we reached the freeway, we were no longer alone. At this hour, traffic was light and fast, drivers intent on maximizing the narrow window before seven million Los Angeles motorists joined them in their daily commute. Stray settled across the back seat. I checked my cell phone for messages, considered placing a call to Marce, and changed my mind. I knew where Edward might be and I knew that I would recognize him if I saw him. That was all I needed to know for the moment.

Twenty minutes later we exited the freeway, crossed town and pulled into the alley behind the Police station. Stray stood up and sniffed at the side window. The back yards along the alley were empty of dogs but he stared on braced legs with his nose pressed against the side glass. The sofa was empty, random encampments silent, hovels of blankets, cardboard and plastic sheeting against the building devoid of activity. If Edward were here, most likely he was sleeping. We drove past, exited the alley, turned right and stopped at the corner. The sidewalk at the front of the vacant buildings was empty. Stray growled and tensed in the back seat and I followed his eyes. Ahead, in the breezeway where I saw it before, was a lean figure beneath layers of ragged clothing. The figure stepped from the breezeway to the sidewalk and looked both directions before it saw me and then jumped back. It was clearly a man, upright, not folded over like Edward, and there was a familiarity in the quick ease of movement. I turned and went back down the alley. Near one hovel, that same man was crouched low on one knee. He rose with his back to me and disappeared into the breezeway as a man emerged. When he straightened, as best he could, there was no mistaking the hunchback posture.

"Edward...."

Edward craned his head to stare at me

"It's Martin."

He watched me and descended the steps along the loading dock to the parking lot. I got out of the car and moved a few steps closer, unsure how near to come. From the shadow of the breezeway came a wounded cry and then a phrase of nonsensical gibberish. Edward raised his arm as if in reply.

"I can help," I said. "I brought money."

Edward grunted with dismissive contempt. Unlike before, this morning his face was scrubbed and clean-shaven, amber eyes clear, his hands no longer laced with dirt, but the knuckles of one were scraped with fresh abrasions. He wore the same clothes with a watch cap pulled low over his ears. He looked up at me from his folded posture, hunchback shoulders twisted, head cocked with earnest curiosity and madman genius grin, his teeth stained yellow with black, gum line crescents.

"What makes you think we need money?"

He shook his head and laughed, shaking with each guffaw, a modern day Quasimodo among the deserted parking grid.

"They're coming," he said. He rotated his upper body at the hips to peer skyward and pointed to the waxing moon. "Money's superfluous to the hegira."

"I don't know what that means."

"No, you don't."

Edward swallowed the madman genius grin and turned away. I touched his arm and he jerked it away.

"Edward, I need to talk to you about your sister."

"My sister."

"Carolyn."

"I know my sister's name."

"She's here, looking for you."

"And?"

"Last night she said something. She said she wants to '*Remove*' you."

Edward straightened his back as much as he could. He pressed the heel of one hand to his forehead and pushed up on the watch cap. His face seemed frozen, amber eyes unblinking and gone with that middle distance stare from high school. We stood in silence, Edward's hand on his forehead, moisture glassing his eyes and pooling along the lower lids. I waited and finally he blinked and wiped at his nose with the back of his hand.

"We need to eat," he said.

"You said 'We'."

He smiled, bared his teeth and laughed out loud as he spread his arms in a gesture encompassing the entire, homeless encampment. The man in the breezeway stepped forward onto the loading dock and Edward turned his direction and pointed.

"John the Baptist is hungry, too."

At the sound of his name, he jumped from the loading dock to the ground and moved a few steps closer. He was wearing the same layers of ragged clothing as before, his hair greasy and matted. One eye was black and almost swollen closed and he touched it when Edward turned to point to him. If I had to put money on it, I'd wager that Edward and John the Baptist settled their disagreements outside of church.

"How about just you, Edward. Just you and me," I said. "Let's talk."

Edward took a deep breath. I took a deep breath. Sunlight was breaking on the encampment and a weak ripple of Santa Anas rustled past. Already this early morning, the breeze smelled of metropolitan waste, that combination of automobile exhaust, industrial emissions and consumptive humanity. But Edward didn't smell. The acrid, urine odor from the last visit was gone. First one and then another mound stirred. A black man crawled out from beneath his pile of blankets, sat upright, and scanned the parking lot with dark, rheumy eyes. Along the loading dock wall a fat, Hispanic man stood and stumbled from his cardboard redoubt. He walked to the edge of the loading dock, arched his back and peed onto the asphalt. The black man yelled something at him in Spanish.

"I can bring some food here," I said.

Edward nodded and watched the fat, Hispanic man. John the Baptist moved closer and stood a few feet behind Edward. He mumbled something to Edward and held out his hand in expectation.

"We are a tribe of fallen disciples," Edward said and looked me in the eye. "John the Baptist wants food."

He put his hands in his pockets, shuffled to the cushion-less sofa and sat down, head back, face lifted to the morning sun. A back door slammed at one of the houses adjacent the alley and seconds later a dog began barking. Stray stood with his nose against the side window. When I opened the door to get in, he was growling.

"I'll be right back," I called, closed the door and twisted the ignition key. Nothing happened. I tried again and still nothing. Stray kept a watchful eye on a muscular gray and white Pit Bull stretched upward against the fence of a grassless backyard while I got out to push. John the Baptist had joined Edward on the sofa. He watched me and I watched Edward pointing his face toward the sun. I bump-started the motor and we drove down the alley, past the Police station, and out to the street. The stores I passed were closed. A gas station on the corner switched on its office lights as I drove by. It was early morning but someplace that served food had to be open. I headed toward the Coco's where Marce and I had talked. Stray watched through the windshield from his post on the center console. I didn't really know why I was getting involved with Edward and his tribe of fallen disciples. I didn't know if I was compelled to help because Edward was a former classmate, or to obstruct Carolyn's revenge because she had obstructed my fantasy, or because I saw in Edward what could have been me. I wasn't clear what my reasons were. I just didn't know. I'm complicated.

Chapter Fifteen

Coco's was closed but caddy-corner was a Norm's restaurant. Two cars were parked at the back and three along the front row. Inside the restaurant, two men sat at the counter, and along the front windows, two of the booths were occupied. I stood next to the register and waited for a middle-aged, redheaded waitress to hang her check on the rotating order wheel. She walked to the register and pointed one finger at me.

"Aren't you in the wrong place?" she said.

"Huh?"

The waitress smiled and stuck her tongue in her cheek. "Where's your friend, Honey?"

"My friend?"

She snickered and stared while I tried to identify her. I'd never been in this restaurant before but I'd eaten at the Coco's with Marce.

"You must mean Marce."

"How would I know her name, she's your friend," she said.

"Yeah, you're right. She is my friend. What are you doing here?"

She rocked back, sucked her chin to her chest with a twist of her neck and gave me a sideways look. "What'a you think I'm doin'? I'm workin'."

I laughed and one of the men at the counter smiled at me. He was leaning over a plate of breakfast with a cup of coffee in his hand. He had on some type of trade service uniform, like a plumber or electrician, and a ball cap.

"Don't mind her, she's always like that," he said.

"Both places?" I said.

"Takes more 'an one to make ends meet," she said and turned to the tradesmen. "Refill Phil, you ready for your refill?"

The tradesmen laughed and looked in his cup while he shook his head.

"You know the type. Sit on his backside all day drinkin' coffee if he could," she clucked with a good-natured sigh. "I should be so lucky. What can I do you for?"

"I need some breakfast, for two, to go," I said.

The waitress shook her head. "We don't do no breakfast to go."

"Well, I need some food for a couple of homeless guys by the Police station. What do you suggest?"

The waitress looked around, took inventory of the patrons at the tables by the window, and pulled her checkbook from her apron.

"Lunch. Two egg sandwiches, should do," she said. "Coffee?"

"Yeah," I said. "Two to go, please."

"Right Oh."

She marked the check and hung it on the order wheel. Then she poured coffee into a cup and set it in front of me.

"You can work on that while you wait," she said. "No refill, unless you're nice to me." She winked and sauntered along the counter, stopping to top up Phil's coffee.

A couple of young guys in short sleeved, white shirts and narrow ties entered and the waitress pointed to the booths along the windows. "Take your choice." The young guys carried messenger bags over their shoulders and one had a bicycling pant's clip around his right cuff. The waitress muttered under her breath as she racked the coffee pot. "Won't need this. No coffee for the seven dayers." I smiled to myself and the tradesman nodded his head with a nasal 'hurumpf' and raised his coffee cup in mocking salute. Ten minutes later I was on my way.

Back at the alley, most of the inhabitants were awake, either standing near their encampments or sitting on the edge of the loading dock smoking cigarettes. Edward and John sat on the sofa. The black man lingered at the breezeway and focused on me with his rheumy eyes as I carried the food from my car. The fat, Hispanic man kept his eyes on the sack of food in my hand. Edward took the sack from me and handed it to John the Baptist. He put one coffee on the ground at John's feet and held up the other. The black man walked over, took the coffee from Edward, and stood staring at the paper-wrapped sandwiches. John the Baptist handed the sandwiches to Edward, and Edward unwrapped the paper and offered half of one sandwich to the black man. First he sniffed it, and then walked back to the loading dock to sit and eat. Edward held up the other half and the fat, Hispanic man scurried over, snatched it and went back to the loading dock. He dug a crumpled paper cup from inside his pants pocket and followed the black man. John the Baptist took half of the other sandwich and sat on the end of the sofa.

"Feeding the tribe?"

Edward looked directly at me for a second and then off into the middle distance. He smiled as the fat, Hispanic man called out something in Spanish and John the Baptist shook his head and ate his sandwich as fast as he could.

"Everyone's hungry," he said. He took a bite from his sandwich and looked at me.

"What do you want?"

I took a deep breath. The Santa Anas had increased with the rising sun. The paper from John's sandwich fell to the asphalt near his feet and skipped a few feet away. There was a foul odor coming off John the Baptist. His face was dirty, hands soiled; he wore the same multiple layers of clothing he'd been wearing the last time I saw him and his shoes were a pair of decrepit Chuck Taylor high tops with electrical wire in place of laces. By contrast, Edward's appearance in decent clothes and boots differentiated him, and the generosity exhibited distributing the food demonstrated benevolence beyond that of his cohabitants. Judging by the way the members of the "fallen disciples" watched Edward, he was the leader of this tribe.

"What's the hegira?"

Edward chewed his sandwich, looked around at the others sitting on the loading dock, retreating into the breezeway, or rummaging within their stash of goods. Everyone was either awake and active or, if not active, watching us from the threshold of their hovel. A tiny woman in a heavy, wool coat and tangled, dirty, gray hair emerged from the breezeway. John watched her stop at the edge of the loading dock.

"Winter solstice," Edward said. "John the Baptist and me and maybe some others. We'll see."

"Solstice?"

"Leaving," Edward said. "On the solstice."

He extended the rest of his sandwich toward the tiny woman. She slid from the loading dock and hurried across the parking lot.

"Virgin Mary's hungry, too," he said.

Edward reached out his hand and she grabbed at the food. She nibbled at it with tiny, rodent teeth, and then climbed to the loading dock and disappeared into the breezeway. Edward leaned sideways on the armrest of the sofa. He closed his eyes and took a long, deep breath.

"I can help you, Edward," I said. "You don't have to go anywhere. I can help you."

Edward lifted his head and swallowed a grunt.

"Look at you," he said. "You can barely help yourself."

He lay down on the armrest again and curled his legs on the sofa. I considered his statement, his uncanny insight into the battle I waged with alcohol, the whole sick mess of mid-life disillusionment, personal regrets, and the piercing anxiety that wakes you in the middle of the night and leaves you pacing in the dark with the realization that your life has more past than future. It was all just too much. Then Carolyn jumped into my mind's eye, and a combination of niggling guilt over a venial offence 30 years in the past and the self-righteousness of the recovered alcoholic made what seemed complicated clear. To help myself, I needed to help Edward. There was no turning back. The only way forward was to go where I had to go.

"I mean it, Edward."

John the Baptist picked up his coffee and took a drink, then held it in front of him and poured it on the ground. Someone from the loading dock cried out. The liquid splashed around his feet, on his Chuck Taylors, and then soaked into the cracked asphalt. He put the empty cup inside his ragged sweatshirt, pulled his knees to his chest and sat staring wide-eyed.

"Edward?"

John the Baptist let loose a smirking giggle and slapped a hand over his mouth. A second later Edward began snoring. I don't know if he were faking or not, but this conversation was over. I got back in the MG, turned the ignition key and it started. John the Baptist followed my progress as he psychotically rocked in place with his arms wrapped around his knees. His mouth hung open like a demented imbecile, another damaged, homeless citizen incapable of taking care of himself, but in his eyes the gleam of clear, penetrating cognition burned brightly as he watched me drive away. He may have been antisocial, autistic and even psychotic, but wheels were turning in his head: some twisted thought process was evaluating what had happened, scheming and extrapolating and plotting the possibilities of what it meant to his future. You can act like you're crazy, but the eyes never lie.

I exited the alley and headed home to drop off Stray. On the drive, I thought about what my expectations had been and what, if anything, to do next. No matter your good intentions, you can't help those unwilling to help themselves; that was the extent of anyone's power. I didn't really believe that Carolyn would act on her declaration, anyway. I didn't believe that she would carry her anger, resolved to its steady comforting presence in her life for three decades, and then for no particular reason, as a result of my self-serving correspondence, chose to travel across the country and commit cold-blooded fratricide. It did not make sense. Notifying the Police was an option, but the reality is that they would probably laugh me right off the phone. In a county rife with homicides, gang violence, assaults, robbery, and more petty crime than law enforcement could handle, how concerned could the Police be over a three-Gibson threat from a well-to-do, embittered sibling with everything to lose?

Chapter Sixteen

By the time I arrived at the shop, Tamara had called. Tom told me that she'd be in after 5:00 to pick up her car. The parts arrived about thirty minutes later and I went to work. I replaced the donut, as quoted, and performed what the dealers sell you as a "29-point" inspection. Mostly, it is a cursory look to find repairs that you may not really need but are the most profitable to perform. We serviced and repaired all makes of older cars at Big Magic Foreign Auto, but usually the type of cars seen in the shop were rare, collectible vehicles kept in perfect condition by fanatical owners who worried every last detail of their considerable investment. These cars were as much physical embodiments of professional success as they were prized additions to personal portfolios and, as such, they had to be correct down to the cross-stitching of the upholstery and chrome plating of the trim. Most of the work we performed was for preservation and market appreciation. Customers were always on the lookout for some way to build in provenance and resale value. The simple addition of a factory option could not only assure exclusivity at an exhibition concourse, but when sent to auction, could inflate the hammer price by as much as 25%. The rarer the item, the greater the increase in net value. Tom specialized in locating those rare, factory options, and via his extensive knowledge and many years spent in the business, profited handsomely buying, reselling, and installing the very items that grew a vehicle's value. He made a good living and was unapologetic at the extraordinary markup on what he offered for sale. 'I only ask what the customer will pay' he'd told me once with a wink of an eye: 'And eventually, they will pay what I ask.'

Tamara's car was old but not considered collectible. Nothing about it was perfect and it didn't need to be, but it had to be safe and reliable. I inspected the drive belts, filled all the fluids, tightened every bolt, lubricated every moving joint, and adjusted the hand brake. I lowered it from the lift and added some automotive snake oil claiming to "restore" worn out engines. I started the motor and while it warmed up checked all the lights and set the inflation level in the tires. After a short test drive around the block, I parked it out front and gave it a quick wash. The car was as well prepared for service as I could make it.

This is one way that men demonstrate affection, ensuring that the women they care for are in a vehicle that is safe and reliable. It was a character lesson that Tom had taught me 30 years ago in auto shop, a lesson overlooked by an emotionally distant father who elected to spend his time brooding in his den with a liquor bottle and menthol cigarettes rather than engaged with the unexpected "surprise" baby. That was probably the reason as an adolescent I'd sought refuge in my own car, trying to put right those things that I could not put right in my home life. My siblings, the nearest in age being ten years older, had fled one by one in self protection, putting behind them the dysfunctional family dynamic I suffered until I came of age to leave. I spent my afternoons with the few friends I had or working alone on my car, ignored by my father in the evenings and around the clock by a chronically depressed mother dependent on gin and prescription medication to navigate morning to night. These parents, fully spent after raising three children, were a duo ill prepared to manage the personal challenges that held them captive to the needs of an unplanned fourth. Astonishing as it seems, they survived to retire, still married, neither one energetic enough to change their marital status, satisfied to maintain their unbroken pattern of self-abuse. I don't think their story is all that unusual.

I spent the afternoon working on the Alfa. Another example of a collectible car owned by a micromanaging, type A individual. Tom fielded his telephone calls, which recurred daily, sometimes two or three times, but deferred to me for progress reports. I had completed all the repairs, and in my mind the car was ready to be picked up, but something else was going on. The customer had run up a bill of more than $4300 dollars, most of which was labor, and I suspected that this was at the heart of the many telephone conversations. The high-end classic cars are usually owned by successful businessmen, and their world is expense and return. More than once I'd seen one of them trying to negotiate the bill with Tom at the time of pick up. As I stepped out of the shop into the sunshine, my cell phone chimed in my pocket.

"She's gone." Marce said.

"All right."

"Really, she is. Just left with that restaurant guy. We went looking for Edward, and when we got back, he was waiting."

The phone rang in the office and I could see Tom's face break into his broad grin almost immediately.

"She didn't even say thank you."

"Did you find Edward?"

"I just wanted her to like me."

"Edward, Marce. Did you find Edward?"

"No, he wasn't at either place."

"Either place?"

"She liked me before."

"Marce, what other place?"

"We went to the alley and then the river camp."

"River camp?"

"She's a bitch."

"The camp, Marce?"

"On the Los Angeles River."

"How'd you know about that?"

"When Bill and I started dating, we went for a walk with Alan along the river. Alan's more than just an aspiring juvenile delinquent. He's a birder, too. The river is full of birds."

"Does Edward live on the river?"

"He has a camp there, in the middle, with some other ones. It's pretty amazing."

Tom stepped out of the office. He was grinning ear to ear. I gathered that his latest conversation had gone well.

"Good thing the Alfa's still on the lift," he said.

"Hold on, Marce."

I lowered the phone to my side.

"Guess what's next?" Tom said.

"I give up."

Tom touched the tips of his fingers together with an exuberant chest heave and beamed like he'd won the lottery.

"Vented brake conversion with finned, alloy drums all around. *Like a fully optioned Veloce!*"

"That's a complicated job," I said.

"That's why I have you."

I put the phone back to my ear. "Marce, still there?"

"Uh huh."

"Can you find the river camp, again?"

"Yes."

Tom walked over and chucked me on the shoulder.

"There's a bonus in it if we can have it ready for this weekend. Expedite charge. Maybe more if I can sell the wheels, too. He wants to show off the car at a meet on Saturday. OK?"

"Marce, I'll call you back." I slid the cell phone into my pocket. "That's a lot of work, Tom. I don't know if I can get it done."

"Sure you can, Martin. You're the only one who can get it done. I'll find the parts and see what else we need. I thought I'd never sell those brakes. I think he'll want the wheels after he sees them. It makes a nice presentation," Tom said, the grin still broad as a box canyon on his big, round face.

Nothing made Tom happier than selling something from his stash of exorbitantly priced, special parts. It was profit on top of profit. For me, it was work more interesting than the usual maintenance tasks, and he always gave me a percentage of the sale as a reward for any additional effort.

"About the expedite, then? Do I share in that?"

Tom laughed.

"Of course! I've been taking care of you since high school. Why would I stop now?"

Chapter Seventeen

Tamara arrived a little after 5:00. Tom had gone to an AA meeting for sponsors. I was as cleaned up as I could be with a lavatory spit bath, had put my work clothes into the washing machine at the back of the shop, and was sitting behind the desk in the office watching the local news. I sniffed beneath my collar for any gamy funk, looked up and there she was, standing in the doorway as if she had materialized from out of nowhere. I hadn't heard a car pull in to drop her off, or seen one exit the property. She could have been watching for some time before I noticed.

"Hi. I didn't hear you come in. Standing there long?"

"A minute."

"Watching me?"

"Yes."

"Oh. Car's ready."

"I know, Martin."

"I gave it a wash, too."

"Thank you."

She continued to stand in the doorway, in blue denim jacket and white jeans, a canvas bag hanging from her shoulder. Sunshine streamed past her, warping along the torso, haloing around her head, and blurring her face. She appeared angelic, framed by the doorway, with luminous orange rays flowing past like one of those swap-meet posters of the Madonna and child that glow under a black light.

"Everything all right?"

Tamara stepped through the doorway into the office and stopped in front of the desk.

"I owe you an apology," she said.

"For what?"

"For my behavior last night. I was rude, sending you home like that," she said, and then looked up at me from under her eyebrows and offered me her flirtatious, high school reunion smile. "Without some dessert."

I stood up and came around the desk. She stepped forward and hugged me as tightly as I've ever been hugged.

"Things that you don't know," she whispered in my good ear. "Give me a little time. Be patient?"

I pulled back and looked deep into her green eyes. They were big, earnest eyes, empty of duplicity, filled with an irresistible sparkle of vulnerability. A line of moisture clung to the lower lashes. I kissed her on the forehead.

"You know, if you want to talk, you can call me on my cell phone. I don't give out the number to everyone, but you're an exception."

Tamara pressed her nose into my neck and her shoulders relaxed. She took a short whiff of me, sighed and her body went limp. I guided her to a side chair and then sat on the edge of the desk.

"That would be nice," she said.

I smiled and wrote out the number on a piece of paper.

"I'm no prize myself, with the manly odor and all," I joked.

She nodded her head and sat up straight.

"It's one day at a time, then, for both of us, isn't it?"

"I suppose it is."

The television news went to commercial and the volume increased. I turned off the set and Tamara lifted her bag to her lap.

"All right, then. What's the damage?"

I pulled the clipboard from the rack and handed it to her. I followed her eyes as she looked at the bill, reading each entry, and then smiling.

"Just that donut thing, nothing more?"

"It's only an hour's labor. And the parts."

"It's not really a donut, right?"

"No. Mechanic's shorthand," I said. "But it needed replacing."

"You mechanics speak your own private language, don't you?" she said with a smile.

I smiled in return and winked like she was in on it.

"You forgot to charge me for the car wash."

"One of the perks," I said. "For special customers."

She opened her bag, pulled out her purse and counted out $132 dollars in twenties, tens and singles. I marked the bill "Paid," tore it off and handed her a copy. I put the money and clipboard in the top draw of the desk.

"That's it for me. What about you? I think it's my turn for dinner?"

"That would be nice."

We left the office and I locked up behind us. I walked Tamara to her car. She stopped at the driver's door, gave me that flirty reunion smile again and made a point to wait for me to open it. She shook her head with a giggle and got in. When the car started, it blew a single puff of black smoke and that was all. Maybe that can of snake oil actually worked. I climbed into the MG, turned the ignition key and nothing happened. I tried again and again, and still nothing. Tamara walked over and leaned in the window.

"You need another push?"

"I may," I said.

She walked around the car, opened the passenger door and sat. Then she leaned across the center console and gave me a deep, wet kiss.

"For luck," she said. I turned the ignition key once more and the engine started.

"Something about you is lucky for me," I said.

"Keep that in mind," she answered as she climbed out of the car.

I exited the lot and Tamara followed. We crossed town and 20 minutes later pulled into the entry drive. A black, Lincoln Town Car limousine was parked at the front gate of the main house. Stray raised his head from his sentry post, and followed me up the entry drive. Tamara parked next to me. I climbed out and Stray trotted over wagging his stubby tail. I scratched him behind his good ear while Tamara joined us and we stood, a mighty pack of three, staring across the front yard toward the mysterious visitor.

"Looks like someone's waiting," I said.

"Who do you think it is?"

"I don't know," I said and took Tamara's hand. "Let's go check the mail."

A driver got out of the limousine, held the back door open, and watched as the three of us walked down to the street. An older man, a little over six feet tall with a full head of white hair, climbed from the limousine and stood straightening his jacket. He walked alone from the front gate to the entry drive wearing a black suit, bolo tie and cowboy boots.

"Excuse me, are you Martin Gardens?" the man asked. I nodded and he stuck out his right hand. On his wrist was an elegant tank watch. Alligator band, gold case, subdued but definitely expensive. Not the type of watch you get after 25 years with the municipal water company; more the type of watch that is handed down from generation to generation, a priceless possession incalculable in sentiment, and fully insured. He leaned forward slightly to take my hand. His grip was firm but the flesh was soft. This was not a hand familiar with physical labor. This was a hand more accustomed to the physical activity of golf links and signing checks. He wore a polished gold band on his ring finger and his nails exhibited the careful treatment of a recent manicure. I estimated his age to be somewhere in the 70s.

"My name's Grant Parker. I'm Carolyn's husband."

At times like this, I am an open book, unable to conceal any reaction. I suspect that surprise showed on my face. In the foreground was Carolyn's husband, in the background, her adulterous behavior. Between the two stood me, the agent of Grant's cuckoldry.

"You seem surprised," he said.

Stray trotted over and butted his head against my knee. I reached down to scratch his ear and Tamara took my arm.

"Fine looking dog you have there. What's his name?"

"Stray," I said. "I named him *Stray* because, well, he was."

"Yes, they make the best companions, don't they? Loyal to a fault, no pretense, no agenda; just food and your good company. Wonderful creatures."

Grant dropped my hand and looked up at the main house, then me, and then Stray.

"He wouldn't recognize me, but judging by your reaction, you must."

"Uh, maybe," I said, unable to fashion a more specific response.

"You're a little young, but do you remember a cowboy, on billboards across the country, and television commercials? That cowboy standing in a corral or posed on a horse with a particular brand of cigarette?"

"You were the Marlboro Man?"

"I was one of them."

"Is that right?"

"It is."

Tamara looked at me and I'm sure that surprise was still on my face. Though she new nothing about my involvement with Carolyn, she said exactly the right thing to deter suspicion.

"Hi. I'm Tamara, Martin's girlfriend. Pleased to meet you, Marlboro Man."

Grant bowed at the waist and lowered his head. He took Tamara's hand and kissed the back of it.

"The pleasure is all mine," he said, straightened to his full height and turned to me. He cleared his throat before speaking.

"A girl gets an idea in her head and there's no stopping her. Carolyn told me that she requested you locate her brother."

My cell phone chimed in my pocket. It was either Tom or Marce, but most likely Marce.

"Mr. Parker...."

"Grant."

"Okay. Grant. Why is it so important, after all this time, that Carolyn find her brother?"

Grant looked me in the eye and held his gaze long enough to make me feel uncomfortable.

"In the two years that we've been married, not one night has passed that my dear bride hasn't woke with her brother on her mind. I've seen her in tears as she tells me about him. I've seen her miserable day and night, and it is time that her suffering stopped. I intend to ensure that it does."

A strain of Frank Sinatra singing 'New York, New York' began to play and Grant reached inside his jacket.

"Excuse me," Grant said. "Uh huh, yes, I'm with him now. No, nothing. Fine, I'll see you at the hotel within the hour. Goodbye, dearest."

I checked my cell phone and decided that Marce's call would have to wait.

"I'd like to report to Carolyn that you will locate Edward?" Grant said.

I considered my answer before I spoke. The timeworn adage to never say more than you have to say had served me well in my stint in the corporate environment and seemed appropriate here.

"Grant, I took her to look for Edward once, and then a mutual friend took her to look again."

"You're looking for Edward?" Tamara said.

I nodded and Grant spoke up: "Well, I know that you haven't located him yet, but if you would continue looking, I'd appreciate it. I'm willing to pay you for your time. I know that Carolyn's your friend but private detectives don't work for free."

Sometimes my compromised hearing misleads me, and on many occasions, what I think I heard is not what was said. I must have appeared confused.

"Carolyn told me you were a private detective. Isn't that correct?"

I felt as though I were backed into a corner. If I disabused Grant's assertion, I'd have to explain more of Carolyn's visit, what had transpired that got her to visit, and maybe even what had happened after she arrived. I didn't want to do that. The sexual encounter with Carolyn was clearly intended to obligate me to her. Any disclosure would reveal that my letter to her had initiated the contact, that I was beholden in more ways than one, and more importantly, might jeopardize my inchoate relationship with Tamara.

"I will do whatever is required to satisfy my wife. Whatever," Grant said and looked me square in the eye. "Do you understand?"

"Yes, I do," I said, not clear on what his declaration actually entailed. For reasons I can't explain, I took Tamara's hand in mine.

Grant smiled, clapped his hands together and nodded in Tamara's direction.

"But you didn't find him?" Tamara said. "He wasn't there?"

"Very well. I'm off to meet Carolyn, then. I'll be in touch. Very nice to have met the both of you," Grant said and pointed toward the main house. "Lovely home," he added as he walked away. The driver was already holding open the limousine's rear door and as Grant entered, he waved to us. Stray stepped forward and wrinkled his nose at the hole in the air Grant left behind. He barked once, at that vacant hole, and then followed us up the entry drive.

"That was unexpected," I said. "Carolyn doesn't wear a ring."

Tamara nodded her head and we climbed the stairway to the apartment. I fed Stray while Tamara, expressionless and silent, sat on a stool and watched me. I refilled Stray's water bow and leaned against the refrigerator. Tamara took a long breath and placed her hands palms down on the counter.

"The thing that I haven't told you, mister private detective," she said and looked into my eyes with pleading intensity.

"Mechanic private detective," I joked.

"The thing is," Tamara said: "I know Edward. More than know. He's, he's…." She searched my face as if looking for a sign, something in my countenance that would provide a sense of trust. "He's Brenda's father."

Chapter Eighteen

Stray shoved his blunt Boxer nose against my shin, and then went and sat by the front door. Animals are direct. Unlike humans, there is no dissembling of motive. I stood up and grabbed Stray's leash from the back of the rocking chair. Unsure just how to respond to Tamara's comment, I thought, movement is my friend.

"Let's take a walk, OK? We can get something to eat at the Mercado by the park. How do you feel about Mexican food?"

Tamara stared at me for a few seconds, slapped her hands on her thighs and slid off the counter stool. I intended to revisit her statement, but Stray needed to go out and walking was one way to provide some clarity when what, in the moment, seemed complicated. Movement, simply putting one foot ahead of the other, freed my mind to put one thought ahead of the other until eventually the thought that I needed appeared. Usually, I'd find that the very solution I was seeking was there all the time; I just wasn't able to see it until I began moving.

"Sounds fine. Give me a minute."

While Tamara used the bathroom, I pocketed a few dog biscuits and hooked Stray's leash to his collar. He was aware of the dog biscuits, since a treat after his evening walk was his regular routine, and kept his eyes riveted on my back pocket. I sniffed beneath my collar and didn't notice any odor. The gamy funk, in check for the moment, had a history of coming on strong at the least appropriate time. Tamara stepped out of the bathroom as I grabbed my field jacket and we headed for the park.

"That is really wonderful. I love the tile."

We walked down the block, across the street and into Herrera Park. Stray alternately tugged on the leash with fierce determination and then abruptly stopped to mark bushes. In the park, the overhead lights were beginning to glow. At first, very dim and then gradually brighter until the pathway was fully lit. The park was closed after 10:00, at least that was when the lights shut down; driving past well after closing time I'd heard shouts and laughter that probably came from gang members determined to tag every surface from retaining walls to park benches. Most of the tagging looked crude and hurried, no more than scribbled gang identification left by a rushed pass of a spray can. Occasionally, some graffiti was artistic, utilizing stylistic fonts with drop shadowing and multiple colors, demonstrating a surprising understanding of foreshortening and perspective. County park crews would arrive and whitewash it all, providing a fresh canvas, and a few days later, the tagging returned. This had been recurring like clockwork for as long as I'd been a neighborhood resident. If those gang members were anything, they were persistent. Repurposing that artistic skill set toward some legal enterprise would find them middle class slaves like the rest of us, paying income taxes, social security, rent or mortgages, and complaining about taggers.

We walked the well-lit pathway along the perimeter of the park. Tamara stayed close to me and draped her arm through mine. I didn't realize that she had been saying anything until she let loose, moved behind me and resumed her position on my other side.

"I forget about your hearing."

Stray followed a scent off the main path so I let the leash play out.

"What were you saying?"

"I said that I was enjoying being with you."

"Me too, Tam. Me too."

She knocked her forehead against my shoulder with a smile. "You call me Tam, now?"

"Is that all right?"

"I told you it was."

"You did?"

She nodded her head and leaned into me.

"Do you think we have a chance?" I said.

She squeezed my arm and let out a pensive sigh.

"Time will tell."

Stray wouldn't come when I called so I followed the leash off the trail. He had his nose buried beneath a shrub and when I pulled him back, I spied an aluminum baseball bat. Too well hidden to have been forgotten after a ball game, more likely a gang member had considered its lethal potential and stashed it for the future. If it had been used in a crime, it would have disappeared someplace. It wasn't the only weapon I'd seen during our evening walks. I had a six-inch folding knife with a saw-tooth blade I'd found at the edge of the sidewalk. Probably it fell out of someone's pocket. I took it home and put it in the center console of the MG for no other reason than I didn't have any idea what else to do with it. The aluminum baseball bat was more than I wanted to explain at the moment, so I left it where it was and rejoined Tamara.

We walked through the park to the Mercado, sat at an outdoor table and ate dinner. Our conversation was light and cheerful, neither one of us returning to the topic of Edward. The air smelled of pine trees and the jagged Puente Hills to the east gradually disappeared in soft, lavender light. The light is unique in Los Angeles: ocean air settles in the basin and gets trapped beneath a blanket of warm air from the desert. The inversion layer creates atmosphere beneath it that is remarkably stable. Objects in the middle distance resolve in forced perspective. It is a condition unique to the area that attracted astronomers at the beginning of the 20th century followed by a wave of fine artists in the 60s. The astronomer's recognized the stability of the air but the fine artist's coined a name for it; they called it *'airlight'*.

Walking back to the apartment, Tamara brought up Brenda and said that she expected her for a visit weekend after next. We climbed the entry drive and she stopped at her car, hugged me and got behind the wheel. As she drove off, she waved her hand out the window. Nothing more had been said about Edward, nothing more about our relationship. Stray followed me inside the apartment and curled up against the front door. I washed up, stuffed some dirty clothes into my gym bag and sat down to read Chandler, but the relationship between Edward and Tamara kept running through my head. Whatever the nature, be it marriage, cohabitation or a one-night stand, it resulted in a child. Tamara hadn't indicated that there was any contact between them at present but I was certain that she knew a lot more than she'd disclosed. Tamara was an open book, but you needed to turn the pages. About 10:30, I switched off the light and got into bed. My cell phone displayed 12:03 when I woke to the chime.

"Carolyn?"

"You met Grant."

I switched on the table lamp. Stray lifted his head off his dog bed, alert and attentive, and cocked it with midnight curiosity. Any time of day or night, he was always ready for adventure.

"Yes, I did."

"What did you tell him?"

"About what?"

"About Edward. What did you say?"

"I didn't say anything about Edward. He said you asked me to locate him."

"And that is all?"

"Yes."

Carolyn was silent. A telephone rang in the background, and then a man's voice answered, *'Lobby.'*

"You owe Carolyn. You wrote it in your letter, remember?"

"That debt's been paid, Carolyn."

"No."

"Yes, it has."

The line was silent for a few seconds. In the background, voices were barely audible. Then Carolyn spoke.

"Carolyn let you inside her."

The background voices got louder and then receded. Listening with my good ear, I could hear Carolyn's raspy stridor over the line. I was a little slow to come up to speed, but there was no mistaking it. Her brief intimacy represented no more than behavior contrived to incur leverage. Behavior refined with practice and executed with perfection like the way she had manipulated Guy at the restaurant to comp the bill.

"You do not know him like I do. Find Edward."

"So that you can *Remove* him?"

"Find him."

I heard people laughing and the distinctive ping of an arriving elevator before the connection went dead. Stray was watching me with his good ear poised upright in that anxious expression dogs get when they expect you to say something.

"It's OK, Stray."

I switched off the table lamp. I wasn't sure just what Carolyn had told Grant. I didn't know any more or less about the relationship between Carolyn and Edward, or about the relationship between Tamara and Edward, or about Edward's relationship 30 years ago with Marce. There was too much to consider and not enough information. I did know one thing: my simple, apologetic missive had caught me up in something that was only going to get bigger before it went away.

Chapter Nineteen

Tom was taking inventory of all the special parts for the Alfa when I arrived at the shop. He'd laid each component across the empty garage bay, neatly arranging them in the order of assembly, starting with the suspension parts, brake parts, and finally a set of rare Italian alloy wheels. He was grinning from one side of his big, round face to the other as I walked into the garage.

"Beautiful stuff, huh? I've been hanging onto those wheels for 15 years and finally a car comes along that's worthy of 'em. By the way, your girlfriend called to thank us for the work you did on her Fiat."

"Girlfriend?"

"That's what she said. Complimentary, too. Another Big Magic satisfied customer."

"Good."

"Claims you're the best *'mechanic private detective'* that she knows," Tom said with a smile. "What are you doing, two-timing on me?"

I put my gym bag down. Tom let me do my laundry in the washing machine we used for shop clothes. I went to the machine and lifted the lid.

"It's a crazy thing, Tom. I've got myself into something."

I pulled work pants and three shirts from the washing machine, and clothes-pinned them to a line stretched above the utility sink. Tom watched me, still grinning, and nodded.

"Life gets interesting when you participate. It can be a new kind of addiction, for an addictive personality, when you stop avoiding it."

I dumped my clothes from home into the washing machine, spilled some detergent over them and started the wash cycle.

"Is that what I'm doing?"

"That's what you've been avoiding doing. Avoiding participation is just another manifestation of alcoholism. The booze is the crutch but the addiction is part of a personality type."

"I hadn't thought of it that way."

"I know. It gets easier after time."

I smiled and shook my head. Tom was one of the clearest thinking people that I knew and usually a reliable sounding board, but he could be irritating at times with his pop psychology assessments. It wasn't that he lacked the insight for the complexity of human behavior, it was that it mattered little to him in the final equation. His worldview was rooted in the empirical consequences of cause and effect. You turn up the heat on a pot of water, it boils; you drink regularly and enough, you're an alcoholic. You are what you do, no matter how many intricate rationalizations you concoct to clothe your actions. The glitch in his thinking was that past behavior doesn't necessarily predict future behavior. The only thing predictable about human behavior is its unpredictability. That's where empiricism and theory diverge. The mysteries of the world can be explained with science, but not the mysteries of the human heart.

"You want me to start installing those parts on the Alfa?" I said as I pulled clean shop pants and a shirt from the bottom drawer of the workbench.

Tom looked up from admiring his collection of car parts. His broad grin had morphed from beaming glee to thoughtful grimace.

"Not yet. I want Bill to see them first. Kind of hate to let 'em go, to tell you the truth."

"Is he coming in?"

"This morning. Don't do anything until he gets here, but take a couple of wheels off his car and put on the alloys for comparison. He wants the brakes, but I may still need to do some selling on the wheels."

"Are you sure you want to sell them?"

Tom chuckled under his breath and shook his head. He pressed the fat fingers of his thick hands together, and drummed the tips against each other.

"Well, I didn't hang on to 'em just for fun. The only question is what I'll take for 'em. Not sure, yet. Participating can be nerve-racking, huh?"

"I guess it can."

I went into the lavatory to change. When I came out, a convertible, British Racing Green, Aston Martin was parked in front of the garage. Everything on the car shined with newness. The paint, the chrome, the polished wheels, even the tires had that just-off-the-showroom-floor patina. I could almost smell the leather upholstery from inside the garage. It was absolutely perfect and my mottled British GT parked in the background seemed to shrink in shame as if humbled by its Emerald Isle brethren. A Newport Beach dealer placard filled the license plate frame. I could see Tom and a man talking in the office. The man kept switching his attention from Tom to the Aston Martin. This wasn't a sales pitch for new telephone service or bottled water. I was removing a wheel from the Alfa when both men entered the garage.

"You met Martin?" Tom said. "Martin, this is Bill."

Bill was in his 50s, average height, slim but wiry, age-lined around milky blue eyes, with a small, hard mouth, short, thinning blond hair, gold frame prescription eyeglasses, and sideburns with some gray hairs that hinted at a recent dye job. A guy with a little edge to him, maybe some hard living in his past, kind of rough once but cleaned up now and outfitted like a successful entrepreneur. He stood ramrod straight, more tough guy attitude than military posture, with a pointed chin that he thrust forward inviting confrontation. He had a friendly but guarded smile and a nose pushed cockeyed that indicated an unpleasant adjustment in the past. If 50 is the new 40, then at the new 40 you get the face you earned. Bill looked like he earned everything he got.

He wore light gray chino trousers, a shiny black sport shirt, black, tasseled loafers and a matching belt with matte silver clasp. I didn't take him for a company man, not with his attitude or in those clothes. He looked more like the independent broker type, something in finance, commercial mortgage, buying and selling; something lucrative enough to meet the monthly nut on a six-figure luxury convertible and the lifestyle its ownership reflected.

"No, but I've heard about you. Tom speaks highly of your expertise."

Bill stuck out his right hand without hesitation. I wiped mine on my pant leg before extending it to shake.

"Nice to meet you."

Bill smiled and a set of gleaming, bleached-white teeth filled his small, hard mouth. He squeezed my hand with conviction and held tightly as he looked straight into my eyes.

"I hear you're also a private detective," he said.

I looked at Tom. He was holding one of the alloy wheels upright against his knee.

"Here are those wheels I was talking about," Tom said. "Martin, put one on the car for Bill to see."

Bill stared at me. "I'll keep that in mind," he said.

"Special, very rare," Tom said.

"I may have a case for you," Bill said, continuing to squeeze my hand and stare into my eyes for another few seconds before letting go and turning to Tom.

"Had these a long time. Wasn't sure that I wanted to sell 'em until I saw your car. They're correct for it," Tom said, "*like a fully optioned Veloce!* Only set I've seen in 15 years."

"That must make them valuable."

"No, that's what makes the car *they're on* valuable," Tom said.

Bill laughed, low in his gut, and pointed a finger at Tom.

"You are a good salesman," he said.

Tom smiled his broad grin, showing most of his teeth, and snorted in agreement. Tom was pretty smooth and Bill recognized a pro when he met one.

"So what's it going to cost me?" Bill said.

"Well, you've seen the product, and can we agree that you're interested?"

Bill nodded his head, looked past me to the street and scanned the background. His eyes swept right to left, hesitating once on the Aston, before settling on Tom's face.

"How about we go into the office?" Tom said. "And talk?"

My cell phone chimed on the workbench. I stepped away and picked it up to view the caller but the number was private.

"Hello?"

Bill followed Tom into the office and closed the door behind him. I saw Tom take the seat behind his desk. Bill remained standing near the front door, obscured from outside view by the doorframe but able to see the entire lot from his vantage point. He looked at Tom, smiled and then looked out the window at his car and the street in front of the shop.

"Hello?"

"Mr. Gardens, this is Grant Parker. Do you remember me?"

"Yes, Mr. Parker, I do."

"Have you a minute to talk?"

I looked across the garage at Tom. He was extending his arms, pointing and gesturing toward the garage and nodding his head in some animated sales rubric no doubt intended to cement the deal.

"I have a minute," I said. "But how'd you get this number?"

"Carolyn. She's in custody. My attorney is handling the matter but we have need for your services. I've dispatched my car and driver to present a retainer. It should be at your home within the hour."

The door to the office opened and Tom and Bill emerged. Bill was chuckling under his breath and Tom had his broad grin pasted across his big, round face. Bill waved at me as he walked to his car.

"It's a done deal," Tom said. "Oops, on the phone. Sorry."

"I'm not sure what to say. She's in custody?"

"We can discuss the details later. I need to speak with my attorney, now. I'll call you, later."

"You've caught me off guard, Mr. Parker."

"I know that I have, but Carolyn requested your help," he said and paused. Tom was still grinning like he'd won the lottery. "By the way, she's being held for questioning in the death of her brother," Grant said and the connection went dead. I held my cell phone in my hand and stared at it. Carolyn's whispered declaration to '*Remove*' Edward sprang to mind. I'm sure that shock must have been evident on my face as I looked at Tom. His broad grin had disappeared and he had his head down, face contorted in personal conflict, open arms spread toward the floor of the garage as if embracing the scattered parts he had sold. He looked at me, clamped his hands together and squeezed them like wringing moisture from his palms. Tiny balls of perspiration clung to his temples.

"Oh how I love it when I make a sale," he said with little enthusiasm.

"Congratulations," I said. "I think."

Tom shook his head from side to side, shrugged his shoulders in a comic imitation of utter resignation, and the broad grin began to tug at the corners of his mouth.

"I'm giving you a new home. I'm setting you free!" he said as he swept his arms over the parts on the floor.

"Tom, I need to take off for an hour to meet a guy."

"Something wrong?"

"I just need an hour. Then I'll get to work."

"All right. You know the deadline. End of the week, remember? I'll do what I can to help out." Tom ran one hand across his face and rubbed at his eyes. "Meet a guy for what?"

I looked at my cell phone in my hand, contemplating how much to tell, or how much that I actually knew.

"I'm not clear on all the details, but I've been hired to do some detective work."

"Detective work, huh.... OK, but we can't miss the deadline."

"Understood, Tom."

"So don't let it interfere. This is important."

"I know."

"Branching out, then, I see," he said in a bad foreign accent, and arched his eyebrows and drummed his fingers together in a corny impersonation of a stereotypical movie villain. He adjusted his stance, spreading his legs and crossing his arms. The mixture of joy and anguish on his face was replaced with thoughtful concern. I'd seen this before. This was how he looked when he put on his AA sponsor's cap.

"Be careful, Martin," he said.

I grabbed my car keys and wallet from the top drawer of the toolbox. As I picked up my cell phone, it chimed in my hand. I checked the caller ID, saw it was Marce, and let the call go to voicemail.

"I will, Tom. I'll see you in an hour," I said and walked out the garage to the MG. My cell phone chimed again: Marce always called more than once. She'd call the apartment next. Her importunate nature was not one of her most attractive qualities. If she had more to tell me about Carolyn, I'd hear it when we met later. There was a lot I still didn't know, beginning with why Grant would allow Carolyn to dictate that he hire someone he didn't know for something he couldn't be sure he needed. Once again, it reminded me of the lengths people go to, to please others. It seemed that he was as much under Carolyn's spell as I had been. We were each beholden to her at some level. The only difference between us was that she was his wife.

Chapter Twenty

Shit happens. That's what everyone says. What began as a self-serving declaration of remorse had become a shit storm of shifting alliances, hidden motives, and alleged felony. All I wanted to do was set right a wrong, maybe unnecessary after so long, but another step toward changing a pattern that had me at loose ends, unsure of which direction to turn and what came next. But that is life. Shit happens whether you're ready for it or not. I'd been a mid-level corporate manager, fiancé, drunk, arsonist at large, automobile mechanic, and now in the most unlikely turn of events, private detective. I didn't need termination to motivate me, rejection to instill self-reflection, or a liquor crutch for support. I needed something to go my way.

Stray lifted his head from his post at the bottom of the entry drive with a quizzical expression in his eyes. He seemed happy to see me, wagging his stubby tail, but the interruption in his daily routine was apparent by the way he stared. Dogs have an innate sense of routine, and anytime it varies, they take notice. It is not so very different for humans: Disruption in one's personal routine can be upsetting. My current predicament could attest to that.

Normally, when I got home in the evening, I'd feed Stray, and then we'd take our walk through the park, past the Mercado, and back to the apartment. He followed me up the entry drive, the stairway, and into the kitchen, his eyes flicking from me to his food bowl and then to the Old Bushmills bottle on the counter. Something in our routine was different. I picked up the Irish whiskey from where it had sat, undisturbed, for two nights. Stray crouched and pinned back his good ear as if he were fearful of what would happen next. I held the bottle at arm's length. Sunlight from the picture windows refracted in the beautiful, amber liquid. 750 milliliters of release, right there, in my hand; 750 milliliters of euphoric, intoxicating incoherence just a screw top away. I turned the bottle this way and that, watching the rays of light bend around the edges. Stray let out a single warning bark. Approaching seven months sober and that had to be worth something. Tom was right; I had an addictive personality. I put the bottle in the cupboard where it was out of sight and tossed a rawhide bone to Stray. No doubt insufficient reward for prescient intervention.

The light on the answering machine was blinking. As I reached for the Play button, there was a knock on the front door. Visible through the glass was the driver that had been with Grant. Beyond him, parked at the bottom of the entry drive, was the black limousine. Stray stood at attention, clutching his bone in his mouth, and watched as I opened the front door.

"Mr. Gardens?"

"Yes."

"I have a package for you from Mr. Parker."

The man handed me a full-sized manila envelope. I took the envelope as he stepped back.

"I tried the house but no one answered."

Before I could respond he pointed to the envelope.

"If you would, please," he said.

I opened the envelope. A business card for Grant Parker, CEO, of Solate Pharmaceuticals, Inc., was inside. Next, was what looked like a pre-printed form letter that could have been used for anything, but $2500 dollars as *"retainer for personal services,"* hand written in large, blue characters, jumped off the page. At the bottom of the envelope sat a rubber-banded bundle of $100 dollar bills and a cell phone. I scanned the form letter looking for some sort of defined job requirement; no specific duties were listed. The entire letter was boilerplate. In the bottom corner was an item number and an address for a forms company. The line where the recipient's name should be was blank. When I looked up, the man was extending a pen to me.

"I sign and that's it?"

The man nodded his head. I signed and handed both back.

"Now what?"

The man folded the letter and put it inside his jacket.

"Mr. Parker will be in contact," he said and clipped the pen to his shirt pocket. Then he descended the stairway, walked down the entry drive to the black limousine and drove away.

"Well, I guess that makes it official, huh?"

Stray sat next to me, rawhide bone in his mouth, staring out the front door.

"My services have been hired. I've accepted a retainer. That means I'm a professional, right? A professional *what* is the question."

I closed the front door and Stray followed me into the kitchen. On the answering machine was a message from Marce, telling me that the police had questioned her. The next message was from a Detective Marsons, of the LAPD, requesting that I return his call. He left a number and I jotted it down on the front of the manila envelope. The final message was a sales pitch from a mold remediation company that promised to rid my home of mold in one single visit. At the moment, mold remediation was the least of my worries.

I grabbed the new cell phone and out we went. I gave Stray a *Stay* command. He watched me climb into the car from the stairway landing, confusion in his face from the disruption of his routine, but content to hunker down and chew on his bone. On the drive to Big Magic, I called Marce. She was on her way into a department meeting, but agreed to meet me after work at a burger joint near the entrance to the Los Angeles River. I needed to start at the beginning. I'd already seen the homeless camp behind the Police station; Marce could show me the location of the river camp.

I could not assume that Carolyn was connected to Edward's death. I could not assume anything. Detective work was a lot like diagnosing a problem on a car. Assume nothing, proceed in a logical fashion, one step at a time, following each symptom like potential leads until all possibilities have been eliminated and what ever remains is the solution. The first lesson I learned diagnosing cars was to forget what the client tells you; their assessment is almost always incorrect and trusting it is guaranteed to lead you down the wrong path. What the client notices is not indicative of what is wrong but simply a manifestation of the root cause. Begin at the beginning, regardless of the client's explanation; people fit what they think they know into what they actually know, and it skews their reality. You have to go back, way back, to find the source of the problem. I revisited this fundamental lesson, in work as well as life, over and over.

All I did know was that Edward was dead, Carolyn was in custody, and that Grant Parker had hired me on Carolyn's request. The scope of the investigation was unclear but without a doubt it had to do with exonerating Carolyn. I drove across town, turning over in my mind possible scenarios, and parked in front of the empty bay at Big Magic. Tom came out of the front office and pointed to a gray, Police Interceptor across the street in front of the coffee shop, and my stomach dropped to the floor. This was it; just what I'd feared would happen. You can move forward but you can't escape your past; you can't set someone's house on fire without suffering the consequences. Insurance companies don't pay out total loss claims without due diligence. They hire specialists, forensic investigators to determine the cause, assign responsibility, and mitigate financial damage to the coverage provider. Then they call the cops.

The driver's door opened and a man emerged. He was skinny, almost emaciated, and tall, wearing a white, long sleeved shirt with maroon knit tie, dark slacks and luminescent silver running shoes. When he walked it was like watching an ambulatory skeleton: Arms and legs moved in what would be a normal stride on anyone else, but on him they looked like bare bones punching inside out at his clothing in rhythmic blows that demarked the presence of knees, hips, shoulders, and elbows. He was about six-six, which made him look all the more like an animated stick figure, mid thirties in age, with a triangular, pointed chin, and a mustache groomed in a pencil thin line centered equidistance between the top of his lip and bottom of his narrow nose. He had a spiked mat of dark hair, plastic coffee stirrer in his mouth, and he wore a pair of oversized, aviator sunglasses that dwarfed his long face.

"Mr. Gardens, I'm Detective Marsons," he said in a high pitch, feminine voice that cut through the street noises.

"Hello."

"I have a few questions to ask you."

I looked at Tom standing in the front doorway of the office with his arms crossed over his stomach. His big, round face was blank, no broad grin or thoughtful grimace, no expression at all in his eyes. But I knew what he was thinking: once a drunk always a drunk. I'd done something and it was time to pay for my crime. Little did he know the extent of my transgression.

"I'm on the job, right now."

"This will only take a minute."

"All right. Follow me," I said and walked inside the garage bay. My heart was pounding, my stomach was in my throat, and my chest had begun to constrict so that my breathing was rapid and shallow.

"Do you know a Carolyn Parker?"

It took considerable effort not to smile. Relief pushed my stomach back where it belonged, and I'm certain that the detective must have heard me take a deep breath. I was off the hook, for now.

"I do."

"How?"

I hesitated and tried to focus on the coffee stirrer hanging from the corner of the detective's mouth while I composed my answer.

"She's an old high school friend of mine," I said, electing to leave out anything that hadn't been asked.

"You know that she's been taken into custody, right? Your friend must have called and told you that?"

Detective Marsons pulled his sunglasses from his face. Light blue eyes bulged from their sockets like someone with acute hyperthyroidism.

"What friend?"

He laughed, fingered his sunglasses and looked me in the eye.

"Let's make it easy, huh? Let's start out knowing that I know of your involvement with Carolyn Parker; I know that the three of you, a …," he removed a spiral bound notebook from his back pocket and flipped the cover open, "… Maria Estrada, you, and Carolyn Parker had dinner Sunday night where she said she was in Los Angeles to 'Remove' her brother. That much we both know, agreed?"

I watched him flip the page in his notebook before looking up at me.

"Her brother was found dead yesterday at a homeless camp. Would you know anything about that?"

"No."

"When was the last time you saw Carolyn Parker?"

"At dinner. She left with Marce."

"Marce?"

"Maria Estrada."

Detective Marsons wrote something in his notebook. He reached with long, bony fingers and ragged, chewed nails to his mouth and removed the coffee stirrer, inverted it, and put it back.

"Did she say anything else?"

He held his pen on the notebook page as if poised to make another entry, looked up, and waited for me to answer. I was on a slippery slope, unsure how much to say, uncertain of just how much was really known. Clearly Marce had spilled her guts to the detective, but how much she had spilled was the question.

"Mr. Gardens? Anything you can add?"

I chose my words carefully. "Not that I can recall."

"And that was the last time you saw Mrs. Parker?"

"I dropped her things off Monday night at Marce's."

The detective flipped the notebook closed and put it in his back pocket. I looked past him and Tom was standing in the doorway between the garage and the office.

"Then that's all for now," the detective said. "Unless there's something else you just *'Recalled'*."

He watched me as he spoke and it felt like he was waiting for me to say the wrong thing. Never say more than you have to say, and if you have to say something, never say all of it. I kept that in mind as I shook my head.

"All right, Mr. Gardens. I'll be in contact."

He handed me a business card, walked back to the Police Interceptor, climbed behind the wheel, and drove off with rear tire's squealing. Tom joined me in the garage bay and we watched the sedan race up the block as if it were responding to an emergency.

"Those guys always have to speed off like they're in a big hurry," he said. "They can be real assholes."

We stood motionless for a few seconds as if transfixed by the detective's departure. I figured that Tom's comment was his way of saying we were on the same team.

"Anything I need to know about?"

I shrugged my shoulders. "More of that earlier stuff."

"You in trouble?"

I wasn't sure how to answer that question, so I just shook my head. Tom reached up one arm to the lift and rested his thick hand on the rocker panel of the Alfa. That familiar AA sponsor look of suspicious concern was on his big, round face.

"You know if you need it, I can still help, bring some heat, show some muscle. I may have grown old and fat, but I haven't lost a step."

Tom was big enough to look imposing. Just by standing up straight and crossing his massive arms he could seem threatening, but in reality, he was more teddy bear than grizzly bear. I knew that he meant what he said, and if I asked, he'd do all that he could to deliver on his boast.

"Remember what I did to Cal. I still got it," he said and assumed a linebacker's squat with both fists clenched, fierce grimace, and throaty growl.

Tom, in a legendary defensive play against Cal High, was renowned for delivering a game changing hit during the playoffs. At the precise snap of the ball in a crucial third down series, Tom exploded off the line of scrimmage and hit the offensive guard so low and with such force that he lifted him off his feet and into the air. Tom carried the guard clear of the ground, balanced on his helmet, into the backfield at a dead run, colliding with the quarterback to halfback exchange, creating a fumble that ultimately resulted in a field goal to capture the division championship. The local sports writer covering the playoffs wrote that when the team needed some 'big magic to turn around this big game', Tom provided it. 'Big Magic' became Tom's nickname and followed him through high school. It was Tom's defining moment and he'd never forgotten it.

"I appreciate that, Tom, but it's not like that."

"Then maybe you should come back to some meetings."

I looked up in surprise. "I'm not drinking."

"But you want to?"

I looked at my feet, the brake parts on the empty bay floor, anywhere but at Tom. He had a way of cutting to the truth of a matter that was surprisingly uncanny and always irritating. He crossed his thick arms over his fat stomach and waited.

"Still sober," I said and looked him in the eye. "I'm hanging on, Tom. Thanks."

Tom stared at me as if he expected more. I bent down to examine the brake parts. Tom continued to watch me. After almost half-a-silent-minute, he turned and took a few steps toward the office.

"We've got this job to finish, right?" he said over his shoulder.

"Right."

"This week, right?"

"This week."

"Fine. I'll leave you to it. Let me know if you need any help."

He walked into the office and sat down behind the desk. What he was thinking I've no idea, but he was certainly thinking something. Tom's nobody's fool and he probably had some ideas about what was happening. Some ideas about my tenuous sobriety, although how he could sense any weakness was beyond me, and some ideas about the visit from Detective Marsons. But he couldn't know anything about the house fire and arson. I hoped that bit of information was unknown to everyone but me. Tom was the type inclined to give you plenty of rope to hang yourself, but he'd never forego our friendship. I knew that I could count on his allegiance if I needed support to stay sober, on track or, worse case scenario, bail money.

Detective Marsons' visit had raised fears about past events, and along with those fears, some paranoia. Not knowing if my cell phone were monitored, I decided that there was no immediate reason to call Marce. We were meeting later, after work, at a burger joint near the Los Angeles River, where we could talk in private. I'd have more information after I spoke to Grant, as well. There was nothing I could do at this point except finish my workday. The immediate task was on the lift above my head. I tucked a shop rag into my pants pocket and got to it.

Chapter Twenty-one

I do my clearest thinking by misdirection. Even before the alcoholic dementia, when focused on some task, unrelated thoughts would rise through the murky water to surface with clarity. Whether it's walking with Stray or engaging my full attention working with my hands, physical movement guides me forward. Working on the Alfa was no exception. The rest of the day, as I removed suspension and brake components, small pieces in the puzzle found relationships to the whole. First, how did the Police get to Marce and Carolyn? Someone must have given the Police their names. The only person who knew Marce was Edward, and he was the victim, but John the Baptist had heard him repeat her full name. Second, Detective Marsons must have interviewed them, and who else? Did he know about Guy? Did he know about Carolyn's trip to the river camp with Marce, and whatever Guy did with Carolyn after they left together? Third, Marce, at the minimum, must have told the Police what Carolyn had said, unless Carolyn revealed what she had said and I suspected that she was too intelligent to let that detail slip through her lips. Somehow there was enough suspicion, if not actual evidence, after questioning Marce and Carolyn and who knows who else, to hold Carolyn. If there were any evidence, Grant had not mentioned it and by this time Carolyn would have been charged. Unless something had changed, the fact remained that Carolyn was being held only for questioning.

At dinner, Carolyn had said that she came back to *'Remove'* Edward. That was just a statement and not evidence that she had committed a crime. People say many things that they never do; people make threats that they never fulfill. Detective Marsons either knew more than I knew or he was on a fishing expedition. I had to proceed without prejudice and unlike my shop clients, not skew reality by fitting what I thought I knew into what I actually knew. Edward could have been murdered by any one of the vagrants inhabiting his small universe. Jealousy, spite, envy, or something as simple as coveting warm clothes were possible motivations. When you have little of your own, even a jacket on a cold fall night can inspire a homicidal act.

Now that my professional services were retained, an ethical question was raised: If I found evidence of Carolyn's involvement in Edward's death, evidence not found by the Police, was I to report it only to Grant? The client and detective relationship was something I knew nothing about, but I knew that withholding information could put me in a position for prosecution. It was up to the Police, and ultimately, a trial by jury, to determine culpability. But if you have information that could be used to convict a person, and you withhold that information from proper authorities, are you any better than the perpetrator? Are you a conspirator or just another collateral casualty swept up in the commission of the crime? Aren't you just as guilty?

Tom went out just after 11:30 to pick up lunch. When he returned with burgers and fries, we sat in the office and ate, making small talk, never touching on Detective Marsons' visit or my involvement in the matter. Tom is pretty good about keeping his nose out of other people's business, and he seemed respectful of my reluctance to discuss my personal life, but he was curious. His involvement as a sponsor with AA had made him a pretty good judge of behavior and he knew when to listen and when to speak up.

"Tom, what drives someone to murder?"

Tom put down a massive plastic tumbler of soda and wiped his mouth.

"Anger and rage, revenge. You want to get back at someone who hurt you or ruined your life. Or protection: someone knows something that could harm your family. Passion. That's a common one. Drugs and money, of course. This have to do with the detective's visit?"

I nodded my head. "It does."

"Someone you know?"

I nodded my head again.

"You involved?"

"It's my first case."

"As a detective?"

"Yup."

Tom gave me a smart-ass grin. Chunks of hamburger stuck between his teeth made him look like a gum diseased, Halloween jack-o-lantern. I smiled back, crumpled my wrapping into a ball and tossed it at him. He head butted the wrapping toward the trashcan in the corner. It missed.

"Detective Gardens," he said, still grinning. "I'm going to enjoy watching this."

The rest of the day was spent working. No new revelations came to mind. I just keep turning over what I already knew and what I didn't. A little after 5:00, I quit for the day, washed up and changed my clothes. Tom was in his office, on the phone, and surfing the Internet. If he had any addiction now, 20 years after he quit drinking, it was buying and selling. He had branched out from auto parts and lately developed an interest in historic muskets and flintlock pistols. I could already see that antique firearms were going to be his next obsession. I waved at him as I walked to the MG and he waved back. During my day, even though nothing new came to mind about Carolyn's case, I did come to a sober and brutally personal realization. The time for dreaming was past: I was a recovering alcoholic devoid of any career path, a clandestine arsonist, and living month to month in a rented apartment with a stray dog. Edward's case and the $2500 dollar retainer might be my only chance to start over. I couldn't afford to screw up. The last stop express was leaving the station and I better not miss it. What Tom called participation was just another word for nothing left to lose.

Chapter Twenty-two

Stray was waiting at his post at the bottom of the entry drive. There was no confusion on his face this time; he knew that he would be fed, walked and given his nightly treat. What he didn't know was that tonight he was also going for a ride. Tonight we were detecting.

After feeding Stray, changing my clothes, and a quick loop around the park, we loaded up the MG and headed across town. I had agreed to meet Marce at a burger joint near the entrance to the Los Angeles River trail. I had a flashlight in the car and the six-inch folding knife as the only provisions for investigation. I was new at this and had no idea what I was supposed to carry. I didn't own a gun, and didn't think that I needed one, but my knowledge of what the well-equipped private detective needed was between zero and none. In fact my actual experience was zero, unless you counted an adolescent addiction to James Bond movies that ended when Sean became Roger. The total extent of any on-the-job-training, beyond the Bond movies, was happening right now. I wore my gym shoes, a pair of jeans and, for no other reason than it seemed appropriate, the black field jacket. It made me feel like one of those edgy types, unpredictable and mysterious, someone who worked the undefined median between the intent of the law and the letter of the law.

I parked at Tempest Burgers and Grill next to their dining patio. The lot was about a quarter full. There were a few customers coming and going, and one guy who looked homeless smoking a cigarette and squatting on his haunches between a row of newspaper racks and the restaurant bathroom. Although the neighborhood wasn't very upscale, surrounding businesses seemed to be well kept without much graffiti or trash. A gas station on the corner was doing steady, mid-week business and directly across the street, in the lot of a Super King grocery store, an unarmed security guard stood sentry near the entrance. At least his uniformed presence provided the illusion of security.

Marce arrived a few minutes later and parked next to a light green Dodge from the 70's. Flaking paint, some rust, and a broken taillight. My ride wasn't the only vintage iron in this hood. Marce stayed in her SUV as I approached.

"We can go in my car," she said.

"Go where?"

"There's a closer place."

"What about Stray?"

She looked around as if she were worried about being seen. It may have been the location, anxiety or just her ADD personality, but her brows were scrunched together and she squinted her eyes as if she were in pain when she talked. Even her voice seemed strained. A few strands of hair had slipped from a black ribbon headband and fallen across her forehead into her eyes. She blew at them, then swiped at her forehead and cursed when they fell back in place.

"Fine. Let's go. But he stays in back!" she snapped and slapped the steering wheel.

I loaded Stray into the back seat and climbed into the front. Stray immediately stepped onto the center console to take his usual position. Marce reached over and pushed at him.

"I said in the back!"

"Stray, back. Back!"

Stray stared at me and backpedaled onto the rear seat. I could see his confused expression in the rear view mirror.

"It's OK," I said. "Down."

Stray turned once in a circle and dropped to his stomach. I snapped on the seat belt as Marce put the SUV into reverse. The MG looked as if it would be safe where it was. The patio lights provided some illumination and there were other cars nearby parked against a chain link fence at the edge of the property. There was nothing in the car of value, not even a radio, and the upside of stealing it to part out was almost nonexistent. But as my only means of transportation, I was circumspect wherever I parked. My greatest worry was vandalism, a worry that I tried to alleviate by never locking the doors. I'd rather someone simply open the door to find nothing inside worth stealing, than break a window to learn the same.

As soon as we began to move, Marce started talking at warp speed. The level of hysterical energy in the cab was enough to force me against the passenger door. I looked back at Stray and he had his good ear pinned flat against his head.

"I didn't know what to say Martin he came to my office how did he know where I worked he was looking for Carolyn so told him I didn't know what to say I didn't know…."

The SUV bounced out of the parking lot heading west. I reached over and put my hand on Marce's shoulder and squeezed it.

"Easy, Marce, easy. Slow down."

Marce continued to accelerate so I squeezed harder.

"Marce? MARCE!"

She lifted her foot from the gas pedal and we slowed. I loosened my grip on her shoulder and kneaded the muscle.

"Good, OK. Just slow down. Take a deep breath, all right?"

Marce seemed to shrink. Her back relaxed against the seat and her hands positioned themselves lower on the steering wheel. All at once she seemed smaller as she slumped forward so that her head drooped.

"Good, good. Where are we going?"

The SUV slowed more and cars began swerving past on either side. A horn sounded behind us. Marce was looking straight ahead, face ashen and poised to crack, and tears were forming in her eyes. She was headed for a meltdown.

"Marce, see that gas station? Right there?" I said and pointed to the corner of the block. "Pull in."

She turned into the gas station and stopped in the middle of the driveway.

"Park by the restrooms over there."

She drove to the restrooms on the side of the station and stopped. I reached over and put the car in Park and she collapsed into a heap. Tears ran down her face and her shoulders began to shake. I got out, walked around, and opened her door. She fell into me from the driver's seat like a rag doll. Her nose pressed against my chest and she sobbed for a long time. Stray was standing on the center console, a much larger center console than the one in the MG, and stretching his head around the side bolster to watch. I reached for the ignition switch, twisted, and removed it to stop the ringing. Marce snorted and wiped at her eyes with her hand. In the door pocket, I found a handful of paper napkins and held them to her face. She patted her eyes and sighed a deep breath that seemed to signal the end.

"All right, that's better. You OK?"

She nodded her head, blew her nose and straightened her sweater. She looked like she was dressed to attend Catholic girl's school. Her hair was pulled back with the black ribbon headband and she was wearing what must have been her office clothes; a tartan plaid knee-length skirt, white hose, Mary Janes, and a salmon pink v-neck sweater. She leaned into me and put her arms around my back.

"I didn't know what to say…."

I held her until she pushed away and looked me over.

"What's with the get-up?"

I spread open the front of the field jacket to show it off. "It's the new me," I said and pulled the flashlight from the inside pocket. "*Private Detective Gardens*. Maybe?"

Marce almost smiled.

"What happened to the old you?"

"The old me is long gone, baby. There's a new me in town."

Marce sniffled again and shuddered as if cold. I looked past her to the back seat, opened the rear door and grabbed her jacket. Stray stuck his head out the door as I helped her into it.

"There you go," I said.

"You're a private detective, huh?"

I nodded my head. "Retained by Grant Parker."

"Grant Parker?"

"Carolyn's husband."

"Carolyn is married?"

"She is," I said.

"Retained for what?"

I wasn't sure just what Marce knew, but I did know that Marce had some past connection to Edward, and since she hadn't mentioned that he was dead, I chose to obfuscate.

"Track down Edward, for Carolyn."

"She left with Guy, from the restaurant."

"All right."

"She never said she was married."

"It was news to me as well."

I led Marce around the SUV and put her in the passenger side. I got behind the wheel and started the motor.

"I never let anyone drive my car."

"What?" I said and pushed my bad ear closer to the center console as if this time I hadn't heard her.

"Nothing."

I adjusted the driver's seat using finger controls mounted on the armrest, and then positioned the mirrors so that I had a clear, rearward view.

The engine speed dropped to an idle and it was so quiet that without looking at the tachometer, I couldn't tell that the engine was running. Outside, it was dark but inside the car interior lights lit the passenger compartment like a jet cockpit. When I began to pull forward, a flat LCD panel displayed our exact position on a backlit street map. This was a vehicle light years away from mine.

"Where to?"

Marce pointed west.

"A little bit farther along this street. There's a cleaners on the corner where we turn."

"Louder," I said.

Marce leaned across the console, kissed me on the cheek, sat back in her seat and flicked her fingers in the direction to go with just a little less impatience than usual. I exited the gas station and pulled into traffic. The SUV accelerated smoothly. Almost no road noise entered the cabin. When Stray stepped forward on the center console, Marce began to object and then stopped short. Stray stuck his stubby nose as far forward as he could and assumed his usual position wedging his shoulder against the passenger seat so that his head was against Marce's head rest. I thought I saw a hint of a smile. We drove in silence for a few miles, stopping and waiting at traffic signals, climbing a low sloping grade through a commercial area on our right. On the left was a steep, barren hillside held in place with stylized, concrete retaining walls. Above them, homes perched on slender columns seemed to hang in space. After half a mile, the street narrowed to one lane each direction. The perching homes went away and multi-story apartment buildings lined both sides of the street.

About a block ahead was the cleaners. I turned right, driving past a Mexican restaurant and a boarded up storefront into a residential area of single-story homes built after the Second World War. There were bars on the windows, front doors with security screens, and chain-link fences enclosing grassless front yards filled with dogs. Stray pressed his nose to the side window watching the assortment of gamboling mutts. They raced back and forth, snapping at their yard mates in manic competition to be the first to reach the other end of their barren confine. I maneuvered past overflowing trashcans of cardboard and Styrofoam packaging that spread like a river delta of consumer consumption. A derelict couch and broke back easy chair occupied a strip of dead, brown grass between curb and sidewalk. A pile of discarded, plastic children's yard toys were stacked alongside. Not a single house had a landscape beyond a handful of dying plants in long neglected planters. Not a single house did not need a coat of paint, or gutters, or window screens, or even a new roof. The average income level looked minimum wage but in each driveway was a shining, late model vehicle. A full-size pickup that sported mud flap women bearing anatomically improbable breasts was parked across the sidewalk blocking pedestrian passage. On each side of the rear window were silhouettes of high-heeled females with angel's wings, serpentine tails and devil's tridents. It rode on huge wheels and sat so high off the ground that access to the cab must have required a step stool. This was once a post war community populated by the same hard working men who had graded the lots, poured the foundations, framed and roofed and finished the family houses that lined each side of the street. A different citizenry populated these homes now; working class as well but less focused on pride of ownership. The decrepit condition of the properties demonstrated that the new cultural ideal began and ended with shiny, late model vehicles and conspicuous consumption.

I stopped at the end of the block and shut off the motor. In front of us there was a small park with two metal benches, a few immature shade trees, and one green trashcan chained to a steel post. A sign stating "Rattlesnake Park" etched on a plank of wood identified a postage stamp of dry grass. Beyond it, the river trail was visible. We got out of the car and Stray began to bark. He ran barking from one side of the rear seat to the other like something was very, very wrong. Marce squinted her dark brown eyes toward me with annoyance etched across her forehead.

"What's wrong with him?"

"I'm not sure. Probably needs to get out of the car," I said as I realized that his leash was in the MG. Marce narrowed her eyes into a reproving glare as Stray scraped his paws against the side glass.

"Get him out of my car. Now!"

A quick look in the cargo bay revealed nothing more than a small gym bag and a pair of clear plastic, platform stilettos. Stray jumped over the rear seat and watched.

"You have a strap for this bag?"

Marce shook her head. I picked up the stiletto and held it in the glow of the interior light.

"Doing a little dancing to make ends meet?"

Marce grabbed the stiletto from me and flung it into the corner.

"I told you, it's a class."

I removed my belt, looped it through Stray's collar, and he jumped out. We walked through "Rattlesnake Park," pausing for Stray to sniff the grass and mark the signpost, and then to the river trail. The park was vacant, as was the river trail, and to the northeast the full moon had broken free of the mountain ridge. Marce pointed to the right and we walked a few hundred feet and stopped at a pipe railing above the edge of the embankment. Stray slunk low in a predatory crouch and growled. We were alone on the river trail with only the distant hum of freeway traffic and a constant, mellifluous tinkle. Below us, the Los Angeles River collected the moon's white light in ripples of slow moving water.

The Los Angeles River, actually a concrete channel, varies in width as it drains the vast San Fernando Valley, Santa Susana Mountains and San Gabriel Valley. Here it must have been 150 feet across. Almost from bank to bank, a low island overgrown with volunteer oaks, cottonwoods and weeping willows, clutches of giant reeds and wild grasses, and dense shrubbery more than head high filled the channel. A collection of mismatched, patio chairs was arranged beneath a willow at the river camp. Around the island, a trickle of water dribbled past. Upstream, one of those miniature, painted lawn jockeys sat atop a rusted barrel, surrounded by half-a-dozen buck naked baby dolls with beckoning arms extending skyward. Downstream of the island, where the river was a wide tabletop of concrete, a slow moving slick of water spread across the channel in a shifting sheen of moonlight. There must have been a hundred cairns spanning the channel, each one purposefully placed forming dual, spiraling rows that looked like a double helix. On each cairn, various kinds of reflective materials caught the moonlight; pieces of broken glass, mirror shards, scraps of stainless steel, almost anything that might reflect light. At the end, on an overturned shopping cart, sat a dented, Victorian gazing ball.

"Why are we here?"

I was uncertain just how much Marce knew and certain that I didn't want to dump any more than necessary in her lap.

"Detecting."

"Oh," Marce said. "The detective stuff."

I nodded.

"Where are all the birds?"

"Birds?"

"When we came here yesterday, there were birds."

"Yesterday? You came here yesterday?"

"I mean Monday, not yesterday. Today's Wednesday, right?"

"This is Wednesday."

"Then Monday. After work. When I showed Carolyn the camp."

"Is that the camp over there?" I pointed to the chairs. Marce squinted and then put her hand across her brow like she was shielding her eyes from the sun.

"I can't see it too well. It was covered, with a blanket or something. It's by those trees."

We walked farther along the river trail and then descended the sloping, concrete embankment. The moon had moved higher in the night sky and was casting more light. Stray stood next to me, good ear racked upward on his head, staring into the distance. He barked and lurched forward against my belt just as a figure darted past the chairs.

"Someone's there," I said. Stray lurched again and I jerked him back on his hunches. He turned and looked at me, then back to where the figure had been, and growled. I pulled the flashlight from my jacket and aimed in the direction of the movement. Someone was definitely hiding in the trees. An arm wearing a dark brown, corduroy coat swept through the beam as a man bolted.

"That looked like Edward's coat."

Stray lurched once more and the belt slid through my fist. I grabbed for the end but he was already out of reach, clearing the water, gaining speed as he ate up the distance to the fleeing figure. Marce grabbed my arm and we splashed through the water to follow. I yelled for Stray as we ran and tried to keep the flashlight beam focused on his progress. He turned with a skid, knocking over one of the chairs, and disappeared into the trees. I let go of Marce and pumped my arms and legs in an all out sprint for the next ten yards. The flashlight caught something moving deep in the trees to my left, so without thinking I charged after it into the underbrush. Branches slapped at my face, my legs, and something stuck me in the thigh and spun me around. About fifteen yards into the foliage I came to an open bower. Marce called out and I answered, telling her to stay where she was. I listened for any noise but there was nothing other than the murmur of trickling water. I called for Stray, listened again, and waited. Marce yelled once more so I retraced my steps to the river camp.

"Did you see him?"

"No. He got away."

"Where's Stray?"

"I don't know."

"What are you going to do?"

"Good question," I said and shined the flashlight on her. She was a mess. Her off-white hose were splattered with water; her Mary Janes caked with mud. The jacket hung open and a vertical line of spots dotted her v-neck sweater. She looked at herself in the flashlight beam and smiled. Then she giggled and I began to laugh with her. She slapped at my arm and then hugged me. I could feel her petite body through the office clothes; the small breasts against my chest, ribs in my belly, her groin where she pressed it snug. Her warm breath on my neck and the aroma of strawberry shampoo caused my mind to wander but the image that filled my head wasn't Marce and the aroma of strawberry shampoo couldn't displace the memory of patchouli.

"I'm filthy," she said.

"And a little soiled, too."

She laughed, pulled away, and sat down in one of the patio chairs.

"What do we do now?"

I dragged a chair up next to her. The full moon was well clear of the ridge and it was almost light enough in the river camp to read a newspaper. I smacked my gym shoes together and mud dropped to the ground. My jeans were splattered with mud as well, and on the back of my left thigh was a diagonal tear in the fabric. I shined the flashlight on the spot. A gash three inches long was weeping blood. Marce gasped and bent closer.

"Does it hurt?"

I raised my leg off the seat and poked at the wound with a finger.

"Not really."

Marce pushed at the torn fabric around the opening.

"You need to go to emergency," she said. "That could be worse than it looks."

The edges of the gash were jagged and beginning to swell but the wound didn't look deep. It was on the rear of my upper thigh, just below my butt, and difficult for me to see well.

"Take them off," she said.

"What?"

"I can't see it with your pants on. Just drop them," she said and motioned for me to remove my pants.

"Yes Maam."

I unbuttoned and shoved the jeans to my knees. Marce took the flashlight and pushed at the wound with a finger.

"That hurt?"

I shook my head.

"It's not very deep, but it could get infected. It should be looked at."

"I can't leave, Marce. When Stray comes back, I have to be here."

"Right," she said. "You and your roommate."

"I'm all he's got and he's all I've got. He's my only family, Marce."

Marce stared at me and I could feel the mood shifting. Her eyes began to shine with tears in the moonlight, her face about to crack again, and she sniffled as we stood alone on the island, two single adults, without offspring, without families. In that comment, I'd reminded her of her childlessness.

Together we had that much in common. Neither of us had created the next generation; neither of us had left someone to inherit our legacy. She took a deep breath, wiped an arm across her eyes and cleared her throat before she spoke.

"There's a first aid kit in my car. I can patch you up for now."

Marce had regained control. She stood up and took my arm with authority. She may not have been a mother, but whatever maternal instinct she possessed had come to the fore and left tearful regret in its wake. She had the motherly impulse to protect and nurture, that was clear, but life had not been so kind to her on that front.

"You have a first aid kit? You surprise me."

I hung on to her, keeping my weight on one leg, and buttoned my jeans.

"It wasn't my idea. That car came with everything. I even have emergency flares," she said with a smile. "If we get really desperate."

"You are something special, Marce."

She pulled my arm across her shoulders for support. I leaned into her a little more than I had to, to let her know she was needed, and we headed back.

"It's about time you noticed, hop-a-long."

Chapter Twenty-three

I was standing with my jeans around my ankles when the car pulled up behind us. Marce was on her knees and had just finished applying antibiotic and bandages to the wound on my thigh. I pulled up my jeans and my dignity at the same time, determined to recover both if possible as the car flashed headlights from low beam to high beam before they went out and the engine shut down. The driver's door opened and even in the dark, with my eyes still adjusting from the headlight glare, I recognized the stick-figure outline.

"I thought I might find you here."

"This may look odd," I said as I tucked in my shirt and reached for my belt before realizing it was gone. "If you didn't know what was going on."

Marce reached past me to pack up the first aid kit. She brushed close and whispered in my good ear, *"That's him."*

"I know what's going on."

Marce put the first aid kit in her SUV and I leaned against the cargo bay.

"What brings you here, detective?"

Detective Marsons was wearing the same shirt, tie and pants, the same luminescent silver running shoes, and chewing on what looked like the same coffee stirrer from this morning. The only change to his ensemble was a dark blue windbreaker with LAPD stenciled above the left breast. His badge was visible on his belt and there was an obvious bulge beneath one arm. He licked an index finger, ran it across his pencil thin moustache, and removed the coffee stirrer to point toward the moon.

"Nice night for an evening stroll."

Marce leaned against the cargo bay, standing close with her shoulder in contact with mine, as if in so doing we presented a united front.

"I suppose."

I looked down at the mud on my shoes, on Marce's shoes, at the dirty spots we'd collected on our clothing splashing through the water and across the wet island.

"Have we done something wrong, detective?" Marce said. "This is public property, right?"

Detective Marsons chuckled and looked down at our shoes.

"Yeah, but you don't get to take any of it home with you," he said with a smile.

Marce looked at herself, me, and then she smiled, too.

"You're funny," she said.

Detective Marsons squinted and with his tongue pushed a bulge in his cheek. A sparkle in his eye and a humorous grunt let us know where we stood.

"This is probably not the best part of town for an affluent, white couple to contemplate the stars," he said. "Why don't you get going?"

"He's right, Marce. Maybe you should."

Marce opened her mouth to speak but I cut her off.

"I need to stay," I said. "The detective can give me a ride back to my car, right detective?"

Detective Marsons crossed his arms on his chest and nodded. The nylon jacket caught in the motion and a long barrel revolver was clearly visible.

"I can do that," he said in his high-pitched voice.

Marce stepped away from the cargo bay of the SUV and I followed. She punched a button on the remote and the deck lid slowly lowered and locked into place with a click that was barely audible.

"Good luck, Martin. I hope that Stray comes back soon."

"So do I."

She walked around to the driver's side of the SUV and I held the door while she hoisted herself aboard. I don't know what it was about Marce and that vehicle. It was the biggest SUV I'd ever seen. The scale was just wrong. The truth is Marce looked like a child playing at being a grownup in her land yacht. Why is a single woman, with no children or even a dog, buying an eight-passenger vehicle? I suppose that the answer was simple. All she had to do was walk into a dealer's showroom, meet a persistent sales person talking a little feminist independence, telling her how much better her life would be in that vehicle, acting like her best friend doing her a personal favor. Appeal to Marce's rebellious nature, add some girl power attitude, and the sale is made. Marce gets manipulated into buying the most inappropriate vehicle on the lot. It's not right. They took advantage of her. She ought to drive it back to that same dealer and park it through their front window. That would show them some girl power attitude. But what did I know. I drove a British relic devoid of the simplest modern conveniences standard in the most entry level vehicles on the market. Just the same, the dealer should have treated her better.

"Call me later, OK?" she said.

"Sure, I will."

She shifted into gear and pulled forward a few feet, then backward, and then forward. She maneuvered the SUV back and forth and back and forth, spinning the steering wheel from side to side, moving a few inches each time. You could see the frustration on her face when she shifted from drive to reverse. Detective Marsons and I watched the huge vehicle as it finally got clear and accelerated down the narrow street. If you're living in a high-density environment, where every place you need to go requires a car, where most of the parking spaces at those places you need to go are downsized for *Compacts Only*, you ought to drive a car that makes life easier than harder. Marce knew better. She's nobody's fool. The dealer must have had one clever sales person to cap that deal.

"I owe you one," I said.

"What for?"

I pointed in the direction Marce had driven. "You left out a few details, didn't you?"

"Like what?"

"Like Edward being dead."

Detective Marsons rubbed his cheek and chewed on the coffee stirrer between his teeth.

"We don't always tell everything we know," he said.

"You mean about Edward and the disciples?"

Detective Marsons nodded.

"John Kennedy shared a lot of information," he said. "No reason to say more than needed."

I guess that I wasn't the only one who held to that philosophy.

"John Kennedy?"

"Our suspect. Edward's partner."

"You mean John the Baptist."

"All right."

"So why are you here?"

"Sightseeing," I said.

Detective Marsons sat back on the hood of the Police Interceptor. He looked at the bike path, the river beyond, and then down at his silver running shoes. I don't know if he was giving me time to say more, but I wasn't volunteering anything.

"Stray get loose?"

"Took off after someone at the river camp."

"Who?"

"I think it was John the Baptist," I said. "I saw an arm in Richard's coat."

Detective Marsons nodded his head and twisted the stirrer between his teeth.

"How's the wound?"

I looked down at the tear in my jeans and lifted my leg a few times to test for stiffness.

"As my father used to say, 'It's a long way from your heart'."

"Wise man."

"He had his moments."

I sat next to him on the hood. The sky was full of stars, at least as many as city light pollution permitted us to see, and the moon silvered everything in icy iridescence. I closed my jacket and zipped it. Detective Marsons crossed his long, skinny legs and stacked one silver running shoe on top of the other.

"What are you really doing here, huh?"

I paused before answering, considering my commitment to never say more than I had to, and decided that maybe it was my turn to make good.

"Grant Parker hired me to help with his wife's case."

"Help how?"

"To investigate Edward's murder."

Detective Marsons watched my face and nodded a few times before he spoke.

"Have you ever done that kind of work before?"

"No," I said. "But the work as a private detective is not all that different from work as a mechanic. You collect information, process it, eliminate false leads, and eventually solve the mystery." I smiled at my succinct summation, thinking somehow that I'd impressed him.

Detective Marsons rubbed his elbow and stretched out the arm with the shoulder holster. He gave the coffee stirrer a twist.

"I suppose the concepts are similar, but first, let's get one thing straight. You're not a *Private Detective*; you're a *Private Investigator*. A Private Investigator is required to have a California State license. I'm not, because I am a *Detective*."

"I didn't know that."

"It doesn't matter, of course, until you enter into a contract for services."

"You mean like accepting a retainer?"

"A retainer can be for all sorts of services, not just for private investigation."

This time I nodded my head.

"Do you know how I found you tonight? "

"No."

"Because I'm a *Detective.*"

He was right, I wasn't a detective, but that wasn't going to deter me. This was a second chance to do something with my life. You don't always get second chances to start over.

"Do you know how I knew your dog's name?"

"Because Marce said it."

Detective Marsons smiled. "Pretty good, but you're not a detective."

"Okay. I'm a *Private Investigator.*"

Detective Marsons removed his coffee stirrer, examined the chewed end in the moonlight, inverted it and put it back in his mouth.

"Being a detective is not about a title or a license."

He paused, twisted on the coffee stirrer, mashing the fresh surface between his teeth, and restacked his running shoes. I stared across the Los Angeles River, into the city lights spreading north, to the San Gabriel Mountains in the distance. If you're going to change your life, reinvent yourself and embark on a new career, you have to learn wherever you can.

"What is it about?"

The detective chuckled, looked down at his running shoes, and crossed his arms on his chest. I suppose that he was thinking about how much to tell, how much of what he knew was worth sharing with someone he did not know. After half-a-minute of silence, he pulled the coffee stirrer from his mouth, folded it in two, put it in his pant's pocket and replaced it with a fresh one.

"Procedure. The way you choose to see the world. Anyone can do it, That can be taught. That's the easy part. Easy, but complicated. Then there's the hard part."

"What's the hard part?"

Detective Marsons straightened his legs and re-stacked his running shoes in the opposite order.

"The easy part is complicated and the hard part is simple," he said and chewed on the coffee stirrer. We looked at each other, his thin, angular face smooth like an adolescent's, the only indication of adulthood the pencil thin moustache and a pinched tightness around the corners of his eyes. I opened my mouth but before I could speak Detective Marsons raised one hand to shush me, then he nodded his head and smiled. I heard him before I saw him. Stray crested the river embankment with his tongue drooping sideways in his mouth and slowly crossed the pathway. I called to him and he lifted his head in acknowledgement but did not quicken his pace. When he got to us he dropped to his belly. I kneeled down and headlights came on. My belt was gone and he was exhausted. I rolled him over in the headlights and there was no blood anywhere. I felt his chest, his back, took each leg and paw in my hand. He didn't wince or yelp. I lifted his head and looked at his face. It was scraped across the muzzle but not bleeding, and when I touched his sensitive, battle-scarred ear, there was no response. All he did was pant. I raised my hand in the air and the headlights went out. Detective Marsons joined me in front of the car and crouched.

"Looks like your boy's come home," he said and stroked his coat.

"He has."

"You take good care of him don't you?"

"He's my partner," I said.

Detective Marsons bent down to ground level, gently lifted Stray's head and looked into his eyes.

"You know something about dogs?"

"I know something about details."

Stray rolled on his side, still breathing in rapid, shallow breaths, but his eyes were alert and his stubby tail wagged when I stroked his coat.

"Not too much worse for wear," he said as he stood up. "Except for your belt."

"How'd you know?"

Detective Marsons smiled and smoothed his moustache.

"I'm a *Detective*, remember?"

Chapter Twenty-four

The Police Interceptor had a full width rear seat. Stray didn't try to climb in. He stood at the open door and I had to lift him. Detective Marsons turned the sedan around, punched the throttle and we sped up the block. As we bumped along, Stray rocked on the rear seat like he was out cold. We slowed at the end of the block to maneuver around a parked car jutting into the street, and then turned east. It wasn't until we'd stopped for a signal that I realized the car jutting into the street had been a light green Dodge from the 70s. The very same light green Dodge I'd seen before with flaking paint, some rust, and a broken taillight. It could have been following me, but that was unlikely. Coincidence: possibly. Entertaining the very idea: Paranoia. The signal changed and Detective Marsons accelerated hard in the direction of the Tempest Burger and Grill.

"Thanks again for the ride."

Detective Marsons smiled. We turned left at the intersection, drove a block and I pointed to where the MG was parked.

"There it is," I said.

We continued up the street.

"You passed it."

Detective Masons nodded his head. "Four Café makes a pretty good patty melt."

I watched my MG recede in the distance and checked on Stray. He had curled his front legs up to his chin and appeared sound asleep.

"If you're hungry, I mean."

"I could eat."

"I'm always hungry," Detective Marsons said. "I know I look like I've missed a few meals, but the truth is just the opposite."

We drove for another mile, approached a five-way intersection, and ducked into an alley behind a strip mall. One hundred feet later, we parked.

Detective Marsons got out of the car and waited for me. Stray slowly raised his head and watched me through half-open eyes.

"Maybe I should leave him here?"

"You can. Or he can come in."

"They allow dogs?"

Detective Marsons pulled back his jacket to reveal the detective's badge on his belt.

"They allow cops."

I opened the rear door and Stray gingerly stepped out.

"Does he heel?"

"We've worked on it," I said.

"Okay, let's go."

I gave Stray a 'Heel' command and he tried to stay close to my side. Each step was an effort for him. His head hung down, swaying side to side with his tongue hanging, and we had to slow for him to keep up. We entered the Four Café from the rear through a hallway that passed the office, bathroom, kitchen door, and then into the dining area. It was a narrow room, with maybe eight or nine tables in a row, a polished concrete floor, exposed HVAC pipes and a long, white, picture-panel wall. An abstract oil painting filled the other wall. The front had a view of the street but the glass door and the window were covered in pastels of animated red, yellow and blue stick figures. Opposite the row of dining tables was the kitchen. Through an opening into the kitchen, a waitress emerged. Detective Marsons signaled her with his coffee stirrer as if he knew her, and we seated ourselves. Stray flopped on the floor in the middle of the aisle. I snapped my fingers, pointed to a spot under the table, and he rolled his eyes. With my help, he crawled under the edge of the table and out of the traffic pattern. The waitress arrived and assumed the slumped-hip posture of the perpetually bored twenty-something bohemian. Her wavy, dark hair was cut short and pulled back into a tight knot with a pink scrunchie at the base of her scull, and one nostril was pierced with a miniscule, gold stud. She wore distressed, low rise jeans rolled up to her knees, a snug, white singlet and no bra, diaphanous orange and purple scarf wrapped around her neck, and those goofy, rubber clogs that all the starving artists favored.

"We don't allow dogs in here," she said.

Detective Marsons smiled. "How are you tonight, Leti?"

The waitress looked from Detective Marsons to me and then to Stray.

"It's not my rule," Leti said.

Detective Marsons smiled again, clasped his hands together and nodded his head waiting for a response.

"Just groovy," Leti sneered.

Stray began to snore. Leti looked down at him and then at me.

"It's like, Health Department rules."

Detective Marsons pulled his badge from his belt and set it on the table.

"This is official. The dog's a material witness in an investigation, so I'm going to ask you to accommodate Police business," he said.

"Police business?"

"Police business, *Leti*."

"Right," Leti said and slumped from one hip to the other.

Stray let out a muffled, dreamy bark. He paddled his rear legs a few times, and then returned to snoring.

"Just so long as I don't get fired," Leti said.

"I can guarantee it."

"All right then," Leti said. "The usual?"

"For both of us." Detective Marsons said and looked at me.

"Sure," I said.

"Fine," Leti said, spun on her rubber clogs and marched away as if the whole incident had been just another petty annoyance in her post-modernistic life.

"What's the usual?" I asked.

"Patty melt, no meat, red potatoes with grilled onions. And a mint lemonade."

"Patty melt without meat? What are you, a vegetarian?"

"Vegan."

"A Vegan detective. Unusual."

Detective Marsons smiled. "Maybe. Maybe not."

Leti returned and put two green, patterned goblets of lemonade on the table. I noticed that Detective Marsons' goblet had two straws. When she leaned in to place the goblets, I caught the fecund odor of putrefying leaves. The scarf gaped from her chest and earth-tone penumbras beneath the singlet outlined her nipples. She caught me staring and I smiled my best 'I'm not a dirty old man but still a man' smile; she seemed to sneer with only her eyes, which I considered a generous concession.

"Nice scarf," Detective Marsons said. He discarded his deformed coffee stirrer, put one new straw in his shirt pocket and the other between his teeth.

"Pagan orange and Ecclesiastical purple," Leti said. "The dichotomy of my displaced Basque soul."

"Haven't seen this one."

"I know," she snorted and walked away.

"Basque?" I said.

"Second generation, but as Hollywood as you can get."

"Exotic beauty," I said.

Detective Marsons nodded his head and chewed on his straw. His eyes followed Leti into the kitchen. "Sweet girl. Fiery, but sweet."

"You know her well?"

"Well enough."

I took a drink of lemonade. The aroma of fresh mint filled my nose before my lips touched the goblet's rim.

"Delicious," I said and took another drink. "Interesting place."

"Everything is vintage. Except the food."

I looked around the room. Another couple, an older man and woman, artsy looking types, with matching short, spiky white hair, sat at the only occupied table. He wore blue jeans, a maroon sweatshirt, and leather sandals with striped wool socks; she wore hunter green Wellingtons, black corduroy pants with a black turtleneck and a green patterned scarf wound around her neck. There were jackets on the backs of their chairs, an open bottle of wine between them, and they were eating from steaming soup bowls. Leti set a basket of bread on their table. The woman placed her hands together, palms touching each other, and made a slight bow. Leti did the same and an image of her, 30 years hence sans rubber clogs, was echoed in the exchange.

"What does the name mean?" I asked.

"The name?"

"Four Café."

Detective Marsons sipped at his lemonade and smoothed his pencil thin moustache. He nibbled on the end of his straw and stared at me for a few seconds.

"Do you know anything about Buddhism?"

"I know a little."

"Do you know the Four Noble Truths?"

"No."

"Four Café is named for them. The owner is a Buddhist."

"Are you a Buddhist?"

Detective Marsons slowly pulled his straw from between clenched teeth and examined the flattened section before speaking.

"I am on that path."

"Kind of conflicts with being a detective, doesn't it?"

"There are no conflicts when you are awakened."

Beneath the table, Stray got to his feet, stretched and started to walk off. He stopped in the aisle and looked at the older couple two tables away, and then bobbed his nose along the air current in the direction of the kitchen. He wiped at the scrape on his muzzle with one paw, slumped to his belly and rolled on his side with a great yawn as if the ambulatory effort had been more than he'd anticipated. As I pulled him back under the table, he didn't even open his eyes.

"He looks exhausted."

He stretched again, reaching out with his front paws to touch my shoe, and then folded them close to his chest.

"I think he's OK," I said. "Just worn out."

"That's what it's like sometimes. You're so tired you don't know if you can go on, but you've got that scent in your nose and despite everything else, you could no more quit than make yourself stop breathing."

"That the easy part or the hard part?"

Detective Marsons smiled before speaking. "The easy part."

"How about the hard part?"

Detective Marsons lifted his goblet, drank it empty, and set it down on the table. He fingered the ornate pattern in the glass and flicked the straw up and down in his mouth.

"The hard part is something else, something else all together. I've been doing it a long time and I know."

"How long is that?"

"Eleven years."

Surprise must have been written in large, flashing script across my face. Detective Marsons swallowed a chuckle and shifted in his seat.

"I know; I look young. Graduated from the academy at 24. Became a patrolman and began to study right away. I knew then what I was meant to do. Took my Detective exam at 29. Eleven years later, I'm still doing it."

"I'd never take you to be 40."

"Next month, officially."

"So what's the hard part, then?"

Detective Marsons smiled. He looked toward the waitress station and raised his goblet. Leti caught his signal and came to the table with a sweating pitcher of lemonade.

"Still like the scarf."

"'Course you do, Mars," Leti said as she filled our glasses. "Patty's coming." She turned to walk away, stopped, leaned down close to me and peered into my eyes as if she were looking to find something. "What about you?"

"What about me, what?"

"You like it, too?" Leti demanded with her own, confrontational, girl power attitude.

The fecund odor of putrefying leaves hung in the air. The distance between us was mere inches. Heat from Leti's body pulsed in waves and a flush ran up my neck and cheeks like my face was about to break out in sweat. Apparently I was being tested in that enigmatic way women have of instant assessment. In times like these, I opt for some clever remark hoping to let me off the hook. It almost always fails, or at the very best leaves me wondering if I've put my foot in my mouth and said something wrong. Detective Marsons was watching me with a sparkle of amusement in his eyes and a tight-lipped grin pulling at the corners of his mouth. He turned over his hands, palm's up, in an amicable gesture that I took as encouragement.

"I like your shirt," I said.

Leti looked down at her singlet and lifted the scarf away from her chest as if she'd been unaware of what the snug fitting material was revealing.

"Humpff," she snorted and walked away.

Detective Marsons broke into a grin. I don't know if I'd passed Leti's test, but I figured that I'd passed his.

"Good one," he said.

"I try."

The older couple was sitting with their hands in their laps. The soup bowls in front of them were empty; the bottle of wine half full. Leti swept past with dishes of food and put them in front of the couple. She collected the empty soup bowls, bowed her head and returned to the kitchen. As she passed our table, she flashed an inveigling, tolerant smile bordering on cordial. I wasn't too far away from that couple's age, and even though I didn't feel old, Leti probably saw me the same way she saw them. She exited the kitchen almost immediately with plates bound for our table. After she set them down, I saw her drop a scrap of potato on the floor and with her rubber clog nudge it near Stray's nose. Stray sniffed, stuck out his tongue, and bit at the scrap without opening his eyes.

"How about this one?" Leti said to Detective Marsons.

"He's all right."

"Humpff," Leti snorted again but this time there was less combatance in her tone and the girl power attitude had definitely shifted from confrontational to almost flirtatious. She lifted the ends of the scarf and flipped them over her shoulders. Her singlet pulled out of her waistband exposing a pierced belly button. "I bet he is."

I stuck out my hand to shake. "Martin Gardens," I said.

Leti took my hand and held it. She cocked her head to one side, looked at Detective Marsons, back at me, and raised one eyebrow. "Oh that is just too easy."

I shrugged my shoulders and mouthed 'Thank you.' She dropped my hand and sauntered toward the kitchen, rolling her hips and dragging her rubber clogs on the polished concrete floor as she went. There was a definite swing in her yard that hadn't been there before. Detective Marsons wrapped a tight-lipped grin around his straw. I opened my jacket, sniffed at my collar, and was surprised that I couldn't smell any gamy funk. It comes and goes without a pattern, for no apparent reason, that much I had discovered. I must have been having a good funk day.

We ate without speaking; me suddenly hungrier than I'd realized, Detective Marsons inhaling his patty melt and side of potatoes before I'd finished half my order. I dropped a few scraps of potato under the table and each time Stray found them. I took it as a sign that he was recovering from his river camp escapade.

"There was the other part," I said. "The hard part about being a detective?"

Detective Marsons pushed his plate away. He dabbed like a dilettante at his lips and moustache with a corner of his napkin.

"Enlighten me, really," I said with a smile. "Since I'm almost a detective, myself."

Detective Marsons just stared and chewed his straw. Then he licked a finger and smoothed his pencil thin moustache.

"Are you sure you want to go down this road?"

"I didn't start out to," I said. "All I wanted to do was make right something I did wrong a long time ago."

"Old business?"

"Yes."

"Did you?"

"I'm trying."

"That doesn't work, you know. You can't undo what's been done."

"I know," I said. "But now that I've started…."

Leti passed by the table on the rolling hips. They caught my attention and she smiled with a sly, alluring glint in the corner of her eye.

"Well, the hard part," Detective Marsons said, put his elbows on the table and held up the straw as if it were a conductor's baton: "The hard part is simple. It requires not what you do but what is meant to be. The essence of who you are. The hard part is the capacity for loneliness."

"Loneliness?"

"Loneliness."

"No friends?"

"Not solitude. Loneliness."

"Then why do you do it? Because you're a Buddhist?"

"No. Seeking the ultimate truth is my nature. Because of that nature, I'm awakened."

"I see."

"No, you don't. That's my point."

"And…," I said.

"It's like this. All you're life you're taught what things are. This is a something; that is a something. You're taught that those things have names. This is a table; that is a chair. Those names begin to define those things. You think 'table' and your brain fills in the details. Certain presumptions are made; level surface, three or more legs, even the size and shape. It becomes unconscious. You do not see things truthfully revealed. You see the definition you've already created in your mind and you miss the reality. To be successful, you must learn to rid yourself of all presumption, see something just as it is, stripped of all the unconscious details you're brain fills in. You see only what is there, exactly nothing more and nothing less. You see each independent detail, and those details have meaning. The smallest detail that doesn't fit immediately stands out. And that sets you apart. You are unique, seeing the world for what it is, devoid of presumption, devoid of illusion. Seeing the world unlike anyone else sees it. That makes you different; that makes you lonely."

I felt Stray's paw against my shin. He held it for a few seconds, as if reassuring himself that I was still there, and then it went away.

"For me, it's natural. I know when something doesn't fit. I can feel it as much as I can see it. That's the difference between us. I'm a professional. I know what I'm doing. You're not a professional. You don't."

A muffled bark came from beneath the table.

"You must have learned that, right? You weren't born that way."

"Maybe, I don't know. It comes naturally to me so I couldn't be any other way. It's like…. Do you know Emerson?"

"Uh, the 'Most men lead lives of quiet desperation' guy?"

"No. That's Thoreau. I mean Emerson."

"I guess not."

"He wrote '*Commit a crime and the world is made of glass. Commit a crime, and it seems as if a coat of snow fell on the ground, such as reveals in the woods the track of every partridge and fox and squirrel.*' Do you understand?"

I nodded my head but wasn't convinced of my sincerity. The image of a landscape coated in snow was fighting for the space where Leti's rolling hips and sly smile had been a minute ago.

"Your sole motivation lies in the pursuit of truth, the truth evidenced in the marks in the snow. Do a sloppy job and you miss the tracks, truth remains buried like history in plain sight, indifferent to weather, time and circumstance. Only you know the difference."

Nodding again, I covered my irritation with a dip of my head, and stalled for time to formulate a response. The remark about not knowing what I was doing had rubbed my ego the wrong way. The implication that I couldn't do what he did was unfair. I didn't have his experience, but experience and capability should not be confused. He spoke in a softer tone, redirecting the thread of the conversation, as if he'd sensed that his remarks might have been insulting.

"If this is your path, and you follow it, you should know that you're going to be involved with bad people, people without consciences, people that live outside of the law."

"You mean sociopaths."

Detective Marsons nodded. "If you have something they want, they'll stop at nothing to get it. If you know something that could hurt them, you become the target. Do you understand?"

"It'll take more than that speech to scare me off."

"I'm not trying to scare you off. I'm preparing you for what *is*. Everyone has some reason for doing this kind of work. Only you know your reason."

I sipped on my lemonade and looked around the room. The older couple was silently eating their dinner, drinking their wine, apparently comfortable in each other's presence without the need for conversation.

"I started something that's become bigger. I'm not going to fight it. I'm going to let it take me wherever it goes."

"That's not a reason, that's passivity."

"Maybe it is," I said. "But it feels right. What's your reason?"

"My reason is who I am. I seek the Absolute. You could say I deconstruct history to reconstruct the truth. When you have been awakened, there is no turning away."

"You're quite the philosopher."

Detective Marsons cocked his head and lifted one eyebrow, neither in agreement or disagreement, and chewed his straw. Leti walked past our table again, her hips like a teasing invitation, and left the check on the older couple's table. She stopped next to me and stood with her shoulders squared and back arched, narrow ribbon of bare stomach almost touching my forearm. The scarf was gone and distinct, pointed nipples pushed with defiance at her singlet.

"Anything else, tonight?"

"Not for me," I said and put my hands flat on the table.

Detective Marsons was shaking his head 'no' at Leti. She bent toward me and put one hand on the table so that her index finger cupped my wrist.

"You ought to come around more," she said looking into my eyes.

She turned my right hand over and dragged her index finger past my wrist, stopped on my palm, and then traced a circle in the soft flesh. The sexual power emanating from her nearness was unmistakable. She stopped tracing and held her index finger in place as if marking me. I stared at my hand and she leaned closer so that her bare waist was against my forearm. Her personal odor filled my nose. Unlike my gamy funk, hers was hormonal. I took a long, slow breath and exhaled. A metallic howl like a jet engine spinning up for takeoff began to grow in the back of my head. A woman at the height of reproductive fertility secretes pheromones that no virile man can ignore. The power is inescapable. They bypass the mind and race unchecked directly to your loins. No amount of deliberate, logical reasoning is possible. The only thought is to copulate. I took another deep breath and felt like I was going to erupt in flame. The jet engine spun faster, the howl grew louder, moved forward in my head, and continued to accelerate. As you mature, you're supposed to learn to resist a fertile woman's pheromones, temper carnal urges with rational thought, exert self-control, but every man is different. I swallowed to drown the noise just behind my eyes and inhaled again but the room was absent of oxygen and the jet engine keep spinning faster and faster and the howl drowned out rational thought. Leti leaned closer to my right ear. Be it the excitement of the evening or just low blood sugar, I could no longer vouch for my behavior. Her fecund scent plus her body heat plus her proximity became excruciating torture and the howling jet engine spinning at warp speed pressed against my temples and threatened to explode out my eye sockets. I clamped my eyes closed, gasped for oxygen and my imagination raced: We were living in a beachfront bungalow, Leti wearing a loose, colorful skirt, an infant riding her hip as I rested in a hammock surveying the breaking ocean waves; why couldn't we do that? What was there to stop us? I didn't have to be childless. Why couldn't I have someone to inherit my legacy after I'm gone? The sun was low on the horizon, sky flaming in red and yellow, something smoked on a grill just beyond view, and nothing else existed but the three of us in that waterfront paradise. Then came another image and she was standing next to me, still young with her arm wrapped around my waist, a school-age child looking back at us from atop a swing set, and I was gray and a little hunched, the difference in our ages more father and daughter than husband and wife. I blinked my eyes and shook my head to clear it, but Leti was just inches away and the restaurant had vanished and she was all that existed. Like a man enslaved by an addiction through proximity and odor, whatever she asked for, right then and there, I was powerless to deny.

Leti stood up and nodded her head as if we'd reached some sort of agreement. Then she collected our empty plates and sashayed toward the kitchen. Detective Marsons chuckled under his breath, licked his finger and smoothed his pencil thin moustache. He stared at me like he knew something I didn't and flipped the well-chewed straw onto the table.

"You should do what she says," he said.

"What'd she say?"

Chapter Twenty-five

Detective Marsons dropped us off about 10:30. I opened the MG hatchback and Stray climbed in with as little energy as I'd ever seen him summon. He swam half asleep over the low seat back and flopped on the rear cushion. I got in the driver's seat and checked the contents. All the instruments were still in place; glove box unmolested, the cigarette lighter and shift knob had not been stolen. I checked the center console. Nothing was missing. The radio was already gone, removed years ago for repair and never replaced, so I was not surprised to see the rectangular hole in the dashboard where it should have been. I inserted the key in the ignition and Leti came to mind. Why was a young woman like her flirting with me? I was old enough to be her … I stopped myself mid sentence and laughed. Who knows what anyone is doing with anyone? Just look at Grant and Carolyn, or Marce and Alan. And Detective Marsons. Leti seemed to know him as if he were more than just a regular customer. Another odd couple.

I twisted the ignition key and like a good omen, the engine turned over and started. I backed out and exited into traffic. Call it pure chance or divine coincidence, the route to the freeway lead me toward Four Café. Leti was probably done for the evening, cleaning up before she left for some artsy loft with shabby-chic Salvation Army furnishings and a double mattress on the floor. As I drifted along in my reverie, I slowed and the car turned itself into the alley behind the Four Café. I didn't process what I was doing until I parked, and when I shut off the motor, my mind abandoned even that processing and the lingering aroma in my nose took control. Detective Marsons was right; I had the scent and I could no more quit then make myself stop breathing. I checked Stray in the back seat where he slept, got out of the car and tried the back door. It was locked and the lights inside were off. I walked to the end of the alley, for some reason staying close to the brick wall for concealment, and skulked with cat-like stealth around the corner. The front door was locked as well. The windows were dark, but a faint light glowed near the kitchen. I returned to the alley and the MG. Stray was snoring on the back seat, so I continued surveilling the premises. I was focused on a single objective, my behavior in response to primal urges and genetic encoding, not Detective Marsons' abstract compulsion to deconstruct history and reconstruct truth. I went to the back door and cupped my hands around my eyes to peer into the darkness. A flicker of light that hadn't been there before shifted in the hallway. That meant someone was inside; Leti was inside. I hurried down the alley, around the corner and back to the front entrance. What was I going to do, smash the glass door like William Hurt lusting for Kathleen Turner in Body Heat? Or better, wait for Leti to exit, fall to one knee and proclaim: 'You are a woman and can bear a child. I am a man and cannot. After I am gone nothing of me will remain in the world but if you are willing to co-operate in procreation, together we can live in a bungalow on the beach and raise our child. Fate brought me here and you've infected me with uncontrollable desire; there is no alternative. It's bigger than the two of us. Does it seem strange that I want to get you with child? Does it?'

Before I did anything stupid, I got back in the MG. Stray rose from the rear cushion and stepped on the center console. He pushed his blunt nose against my neck, sniffed a few times, and then returned to his position on the rear seat. I lifted my shirt away from my chest and took a deep breath. No rank odor, no gamy funk, nothing unusual: just the salty man odor to be expected after a full day's activity. I didn't know what I was doing. The fine distinction between want and need was slipping away. With Leti's flirtatious behavior, the irresistible power of female pheromones, and a sudden sense of mortality, the mystery unfolding as my life approached the half-century mark wasn't going to be solved tonight. I wanted a drink but what I needed was perspective.

The engine started right away, another clear sign seconding my decision to leave, and I backed out of the parking slot, drove down the alley and pulled into the street. This was the time to think with my best clarity. *What you do without hesitation in your twenties you give due consideration in your forties.* That much I could remember. This much I knew: I had a client, a retainer, and my first case. I checked my cell phone in my jacket pocket. No calls from Marce. As I set my cell phone on the passenger seat, I remembered the other one. I pulled it out and flipped it open. Two missed messages were displayed. One was from Grant and the other from Carolyn. I suppose that Grant had advised her to use that cell number instead of my personal number to ensure privacy. Grant didn't miss a trick. As if the forgotten cell phone were a memory trigger, I checked the MG for my flashlight. Gone. Stray's leash was gone, too. OK, I reasoned, someone stole the leash from the car when it was parked. But the flashlight, I had that with Marce when we visited the river camp. Either it was in her SUV or I'd left it behind. Quite the night for the novice mechanic private investigator. One day into my first assignment and between the gash in my thigh and stalking Leti, any semblance of professional focus had been derailed. And the image of Tamara, present just a few hours earlier, had somehow slipped from my mind. I'd already missed my client's call and lost personal assets. At best, a tenuous beginning. The departing whistle for the last stop express was blowing. If I were going to succeed, I better get serious. You can't undo what is done; you can't let the past undermine the future. History need not be predictive; it is simply more information to mix into the present. I had been hired to find out what had happened. I knew that Edward was dead. I knew that he was waiting for the winter solstice; and I didn't think that he died naturally. That meant someone else had perpetrated his death, but the killer could be almost anybody. And for no reason more persuasive than a feeling in my gut, I had an idea who was responsible. It was as plain as tracks in the snow. All I had to do was learn how to see them.

Chapter Twenty-six

Grant's message was clear: If I'd learned anything, call as soon as I could. If not, meet him tomorrow at 7:00 at his hotel restaurant. The message time stamp was 8:45. It was now almost 11:00. There was nothing to report that couldn't wait until tomorrow morning.

Carolyn's message was importunate: *'Call Carolyn immediately.'* That sounded like her; demanding as ever. That she and Grant had found a level of compatibility was pure mystery. In addition to the difference in ages, where he was loquacious and steadfast, she was curt and mercurial. It's curious what people see in each other. Grant and Carolyn: She was too successful and too smart to be a trophy wife. Me and my ex-fiancée Susan: I should have seen that train wreck coming long before I poured myself into a bottle. And then Tamara and Edward: Another oddity. Tamara had said that Edward was Brenda's father, and that meant, even if he were not a part of their lives for many years, she still had some tie to him. I couldn't imagine that she'd been unaware of his living situation. Even though love can shatter as easily as fine crystal, shards lodge in your heart forever. Tamara knew more about Edward than she had shared.

I turned the car around at the next intersection and headed back the other direction. Tamara's salon and apartment were only a few miles away. I continued east across town. The sidewalks were deserted and the street empty of vehicles. I could have driven on either side of the road for all that it mattered. A neighborhood liquor store was closing. The illuminated sign above the entrance went dark as I approached, and then a man stepped out the front door and locked it behind him. In my rear view mirror, I could see him pull a rusty scissor gate across the entrance and wrap a chain through the bars. Not much activity of any sort on a cool, midweek night. I drove for another mile, turned on La Sombra and slowed in front of Tamara's salon. It was dark and upstairs, in Tamara's apartment, a muted candescence from behind the kitchen curtain lit the street-side window. I drove past the salon to the end of the block. An alley behind the salon ran parallel to La Sombra so I turned into it. Two-story buildings, some with windows covered in plywood, others with curtains or blinds that indicated occupancy, lined the alley. On one side was a windowless Quonset hut. The arched metal roof was corroded at the bottom with rust tracks like gnarly roots reaching toward the apex. On the other side of the alley were rear entrances with iron railed stoops and loading docks; dumpsters flanked the loading docks or tucked in close to the stoops. A telephone pole radiated a spider web of power lines, cable, and telephone wires that sagged across the alley to each building. Commercial signage was nonexistent, but street addresses were painted above some of the rear entrances. Behind one building were two occupied parking stalls. Tamara's Fiat was in one and a very dusty, dark blue Crown Victoria sat in the other. Either Tamara had a roommate, which, since I'd been in her apartment on two occasions, seemed unlikely, or a visitor. And that visitor was probably male. It doesn't take much investigative experience to know that a Crown Victoria is a man's car. That could explain her reluctance to push forward in our relationship. I took a slow, deep breath as my heart sank to my stomach. Investigative curiosity had brought me here but now I'd learned what I didn't want to know. I looked at Stray stretched across the rear seat. Where he had become a constant, the women in my life were a variable. You never really know if what you want is what someone else wants, or the level of attraction you feel is equally reciprocal. My personal history was one of failed relationships, and the most recent and most promising appeared to be another.

In the bathroom window above the parked cars, a candle burned. I stopped behind the Fiat and let the engine idle. As I sat and watched the candle flickering inside Tamara's apartment, Stray rose, climbed unsteadily over the console and settled into the passenger seat. His usual place was in back or posted on the center console leaning against the passenger headrest when we drove, but never in the passenger seat. He reached out one front leg, stretched his paw ahead of the stick shift and pushed at my knee. Animals have an uncanny sense of the immediate. It is thickheaded humans who are blind to the obvious. Stray was safe with his master in a place that was familiar, and he was sensing my sinking spirit. A gentle push meant to reassure was his compassionate expression. How could he know just what I needed?

Except for the slow idle of the MG engine, around us it was quiet. No radio or television, no traffic noise from the street at the end of the alley. An hour from midnight and all good people were home asleep or in preparation to do so. I checked the bathroom window again and Stray exhaled with a sigh. He was a good companion on this lonely night. Everyone needs a companion.

Everyone needs someone. I scratched at his good ear as the thought came to me: Edward had fathered Tamara's child and they may have been cohabitating, engaged or married at one time. That was the past. Tonight, legally defined or not, Tamara had lost the father of her child. Solving the mystery of Edward's death had left me oblivious to the impact of his passing. Edward had a sister, a daughter, and Tamara, whatever their relationship had been. He dated Marce in high school, a long time ago, and probably had parents still alive, maybe some friends, and the fallen disciples, as well. He may have lived homeless on the streets, but he did not live in seclusion. There were people who loved him and would miss him. The event is not devoid of human cost; deconstructing history cannot be separated from the emotional damage involved. I checked the bathroom window again and considered making the call. Waking someone up in the middle of the night to tell them that they'd won the lottery was one thing; waking someone up in the middle of the night to tell them they'd lost someone was another. Such terrible news should only be delivered in the light of day.

I pulled forward and drove to the end of the alley, turned right and headed toward the freeway. Normally, I'd put Stray in the back seat, both for his comfort and his safety. As it was, he looked too tired to move so I let him stay next to me. We passed the locked down liquor store, drove another couple miles across town, and entered the freeway onramp. On a Wednesday, at midnight, you'd expect traffic to be a non-issue. But this is the Los Angeles basin and here, at all hours of day and night, people are on the road. We slowed as traffic grew heavier, and half a mile ahead I could see emergency vehicles and flashing lights near the shoulder. Cars bunched around me, packing together, creeping forward until we came to a complete stop. The flashing lights were at least a quarter mile off. A man in a pickup truck next to me opened his door. His radio was blaring something in Spanish. He climbed into the bed and scanned the distance, shook his head in frustration and leaned his elbows against the cab. More people began to emerge from their vehicles. I was reluctant to shut off the engine, knowing that restarting was problematic, but as people exited their cars and began to mill around, I took a chance. Stray lifted his head, got to his feet and climbed over the center console and on to the rear seat. Around us, in the middle of the northbound freeway, not a single vehicle moved. Cars, trucks and motorcycles rushed past us on the southbound side of the freeway, but we were a parking lot. A woman from behind us walked past with a King Charles Spaniel on a leash. She led her dog across three lanes to the shoulder where he lifted a leg against a roadside marker. I got out of the MG and stood next to the car with my arms on the roof. The woman led her dog to an unoccupied red minivan and opened the door. She reached inside, turned her back toward me and then walked away with a purse over her shoulder and cell phone at her ear. Now if I were guessing, I'd think that she had taken her dog to do its business. I'd think that she'd decided to get back into her van, and then for some reason changed her mind. That was obvious. But that was not thinking like a private investigator. As a private investigator, I'd assemble the facts and not let presumption shape the observed behavior. I'd read the tracks in the snow like Emerson had written. She could have been retrieving her purse and cell phone from the empty minivan, or she could have been stealing a purse and cell phone from an empty minivan, or something altogether different. That is how an investigative mind should think; that is how I needed to learn to think. For instance, take the Crown Victoria at Tamara's apartment. I couldn't be certain that it belonged to a visitor because of where it was parked. I had leaped to that conclusion. Actually, I couldn't be certain of anything about the car. All I knew was that it was dusty; not dirty, but dusty. The difference was important: Dirt comes from use, dust comes from disuse. That could mean it had been parked in that spot for an extended period of time. Maybe Tamara rented the space to someone to store a car, or maybe it had no connection to Tamara at all. An observant private investigator would have noticed if the license plate tags were current. I had missed the tracks. It was going to take more than one night to learn how to be good at this.

In the distance, a helicopter approached. It flew low over the northbound lanes and landed on the freeway adjacent the emergency vehicles. The man in the pickup bed had a pair of binoculars and was watching the activity. A few minutes later, the helicopter lifted into the sky, dipped its nose toward downtown and flew off. Around me, people began getting into their vehicles. Engines started in anticipation of moving. I climbed into the MG and it started right away. The engine idled and in my mirror I watched the red minivan. No one was behind the wheel. No sign of the woman or her dog. The car in front of me began to move. I put the MG in gear and followed. As I drove away, the red minivan sat unoccupied. Maybe the pair was stuck on the shoulder, unable to cross moving traffic to get back to the minivan; maybe she had abandoned the minivan and walked home. Maybe it wasn't the woman's minivan at all. That was another mystery.

Chapter Twenty-seven

When I parked at the apartment, Stray didn't lift his head from the rear seat. I reached back and tried to rouse him. He was breathing normally but disinterested in moving. I left the passenger door open and went inside, flipped on the lights, and got his bowl. From the picture window I could see Stray slowly ascending the stairway. I made a point to bang his food bowl a few times for encouragement as I rinsed it in the sink, filled it with a few tablespoons of wet dog food, and tapped the spoon on the rim. Sure enough, moving with glacial speed, Stray summitted the kitchen threshold and slumped on the tile floor. I put down the bowl and he found the energy to crawl to it, lift his nose over the rim and eat. I went out to close the door of the MG. When I returned, Stray was stretched out on the kitchen floor. Once again I felt his body and then lifted his head and looked into his sleepy eyes; he licked the edge of my palm and closed his eyes. I could not imagine how far he had run at the river camp, but for the moment, it was clear that he was spent.

I put the cell phones on the counter and stripped down. Marce had done a pretty good job with her field dressing so I left the bandage alone and showered. When I got out, Stray was on his dog bed snoring. I stood in the kitchen, opened the cupboard and studied the bottle of Old Bushmills. The idea of a drink seemed like the perfect finish to the day. Wasn't that what private investigators did? Slammed down hurtful shots of liquor in the evening to dull the gruesome images of what they'd seen during the day? Or was that just a rationalization to defend a self-destructive addiction? I'd started that direction once before and from what I'd witnessed at the homeless camp behind the Police station, the next destination on that journey was one I intended to skip.

I climbed into bed, set the alarm for my breakfast meeting with Grant, and sat with a yellow pad to make some notes. A lot had happened to me in the past four days and keeping it straight was a challenge. I divided 'Known' and

'Unknown' into two columns on the yellow pad. One column had far more entries than the other but that was just a matter of time. I closed my eyes and leaned my head back to puzzle it out. Tomorrow, Grant might shed some light on Carolyn's relationship with Edward. Tamara might add something as well. I could start putting some entries into the 'Known' column. Delivering the news of Edward's death to Tamara, although probably not a complete shock considering how he lived his life, was going to be difficult. I had seen Edward twice in two days and only knew him from high school, but I was saddened by his death. And I was angry. Angry that for some reason, parental, societal or circumstantial, he had fallen between the cracks, never received the help he so desperately needed, never progressed to a school where he could use that huge brain of his. Not many of us are born with intelligence like his; he could have done something significant. It was such a waste of a life. The people who loved him would suffer for his passing. They would endure days and months and years of guilt, regret, and if not remorse, than endless sorrow. Questions of 'why?' and 'how come?' would plague their waking hours and haunt their dreams. I could not imagine what it would do to Tamara.

I woke just before the alarm went off with the yellow pad next to me on the bed. Stray was already up and he pushed his head across the mattress as he wagged his stubby tail. After our morning ritual of side rubs, he walked unsteadily to his food bowl, stood with head down, and then flopped on the floor. I filled his bowl and was relieved to see that his appetite was normal. I gave him some water, which he slurped down without stopping, and then he dropped to the floor again. It occurred to me that I had no idea how old Stray was, and maybe, after what he'd been through, it would take more than one night's rest to recover. He was probably still sore from his river chase, but he didn't seem to be in any pain. He didn't whimper or whine but still looked very, very tired.

My leg was a little stiff when I walked but it did not hurt. I peeled back the gauze on the wound and it was clean and dry. It wasn't much to brag about, but in the right circumstances I might be able to milk it for some sympathy. I didn't have any medical supplies, so I left the dressing alone. I could change it at the shop where Tom had the OSHA required First Aid kit. I let Stray out the door and watched from the veranda. He moved with some hesitation when he descended the stairway, deliberately placing each paw on the next lower step, and was shaky when he did his business. I decided to take him with me. Tom wouldn't like it much, due to his allergies, but that was too bad. He was my partner, a material witness as Detective Marsons described him, and I wasn't leaving him alone until I knew he was better.

In a day's transition, fall, the best time of year in Southern California, had arrived. After a mild summer, in which temperatures had stayed below normal, we'd suffered through two weeks of record setting highs in the valleys, inland empire, and even the beach. No area had been spared. Downtown, the high had been 113 degrees; the inland empire had almost hit 120, and the beaches, usually the escape destination, had reached 101 degrees. The normal cooling trend in September never occurred and we baked in summer heat into mid October. Now, nearing the end of the month, this morning had that crisp, fall texture that you can almost pinch between thumb and finger. In more ways than one, there were clear indications that change was in the air.

Standing on the stoop, I looked down the long driveway. Beyond the MG, in the main house, lights glowed in only two lower rooms. It seemed unusual, but that didn't mean anything. It could have happened many times before without me noticing. I hadn't been as observant in the past as I was learning to be now. Mostly I'd been thinking about myself. That was another aspect of recovering from alcoholism; the self-absorption necessary for successful abstinence can isolate you. In an effort to remain removed from corrupting influences, you cut yourself off from a good portion of the rest of the world. They talk about it at the meetings, how to re-enter familiar patterns without falling back on old habits, and how to resume your life. Learning to fit the temperate you into the world is a wakening to what exists beyond the alcoholic haze of constant inebriation. What follows is an excruciating and slow acclimatization to a sober reality. Like all things worth doing, it takes time. The self-transformation to private investigator, for whatever it was worth, had opened my eyes. Maybe this was what Detective Marsons meant by being awakened. It seemed that everywhere I looked, I saw what I'd never noticed and was probably there all along: a continuum of inexplicable scenarios and mysterious situations each more compelling than the last. Seeing without presumption was as much a result of sobriety as it was the coincidental events that brought me to private investigation. For some reason, at this time, the two had combined. If there are wake up calls to our lives, this one was mine.

I locked the front door and we loaded up. Stray needed a little help getting in to the car, but he took his sentry position on the center console as if nothing were different, and focused his gaze through the windshield like always. I had one resolute partner, undeterred by minor discomfort, ready to go wherever I was going, whenever I went there. I had my first consolation with my first client. I had prospects for the future. All I needed was a plan.

Chapter Twenty-eight

The entrance to a high end, luxury hotel is designed both to impress and intimidate; the Royal Arms was no different. In high school, all the students knew that this was no place to fool around. Liveried doorman flanked the hotel entrance and dissuaded smart aleck teenagers from entering regardless of how mature they pretended to be, regardless of their family's social prominence, regardless of their best efforts to circumnavigate the doorman, valet or concierge. There were rules and this was not a place for reckless behavior.

When you drive into the Royal Arms courtyard beneath the two-story porte-cochere, and someone steps out of nowhere to open your door and assist you from your vehicle, an attitude of civility and decorum is established. You have been granted entrance to the domain of the genteel, to breathe the air of the privileged, experience the perks of exclusivity, and rub shoulders with the elite. No other place in your life are you afforded such instant, unearned respect. But with every courtesy you are shown, it is clear that beneath the affected deference, the attitude is tolerance and not gratitude. Staff members may claim to offer any assistance, providing that you are a registered guest, but their courtesy is provisional. Let it never be forgotten, the tables have been turned: they have what you want. The charade of master and servant is no more evident than at the front desk. With a shake of the concierge's head, you can find yourself denied access. Appear unworthy, behave unruly, lack the necessary credit, you are out of luck. This is a place where presentation and deportment make a difference. You are not a paying customer, entitled to whatever your pocketbook can afford. You are a visitor subject to management approval, and it is expected that you will treat the Royal Arms with the same care and consideration you would as a guest in someone's home. Though you may believe that the customer is always right, never forget that it is they who are doing you the favor of accommodation.

I stopped beneath the porte-cochere. A doorman leaned down to my window as I lowered it, but did not reach to open the door.

"May I help you, Sir?"

He was Middle Eastern, evidenced in a pronounced accent with phlegmy consonants and forceful delivery. He kept his gloved hands at his sides, unwilling to soil them on the dusty surface of the car, bending rigidly from the waist like a wooden soldier of hostelry. Dark, hooded eyes assessed the MG with the guarded gaze of the cynical proletariat. Stray stood on the back seat and growled.

"I'm meeting a guest."

The doorman scanned the perimeter of the courtyard. Three Mercedes and a Lincoln Town Car were parked on one side, and on the other side, a BMW and some empty spaces. I could almost see the thought emerge before he spoke.

"Around corner, down hill, is parking. Have good day, Sir," he said and stepped back.

There is nothing more revealing of an individual's character than how they treat the less fortunate. In this instance, the doorman had maintained the dignity of the hotel without offending a guest. Omitting the obvious, he had made his point: this mottled, old car had no business parked at the front entrance of a luxury hotel and, rather presumptuously, the guest was probably not affluent enough to afford valet service. Understandable, of course, but it put me off any good feelings the fall weather had triggered.

I saw him watching us as I exited the porte-cochere and rounded the corner. Stray barked once and then settled into a wary crouch on the back seat. I drove along the side of the hotel, down an incline, to the rear of the property. Just past the delivery entrance were designated parking spots for the cars of guests. The cars of hotel employees were parked along the far fence at the outer perimeter of the lot. The location of the vehicles was a socio economic indicator of status. The classic standoff between the haves and the have nots. Nothing about that had changed since high school. My socio economic indicator was somewhere between the two, consisting of behavior driven by a modus operandi of one day at a time. I backed into a parking stall on a slight rise in a sort of no-man's-land next to a low walled enclosure for trash dumpsters. Stray lifted his head in expectation as I shut off the engine.

"I'll be right back." Stray sank back on the seat and sighed in disappointment. As always, his preference was to go with me. I flipped the driver's seat forward and he climbed out. We walked to a nearby bush and he peed. When we got back to the car, he gave me a long look. I pointed to the rear seat. He hoisted himself inside without assistance and dropped to his stomach.

"Stay."

I walked past the delivery entrance, up the incline, and under the porte-cochere. The doorman eyed me with suspicion as if he'd never seen me before. As I approached the hotel entrance he stepped into my path.

"May I help you, Sir?"

Standing toe to toe, he was short in stature by maybe half-a-foot of me, and beneath the long, burgundy coat bearing the Royal Arms logo in gold thread over the breast, a definite paunch pushed at the fabric. He'd shaved recently but stubble had already begun to show on his cheeks. Coarse black hair poked from beneath his doorman's cap. He wore an elaborate badge with the name 'Hamlet' in cursive letters.

"You don't remember me, Hamlet?"

He squinted, glanced from where I'd come, and a hesitant smile spread his mouth.

"Excuse me, Sir. Meet guest?"

Up close, he must have been in his fifties, not a recent immigrant, somewhat acclimated to western ways of behavior. His command of basic salutations was passable, but when off script, it was apparent that English was not his mother tongue.

"Yes, Hamlet. I'm on my way to meet a guest now."

On a good day, I can be charming, extend niceties with the best of them, and even win over a person if given a chance. I'd found this skill invaluable in the corporate world, where walking the fine line between ass-kissing and insincere congeniality is a learned skill.

"Where are you from, Hamlet? You have good English, but I hear an accent?"

Hamlet scanned the empty courtyard and then looked toward the glass doors of the hotel entrance, as if fraternizing with guests like me might have been discouraged. Then, in a gesture I had not anticipated, he extended his gloved hand to guide me toward the front doors.

"I am Persian, 24 years in USA. This way please."

We walked side by side, up the wide, front steps to a broad landing covered with a doormat the size of a living room rug. Hamlet opened the front door and bowed.

"Thank you."

"It is pleasure"

He held the door as I entered the lobby and then let it close and descended towards the courtyard. When he reached the lower step, in a moment he must have thought would be unnoticed, he shot his left leg and arm to the side, hesitated, and drew his leg inward in his Persian version of the Motown electric slide. He snapped his head upright and with one hand traced the bill of his doorman's cap before locking his arms behind his back in military precision. A decent guy with a little attitude. I smiled at the performance, and for the second time since Carolyn's arrival, I felt as though I'd channeled my former, confident self. I would need all the confidence that I could summon if I were to convince Grant that his retainer had been wisely spent.

The hotel lobby was typical with an upscale, commercial interior design, but it reeked of industrial cleansers and synthesized pine as if someone with a bucket and mop had just swabbed the floor. To the left was the front desk, straight ahead a tile corridor that terminated at the elevator vestibule, to the right a seating area. Armchairs and loveseats were grouped in polite distances from one another and upholstered in soothing, pastel earth tones over a densely patterned dark carpet. The walls were painted forgettable beige, and strategically placed planters provided separation and privacy for seated guests. The front windows overlooked the courtyard and heavy burgundy drapes tied back at each window hung to the floor. All the visual input of the seating area was designed to nullify the chaos of travel, pacify the weary, and subdue the anxiety of unfamiliar surroundings. It looked like a nice place to take a nap.

Opposite the elevators was an unobtrusive sign for the dining room. The entrance was blocked from view by two exceptionally tall palms. Their fronds reached to the full height of the two story vestibule lending an exotic, resort feel as if stepping past the palms you might enter a foreign land of forbidden delights. As I walked through the entrance, what I entered was a generic dining room with all the exotic charm of a franchise restaurant. Potted plants lined the walls, the tables were covered in linen, the coffee cups had saucers, but it was simply more of the pompous charade. Just because you couldn't see the kitchen from the dining room didn't make it special.

Grant was seated at a table near windows that overlooked the hotel swimming pool. He saw me as I approached, stood up and reached out to shake my hand.

"Good morning, Mr. Gardens. Please, sit down."

Grant remained standing while I sat opposite. He was wearing a butterscotch tan blazer of smooth hide that looked like deerskin, faded denim shirt with bolo tie, black trousers and black alligator belt with a modest, silver buckle. I couldn't see his feet but I assumed he had on cowboy boots. This was the former Marlboro Man and on him his attire, even in Los Angeles, didn't seem the least bit affected. Some people can dress that way and never seem out of place regardless of where they are. Grant was one of those people.

"Have you had breakfast?"

"No."

Grant lifted his arm and a waitress approached. She took our order as unobtrusively as possible, maintaining what must be the professional food server monotone, asking the necessary questions, turning and leaving without additional remark. Apparently Grant wasn't the type to ask for a menu.

"Thank you for joining me. Have you made any progress?"

"I have. I visited the crime scene yesterday and spoke with the detective assigned to the case. He said...."

Grant waved his hand in front of his face and shook his head.

"I know that. I'm not interested in those details. That's your job. Tell me, have you found evidence that my attorney can use?"

"Evidence?"

"To exonerate Carolyn."

"Nothing yet," I said.

The waitress returned with glasses of orange juice and a coffee pot. She filled my empty cup and topped up Grant's. Without saying a word she turned and walked away.

"What do you like, Mr. Gardens?"

"What?"

Grant held up one hand between us.

"Wait, let me guess. I bet you're a modern type, prefer an automatic...a Colt, no, that's the wrong generation. Glock or Sig Sauer, then. Am I right?"

Grant leaned forward and lifted the lapel of his blazer. Under his arm was the butt end of a polished, nickel revolver.

"I prefer something portable, myself, when I'm away from home."

He let his lapel fall closed and patted the outside of the material.

"No bulge, no annoying lump. Smith and Wesson Airweight, .357 magnum with hollow points. Reliable and simple with enough stopping power to end the argument. So, what's your preference?"

The idea of a gun had occurred to me but only after seeing Detective Marsons long barrel revolver at Rattlesnake Park. I knew little about handguns, and less about ammunition. But Grant was no fool. He expected a private investigator to be knowledgeable if not armed. Maintaining my professional image required a calculated response.

"I don't have a concealed weapon permit," I said to dodge the issue.

Grant smiled and took a sip of his coffee.

"You don't need a concealed weapon permit, Mr. Gardens. All you need is a holster." He laughed to himself as the waitress put down a creamer and a caddy of jams and jellies in cut-glass pots rather than plastic packages. Who did they think they were they fooling? They probably filled the pots from gallon jugs of institutional condiments. I looked at the waitress but she kept her eyes on the table and hands occupied arranging the plates. After twice visiting our table, I could only describe her as unremarkable, at least in comparison to Leti, whose scent had left me turning in my sleep.

"Then how'd you fly with that?" I said.

Grant shook his head as if he found my question amusing.

"Like anybody else. I checked my bag with an airline approved gun box inside, and declared it at the counter. Perfectly legal."

I nodded and sipped my coffee to cover my surprise. I suppose that many people travel with weapons; hunters, sportsman, competitors. It shouldn't be news that it could be done within the law.

"At some point in a man's life, he has to make a decision. Am I going to be a victim or a survivor? Can I do what I have to do? Men like us accept that as a way of life. We do what needs to be done and let the attorneys work out the details after the fact. Right?"

I stared silently at Grant.

"But look who I'm talking to."

Grant nodded his head as if he'd dispatched with the topic, and sat back in his chair. I didn't know the story behind his selection to play the Marlboro Man in print advertisements and on television, but there was no denying he brought a little of the Wild West attitude to the role. It was perfect casting.

"So, what can I tell you, Mr. Gardens?"

"How is Carolyn?"

"Sleeping. This ordeal has been hard on her."

Grant lifted his coffee cup to his lips and looked at me over the rising steam. They say that the eyes are the windows to the soul, and if that's the case, Grant's soul held experiences that his eyes would not reveal. He held his cup motionless, staring at me with bland skepticism that meant he had me figured out. He knew who I was, the loser, impersonating a private investigator, faking my way through my first case, trying on yet another identity in an attempt to find a fit that I had failed to find with a corporate career, a fiancée that I didn't love, liquor, arson, sobriety, auto repair; wishing all along that something in my life would make some sense.

"You two have some history, together, I gather," he said.

I nodded and drank my coffee.

"From high school."

"That was a long time ago," he said.

"It feels like a long time ago."

"People don't really change, much, do they? Circumstances require that different aspects of their personalities emerge, but no one really changes. Carolyn is very fond of you."

I set my cup on the saucer and waited. Grant lifted his coffee and cupped it with his hands as if trying to warm them.

"Carolyn is innocent. She didn't do anything. Either you will provide the evidence to clear her of the charges or the police will. I know that. She wants you to keep the retainer, regardless. Do you understand?"

This was my turn to stare at Grant. I fixed my gaze and projected all the confidence that I could summon.

"I was hired to perform a service. This isn't a charity, this is my profession. *I am a private investigator.*" And like that, with the affirmative declaration, I felt the full force of commitment. I wasn't anything other than what I said I was. Tom was right: You are what you do.

Grant lowered his cup and nodded. In his eyes a hint of respect seemed to replace the bland skepticism. I didn't know him well enough to place any bets, but my gut told me that we had crossed a threshold to a new understanding. The waitress arrived with plates of food: Bacon and eggs for Grant, eggs and sausage for me. She placed a plate of wheat toast and one of English muffins between us. Once again she turned without speaking, walked away, and returned with the coffee pot to refill our cups. We fell to our meal, eating in silence until each had cleaned his plate. Grant was the first to push away from the table and stand up. He reached out his hand as his cell phone rang in his pocket. I took his hand and we shook.

"Check in when you know something," he said.

"I will."

Grant lifted his cell phone as the waitress stopped at the table.

"Suite 767," he said, raised a hand in parting and walked away with his cell phone to his ear. The waitress looked at me and then at the table. There was a $20 bill beneath Grant's coffee saucer.

"I guess that he took care of the tip," I said.

"He sure did."

Chapter Twenty-nine

I walked out the front doors of the Royal Arms into the wind and the hair stood up on the back of my neck. The Santa Anas were back and the air had a portent of uncertainty. Something was going to happen, sometime soon, and the positive charged ions swirling through the porte-cochere were ripe with warning. As I descended the steps to the walkway, Hamlet gave me that suspicious look again like he didn't recognize me.

"See ya, Hamlet."

He touched the brim of his doorman's cap and bowed slightly at the waist.

"Good day, Sir," he said.

When I got to the MG, I let Stray out to stretch his legs. He sniffed around the side of the trash enclosure while I watched a chef in checkerboard pants and white coat smoking a cigarette outside the back door. The chef tipped his chin toward us, flipped his cigarette butt into the bushes, and went inside. I put Stray in the MG, climbed behind the wheel and twisted the key. Nothing happened. I twisted the key again and nothing. A slight annoyance, but I was riding the personal wave of confidence from my breakfast declaration and was not about to let a minor inconvenience knock me off my center. I selected second gear and rolled out of the parking stall. When I released the clutch, the engine fired. It was going to take more than a balky starter to bring me down. *I Am A Private Investigator.*

At Big Magic, Tom wasn't in. I changed my clothes and dragged the doormat to the garage entry so that Stray would have something to lie on that would get him off the concrete floor. He still wasn't his old self, moving with obvious care, and probably needed more time to recover. With very little encouragement and only a quick glance my direction, he flopped on the doormat, tucked his front paws to his body and closed his eyes. I got to work on the Alfa, removing the remaining brake parts front and rear. Focusing on the task at hand helped put the imminent meeting with Tamara out of my mind. The thought of telling her about Edward's death worried me. I had honest feelings for Tamara and didn't want to do anything that might hurt her, but it was better that the news came from me than from Detective Marsons. Bad news is still bad news, but coming from someone you know can soften the blow.

Tom arrived about 10:30. He parked his Suburban in front of the office and unloaded two cardboard cartons from the back. Stray watched him but didn't move from his spot on the doormat. Tom stepped over Stray into the garage with a big smile on his face.

"How's it going?"

I pointed to the vacant wheel wells of the Alfa and to the parts on the floor.

"Making some progress," I said.

"Wait until you see what I bought," Tom said and disappeared into the office. A few minutes later, as I was fitting the backing plates to the rear axle, he stepped into the garage. He had two flintlock pistols shoved into a wide, weight lifter's belt, and a long barrel musket in his hands.

"What do you think?"

"Uh, I don't know what to say Tom. What are you doing?"

"History my friend. The history of armed combat on the great American frontier."

"Are those authentic?"

"You bet. Matched set of original Kentucky pistols," he said and patted the pistols in his belt. "And one Revolutionary War musket. She's the real deal. I'm a Minuteman."

The smile on his big, round face was as lunatic as it was genuine. How could I point out the improbability of a 400-pound, middle-aged Minuteman in a weightlifter's belt and Nike tennis shoes in the 21st century?

"That's really great, Tom. A new interest."

"You got that right. I bought a uniform, too. I'm going to be a re-enactor." He leaned the musket against the wall and pulled the pistols from his belt. "And these babies actually work," he said. "Trust me, my ancestors were highland warriors. If you need the heat, I can bring it!"

The childlike sincerity was endearing. When Tom got into something, he went all the way. Back in high school, he was the guy who celebrated his Urquhart heritage by coming to class on Halloween in costume. Freshman year, he wore a Scottish outfit with tartan kilt of family heraldry, a sporran, and knee socks. Every year the costume progressed in authenticity and effect. By his senior year, he had added black, brass buckle brogues, Jacobite shirt, a wool fly plaid, and a foot-long sgian dubhs and sheath that sent him to the principal's office. He was a big guy then, a Varsity football team athlete four years running, and no one that I saw took the opportunity to poke fun at his outfit.

"I'll keep that in mind," I said.

Tom pointed to Stray. "He sick or something?"

"Had a tough night. I want to keep an eye on him."

"Just today, right? I've got allergies."

"Just today."

"Only out here, so I won't need my nose spray?"

"Only out here, Tom."

Tom shook his head with a frown and then extended his arms. The smile on his big, round face returned as he examined the pistols in the garage light.

"Aren't these something? Can you imagine, going into battle with 'em?"

"They're very nice."

"I can hardly wait to try 'em out. What are you doing later?"

"Well, since you mentioned it, I'm taking off early today."

Tom frowned, looked at the Alfa, and then at me. I could tell what he was thinking, so I pre-empted his question.

"I'm in good shape, here. The rears will be done today, and when the swivels come back from the machinist, I'll be ready. We're right on schedule for Friday."

Tom tucked the pistols into his weight lifters belt and picked up the musket. The frown morphed into a smile as he hefted the musket to his shoulder and pointed it across the garage.

"You still involved in that other stuff?"

"I'm on a case."

Tom sighted along the long barrel. He cocked the hammer, closed one eye and pulled the trigger. The metallic snap brought Stray's head upright and he looked around the garage as if unsure of his surroundings. He saw me, wagged his stubby tail and set his head back on the mat with a sigh. Tom looked at Stray and then leaned the musket against the garage wall.

"Remember what I said about bringing the heat. One look at these babies and anyone would think twice. A little firepower can bring a lot of discouragement."

Tom pulled the pistols from his weightlifter's belt, pointed them at the far wall and fired each one.

"You can't go around threatening people with firearms, Tom. You get arrested for that behavior."

"I know."

"People go to jail, right?"

"Not Jim Rockford."

"Who's Jim Rockford?"

"Detective like you."

"I'm a *private investigator.*"

"Same thing, on TV," he said as he snapped the hammers back and pulled the triggers. He smiled and blew across each empty barrel in a theatrical gesture right out of vaudeville. "I'm ready."

"Got it," I said.

Tom was an odd guy but completely genuine. When he made a commitment to something, it was for real. Participation had been his mantra ever since he got sober two decades earlier, and he hadn't so much as changed with the sobriety as he had evolved on a grander scale the person that he was all along: eccentric, at times a little delusional, and loyal to a fault.

I worked through lunch and into the early afternoon as Tom stayed in the office on the phone or his computer. Every now and then, he'd stick his head into the garage to tell me something he'd learned about being a re-enactor. Stray slept soundly, barking a few times in his dreams, twitching and paddling his paws like he was still on the chase at the river camp. Around 3:00, I had the rear brakes finished and had gone as far as I could go without the other parts. Looking around, there was nothing left to be done; I couldn't avoid Tamara any longer. I cleaned up in the washroom and changed my clothes. The gamy funk was back. I don't know if stress, worry, or excitement were the root cause, but even after I removed my undershirt and washed my armpits in the sink, I still stank. It wasn't the worse that it had ever been, but it was noticeable. I poked my head in the office as I was leaving.

"Tom, I've gone as far as I can, today."

Tom was thumbing through a magazine. Next to the Kentucky pistols, there was a stack of them on the table in front of him with covers featuring Redcoats and Minutemen. I had a strong suspicion of what Tom's Halloween costume would be next year.

"Huh? OK, right."

"See you later," I said.

"What time you coming in?" Tom said and looked over the top of the magazine.

"The swivels should be here when, about 10:00?"

"Probably earlier."

"You going to pick them up?"

"No, drop off."

"Then I'll be in around 9:00. See you later."

"You working your case?"

"I am."

Tom lowered the magazine and got his serious, sponsor look on his face.

"You know, that detective stuff can be dangerous. Why don't you forget about it, come on full time with me. Before you get hurt."

I reached down to scratch Stray's good ear. Tom was right, and his offer generous, but it did not feel like the direction I was supposed to go.

"I appreciate that, Tom. But I started this and I need to see it through."

Tom nodded, dropped the magazine and lifted one pistol from the table.

"No good deed goes unpunished, huh?" he said.

I chuckled and shook my head. Truer words have never been spoken.

"Remember what I said. I can bring the heat."

"Right. I'll see you tomorrow."

Stray followed me to the MG. I opened the hatchback and he climbed in with a little more energy than he'd shown this morning. I got in the car and the engine started with the first try. Tom stood in the office doorway and watched. His body filled the entire opening and with the pistols stuffed in his weightlifter's belt, he cast an imposing presence. If you didn't know any better, he might seem intimidating even without the archaic small arms. I waved as I exited. Stray put his front paws on the center console and leaned into the passenger headrest. He was back at his post, ever vigilant, eyes straight ahead peering out the front windshield, apparently on the mend.

We drove across town to the apartment. I fed Stray, showered and changed clothes. Even after applying deodorant and baby powder, some body odor remained. I grabbed my field jacket with both cell phones and an improvised leash I'd cut from a length of laundry line at the shop. We rolled down the entry drive and into the street by 4:20. Along the route to the freeway, Santa Anas gusted and whipped the high branches of trees. Traffic at this time of day was always jammed so we took an alternate route, past Rose Hills Memorial Park along the Puente Hills. The Puente Hills are just that; a transverse range of hills along the northeastern edge of the Los Angeles Basin. The Santa Anas funnel through mountain canyons and blast past the hills. The wind rocked the MG and a tailwind pushed us. By the time we got to Tamara's salon, it was almost 6:00. I parked in front of the salon and left Stray in the car. A teenage girl was in the first stall with a female stylist at work on her hair, and in another stall, a middle-aged woman was having her hair washed by a tiny Asian man with orange hair. This was the unavoidable moment of truth.

Tamara was sitting on a tall stool at a front desk near the entrance. She was wearing white jeans, the red pumps, a silk, button down blouse in peach with gold chains around her neck and her hair was pinned on top of her head. Loose strands drifted across her forehead giving her a look of dreamy, adolescent innocence. She smiled when she saw me, came around the desk and gave me a hug and long kiss. When she leaned back her head, she kept herself pressed tight against me and looked over her shoulder to the stylist as if to demonstrate that I belonged to her. It seemed unnecessary, but in this competitive feminine environment for attention, possession is paramount.

"This is a nice surprise," Tamara said.

The female stylist was mid 40s, Latina, wearing black combat boots, gray leggings over black tights, and a gray sweatshirt with a gapping, ragged neck and cropped sleeves. She had short, black hair rising above a lavender headband and painted on, lop-sided eyebrows with an acute arch at their center. She could have stepped right out of an 80's music video, a period in which she must have reached her height of glory and was reluctant to let go. She fixed me with a long, cold look that meant she'd seen too many men in her life to give me the benefit of doubt. She was cutting her client's bangs, but I sensed that her ear was tuned to overhear my response. I chose my words carefully so as to make my affection clear.

"I've been thinking about you all day."

"Something a girl always likes to hear," Tamara said. She pulled back, smiling with bright, green eyes, and took my hand. "Are you here for a haircut?"

"Do I need one?"

Tamara dropped my hand and looked at my hair. She turned my head around with one hand and poked at my neckline.

"You could use a trim. Do you want to sit down?"

"Not now. There's something I need to talk to you about."

Tamara's face became serious. She tilted her head to one side and raised a hand to her throat. The fingers cupped the point of her chin and her eyes narrowed with dire expectation.

"What is it?"

"Can we go somewhere private?"

I followed Tamara through the salon, past the tiny Asian man with the orange hair and the woman at the shampoo bowl, past the bathroom, past a sideboard with coffee maker and plate of crumbs from what must have been an afternoon snack, and into a small alcove with cabinets and shelves filled with folded towels. Tamara stopped by the cabinets, crossed her arms and hugged them to her chest.

"I've been a real pain. I know that. You're probably frustrated with me, aren't you?"

"No, Tamara. I'm not frustrated. This has nothing to do with you and me."

She loosened her arms and lifted her chin. I could see relief mixed with curiosity on her face as her posture shifted to one foot and she leaned back against a cabinet. Her heel slipped out of one red pump and she let it drop to the floor.

"Then what is it?"

This was the moment that I'd been dreading. I've never been good in situations like this. I don't know what to say, and when I do say something, it never seems to be the right thing.

"There's no easy way to say this, so I'll just say it. The police found Edward's body Tuesday night. I'm sorry, Tamara. Edward's dead."

Tamara nodded her head three times. Her green eyes went glassy and she blinked once before speaking. They cleared for an instant, and then began to glass over again.

"I knew that it was only a matter of time."

She caught a sob in her throat and took a deep breath, clasped her hands and raised them to her mouth.

"I'm sorry, Tamara."

She sniffled, straightened her back and stood up straight. This was going to be her brave show, facing the moment, but the personal collapse would soon follow. If she had anything that I could learn, I needed to learn it now.

"He was doing so much better, sometimes sleeping here, using the bathroom."

"He slept here?"

Tamara tilted her chin over her shoulder.

"He had a key for the back. He slept in the utility room."

"Show me," I said.

Tamara led me along a narrow hallway. On one side was a laundry room that backed up to the bathroom wall. On the other side, an area with a few chairs and a television on a low shelf. Beyond this room, there was a single door with a hasp and padlock on it.

"I don't have a key," she said. Her voice was weak, as if it began in her throat instead of her diaphragm, and I could see tears pooling at her lower lids.

"Are you all right?"

Tamara sniffed, took a deep breath and nodded. "I don't know."

I lifted the padlock and gave it a tug. The hasp had been installed incorrectly with the mounting screws exposed. Whoever did the installation was no handyman.

"Do you have any tools?"

"A few," Tamara said. She went past me to the laundry room and returned with a plastic toolbox. Inside were a few screwdrivers, hammer, pliers, and some loose hardware. I selected a screwdriver and began to remove the hasp.

"That was his private place," Tamara said. "He never let me see it."

"You said he slept here. Alone?"

Tamara nodded.

"Did his partner ever come here with him?"

Tamara shook her head 'no.' I removed the last screw and pried loose the hasp from the doorframe. The door swung open to a narrow room, just big enough for a cot. Some new clothing, with purchase tags attached, was stacked on the end of the cot. I twisted a switch on a bare bulb socket hanging from the ceiling.

"Oh!" Tamara said.

'Oh' was right. On the end of one wall was an electrical breaker panel. A photograph of a skinny young girl, about five years old, with dark hair and amber eyes, was tucked beneath the edge of the panel door. The long wall had half-a-dozen water pipes running horizontally. Those were the only utilities in the room. The rest of the wall space, carefully segmented and boxed in red outline on all sides, was covered with mathematical equations, a diagram of the solar system across the ceiling with intersecting lines, arcs and arrows connecting the planets, sketches of alien figures with oversized heads, and a string of characters comprising an expansive equation. The complexity of the calculations alone was overwhelming: Continuous strings of characters stretched from floor to waist height in a precise horizontal band like alphanumeric wainscoting. Each group of equations terminated at the box edge of a segmented section, and an arrow transitioned them to the next box. The intersecting lines began above where the boxes ended. In the center of the ceiling was a drawing of a human eye, as if some otherworldly entity were staring downward from outer space. The solar system on the ceiling projected lines down the walls to join the alphanumeric wainscoting. A single, thick black line terminated at a red 'X' above the cot with a polygon outline that looked like California. Written in small characters were 'Solstice' and the date, '21 December' bracketed with parentheses and underlined. Beneath the date in block letters were two names: Edward Lee Cochran and John Kennedy. There was a clear, organizational component to the whole thing. The intent had been considered and exact. If Edward were anything, he was some sort of mathematical genius.

"Did you know about any of this?"

"No, I don't have a key."

"Where'd these come from?"

Tamara looked at the clothes. A heavy sweatshirt, long sleeved undershirt, and two pairs of thick socks were neatly folded.

"I left them outside the door," she muttered as her eyes filled with tears.

"When?"

She began to cry, the tears running down her cheeks and dripping from her chin. I put my arms around her and she sobbed against my shoulder. The horrible news had found its way to her heart, transformed from abstract, spoken words into concrete, overwhelming sorrow. The collapse had begun and there wasn't much to do except hold her and wait. A voice called down the hallway from the salon.

"Everything all right, Tam?"

Tamara sniffled and wiped at her eyes with the heel of her hand. I picked up a sock and blotted the tears from her cheeks. Her face was pale and in her green eyes guileless grief stared out at me with an unanswerable plea.

"Yes," she mumbled.

I turned off the light and closed the utility door. Tamara leaned against me, put her arm around my waist and we walked passed the stylists at their stations toward the front door. The tiny Asian man glanced my direction and then returned to rinsing his client's hair. The Latina stylist looked at me as if I were some kind of monster, the sole agent of Tamara's sadness, another male intent on ruining some innocent woman's life.

"Lock up for me, when you leave, Carla. Please?"

Carla scowled as we walked past and I elected not to point out the lop-sided eyebrows. She didn't look like the type to respond kindly to constructive criticism.

"You OK?" she said.

Tamara sniffled again and cleared her throat.

"We're going upstairs. I'll see you in the morning," she said.

We exited the front door, walked the few feet along the sidewalk to the street-side entrance to the apartment, and went upstairs. At the top of the stairs, Tamara just stared at the door lock.

"Do you have your keys?"

She shook her head and looked down toward the salon.

"OK, just sit here. I'll get them."

I went down the steps and back to the salon. Inside, I asked Carla for the keys to Tamara's apartment.

"What'd you do to her?"

I looked around the front desk and saw a purse on the floor.

"This Tamara's?"

Carla scowled with open hostility. I caught the eye of the tiny Asian man watching from his station. He nodded his head while combing his client's long, wet hair.

"I should call the police on you," Carla said.

I grabbed the purse and started out the front door.

"Go ahead. Ask for Detective Marsons. Tell him Martin says *'Hello.'* "

Tamara was sitting on the landing in front of her apartment door, hunched over with her hands tucked to her chest and staring straight ahead at the stairway wall. I dug through the purse and found her keys. We went inside and she sat on the sofa in the front room. I went into the kitchen and put on a kettle of water.

"I'll fix some tea, all right?"

Tamara lay down with her knees to her chest. There was a woven quilt across the back so I spread it over her. Someone downstairs pounded on the street-side door. The color was returning to her face but streaks of mascara spotted her cheeks. That same someone continued pounding. When I got to the door, the sidewalk was empty and Stray had his nose against the window of the MG. His eyes twitched between me, the street-side door, and something out of my view. I went to the car to let him out and surveilled the neighborhood. Most of the shops had closed for the evening. Lights were beginning to glow in the streetlamps that lined the block. A few cars were parked on the opposite side of the street, but there was no one around. The teenage girl exited the salon and smiled as she passed us. Her dark hair was short and cut in an asymmetrical fashion that must have been popular on some planet. Stray followed me up the stairs and into the apartment. I put him on a 'Down' command while I located cups and selected tea bags from an assortment of boxes. The street-side door rattled once more with what sounded like a kick. Stray lifted his head, anxiously looking around, mangled ear turned toward the noise. I pointed to the floor with my finger and he rested his head on his paws but kept his eyes on me. Tamara was asleep on the sofa, in her apartment, with man's best friend near her feet and me, in the kitchen, preparing tea. At another time, under different circumstances, this domestic image might have been something right off a Norman Rockefeller canvas. If Norman had painted Boxers.

Chapter Thirty

Santa Anas rattled the casement windows with each gust and slipped between sash and sill to flutter the kitchen curtains. Tamara slept unperturbed by the rattling or the wind. My cell phone chimed with a number that I didn't recognize, so I went into the bathroom and closed the door to muffle the conversation.

"Hello?"

"You busy?" a high-pitched voice asked.

Below the bathroom window was Tamara's Fiat. The parking space next to it was empty; the dark blue Crown Victoria I'd seen before was gone. Santa Anas ripped through the alley with a horsetail of dust, whistling past power lines, bending back a loose shingle on a roof across the way. The waning moon was low on the horizon and the air, cleared of smog, seemed to vibrate like millions of charged particles in constant motion. Venus, unmistakable in the dusk, shined dimly against a fading blue backdrop. More planets, distant flickering bodies in the Milky Way, would pop out as the sky grew dark. Beyond the Milky Way, even more planets, light years away; unknown and unimaginable planets in galaxies with solar systems all their own; unknown and unimaginable civilizations populated by alien beings with oversized heads and a keen interest in American citizens; who could know what existed in outer space? Who could really know? On this charged night, Edward's alien images seemed plausible.

"Remind me who this is," I said.

"How is Stray?"

"You are?"

"One meal and already forgotten."

It had taken a few seconds, but the 'meal' clue was what I needed.

"Hello, detective. How'd you get this number?"

"I'm a detective, remember?"

"Right. What do you want?"

"I have some information for you."

"You do?"

"I do."

"And you can share this information with a *nonprofessional*?"

The line was silent, my remark hanging in the electric air between us. The wind gusted again and the windows rattled and Detective Marsons cleared his throat and spoke slowly.

"I'm extending professional courtesy."

From the bathroom doorway, I could see the end of the sofa. Tamara's foot twitched as if she were dreaming, and then disappeared from view. I checked Stray on the floor. His paws were still. If he were dreaming, he wasn't chasing anything.

"I'm busy," I said.

Another pause before a response.

"I mean it. Professional courtesy. Maybe you're not busy later?"

"Maybe."

"It's up to you."

"OK."

"Meet me at Four Café. 9:00?"

"I'll be there."

The line went dead. In the front room, Tamara sat upright with the woven quilt drawn across her lap. She reached down to pet Stray as I walked into the kitchen. From the curtained window, I could see Carla and the tiny Asian man climbing into their vehicles. They drove off, one following the other, Carla in a mid-nineties Toyota Z-car, the tiny Asian man in a full-sized pickup truck. My cell phone chimed again. Marce was calling. I let the call go to message and poured the kettle, shut off the stove and went back to the front room. Tamara was staring at her hands, face composed but vacant of emotion. I set the tea down and sat beside her. She leaned over and rocked her shoulder against mine. I handed her a cup and we sat next to each other, drinking tea on the sofa, listening to the wind rattling the loose casement windows, listening to our private thoughts, each of us processing the personal loss, unspeaking the unspeakable words present in a room overfilled with a widow's sadness.

When I opened my eyes more than an hour had passed. Tamara was curled against me like a child, legs tucked up on the sofa, quilt across her shoulder and chest. Stray was asleep on the floor. I straightened my legs and Tamara's eyes opened.

"I fell asleep," she said. "Again."

Tamara stretched her arms over her head, saw Stray, and stood up. She bent down and gave him a scratch along his back, picked up the cups and carried them to the kitchen.

"How do you feel?"

I heard her rinse the cups and put them in the sink.

"Exhausted," I think she said. She came back and stood in front of me stretching her arms. Then she loosened the button of her jeans, unzipped the fly and pulled out the tails of her blouse. She hesitated, pulled pins from her hair and twisted the loose strands in her fingers. There was no 'come hither' look in her eyes; just something undeniably primal, raw and needy.

"I'm going to bed," she said and started for her bedroom. "Stray can stay, too."

She didn't so much make love as she violated me. She was savage and animated, grinding her teeth and pulling at my hair, moaning like a feral cat and mouthing syllables outside the English language. When we finished, she curled up in a fetal position, closed her eyes and did not utter a single word. As I slid from the bed to gather my clothes, I pulled the covers around her shoulders and tucked her in. She clasped the material in her fists like an infant clutching a security blanket, and by the time I'd dressed, she was sound asleep. Her face was quiet and peaceful, the immediate pain disposed within the shared coupling, where she'd found whatever temporary solace she could. Tomorrow would bring a new perspective on Edward's death. How the finality of his absence would shape her reality could only be understood one day at a time. There is no script for the immensity of human loss. You cannot prepare yourself for what is beyond the limitations of imagination. The only known constant is time. It may heal all wounds, but at what cost? Something of one's self is gone. The world is forever changed for those who have lost someone they loved.

Chapter Thirty-one

I reached the parking lot of the Four Café restaurant around 9:30. Detective Marsons sat, with an empty dinner plate and coffee mug in front of him, at the only occupied table. His expression gave away nothing as I passed the front register, crossed the floor to his table and dropped on an empty chair. A windbreaker was hanging across the back of his chair, and he was wearing a blue, long-sleeved shirt, the maroon tie, the same slacks and running shoes as before, and the ever present coffee stirrer clenched between his teeth. He crossed his arms and waited for me to speak.

"Sorry I'm late."

Detective Marsons picked up his coffee mug, drank and set it down. He smoothed his pencil thin moustache and then twined long, bony fingers together on the table.

"No, you're not," he said.

He couldn't have any idea where I'd been or what I'd been doing, but as a detective, he was a shrewd observer and saw right through my insincerity.

"You're right, I'm not. But I'm sorry that I made you wait."

"That may be true, but I didn't wait," he said. "I *chose* to eat dinner at 9:00 and you happened to arrive before I left."

"OK."

Detective Marsons stared at me over the rim of his coffee mug. His eyes were flat but with no indication of annoyance. He searched my face for almost half a minute in a silent stand off, as if he wanted me to be the one to speak first, as if by speaking first, I would somehow defer to him, the victor in this grownup impasse of childish petulance.

"You said that you had some information?"

Detective Marsons nodded his head and sat back in his chair.

"Look who decided to stop by."

I turned and Leti was standing at my left shoulder. She leaned down and spoke into my good ear.

"I thought that you forgot all about me," she said.

She wore a server's apron, the familiar rubber clogs and low-rise jeans with a tailored, blue vest from a man's suit over a white, button down shirt. The cuffs were folded back to her forearms, and the shirt was unbuttoned to the vee of the blue vest exposing a shiny, orange camisole underneath. Her short hair was loose, and renegade strands of gray that I hadn't noticed before mixed with dark, wavy curls. On top of her head was a pair of heavy, black-framed eyeglasses. She stepped around to the other side of me and said something that made Detective Marsons smile.

"What? I didn't hear that," I said.

Leti smiled and put her hands on her hips: "The regular?"

I nodded. For some inexplicable reason, there was no howling jet engine behind my eyes, no pheromones locking my attention on her. And there was no rolling gyration to Leti's hips as she shuffled her feet without lifting them from the floor. It may have been an off night for her.

"What did she say?"

"Asked about your four legged friend. I guess that he's at home?"

"No, he's in the car."

"Recovered from his adventure?"

"Getting there," I said. "So, what do you have to share with a *nonprofessional*?"

Detective Marsons drained his coffee mug, set it down and put the coffee stirrer in his mouth. The front door of Four Café opened and a gust of wind surged inside, circled the room and over our table. The back of a man's head with dark, wind-fanned hair appeared in the doorway and then the door closed.

"Strong winds, those Santa Anas. I could feel them driving over," I said.

Detective Marsons cleared his throat before he spoke: "*It was one of those hot dry Santa Anas that come down through the mountain passes and curl your hair and make your nerves jump and your skin itch. On nights like that every booze party ends in a fight. Meek little wives feel the edge of the carving knife and study their husbands' necks. Anything can happen.*"

"You read Chandler?"

"I read," he said and peered inside his coffee mug before setting it down.

"Detective stuff?"

"I read all sorts of 'stuff'.' "

I nodded my head. It seemed that each time I talked with the detective, it was like uncovering another layer of his personality. He was no ordinary cop. The Buddhism, vegan diet, literary knowledge, and even his attention to my career path attested to that.

"I spoke to Grant, uh, Mr. Parker, earlier, and he said something that I can't figure out."

Detective Marsons fingered his empty coffee mug, rotating it on its base, and then holding it up in the air and looking toward the kitchen.

"What's that?"

"I told him that I'd been to the river camp, and he said he knew that. How could he know that? "

"Maybe he's having you followed?"

"I don't think so. I noticed an old Dodge that I'd seen before parked near there, but it was empty when we drove past."

"No one else? "

As I shook my head, my cell phone chimed in my pocket. I checked the display and it was Marce. Detective Marsons pointed to the cell phone.

"That your only phone?"

I nodded.

"Been in your possession all the time?"

I nodded again.

"People put tracking software on phones. It let's them pinpoint the phone's location."

"Not on this phone."

"They can put it on anyone's phone."

Leti brushed my shoulder as she walked past with a coffee pot in her hand. She turned her head and the sly, alluring smile from the night before was back as she bent to refill the detective's coffee mug. Detective Marsons winked at her and then looked at me as if the two shared some secret. Leti patted my shoulder and walked off as I was thinking about what the detective had said. The only time my phone was out of my sight was when I left it in the toolbox at Big Magic, and no one ever came into the garage.

"We have the suspect in custody."

"You do?"

"We do, but he won't be charged with any crime. Claims he found Edward dead at the camp. The two of them had a death pact, only one of them backed out."

"Death pact?"

"That's right. There was supposed to be an encounter with a spaceship that would pick up both men. Edward Lee Cochran had planned the event to coincide with the full moon, and laid out markers in the riverbed so the spaceship could find them. There were detailed documents in his car describing the encounter. I've seen it before. Remember the 'Heaven's Gate' cult down in San Diego? It's the same thing."

"Who's the suspect?"

"John Kennedy. We found a syringe at the crime scene. One set of prints on it. Some kind of poison. No indication of foul play. Case closed."

"Syringe?"

"That's right."

More tracks in the snow. But there are different types of tracks. The tracks made when a creature walks, trots or runs are not the same. It's the track inside the track that reveals the truth.

"So you assume Edward injected himself?"

"The evidence leads to that conclusion."

"What if someone else injected him? What about John?"

"Possible, but it doesn't feel right. No motive."

"No autopsy?"

"On a homeless person?"

Detective Marsons leaned into his chair and pushed at his coffee mug with his long, bony fingers. His lips pulled back with irritation and he bounced the coffee stirrer against his teeth and exhaled.

"The county's broke. Don't you read the papers? No autopsy or toxicology. Coroner writes suicide as manner of death on the death certificate. Lab confirms the substance in the syringe. That's it."

"So you'll never really know, will you?"

Detective Marsons stared at me, the coffee stirrer motionless, clenched lips now a thin ribbon of suppressed frustration, not so much at me, I imagined, but at a system that thwarted his professional and spiritual aspiration.

"Captain's directive. Case closed. Move on," Detective Marsons said.

"And deconstructing history to reconstruct the truth. Where does that fit?"

Detective Marsons smiled, stood up and put on his blue windbreaker.

"What about his sister?"

"Charges dropped. The body will be released tomorrow morning. She can contact the coroner's office. Her attorney probably already has the details."

"You said Edward had a car?"

"At impound."

"What kind of car?"

"Crown Vic."

Leti arrived with a goblet of lemonade, napkin and flatware. She positioned everything without saying a word, turned and walked back to the kitchen.

"What about John?"

Detective Marsons put his hands on the table, body hinged forward at the waist, the blue windbreaker hanging loose off his skeletal frame. He enunciated each syllable as if he were talking to a child.

"John will be processed out, provided clean clothes, pocket money and a ride wherever he wants to go within the county. The case is closed."

"Just like that?"

"Captain's directive."

Leti set my dinner in front of me. She smiled at Detective Marsons as he straightened and stepped back from the table.

"I found some…."

Detective Marsons held up his palm and shook his head.

"The case is closed."

"I figured being who you are, you'd want to know," I said.

I watched him, not indifferent, not callous, just better informed with years of experience, the kind of experience that teaches you when to back off, the kind of experience that tells you when it is time to let go and move on. This was simply the death of another homeless citizen already given up for lost by society. With all the other crimes in this county, I suppose a professional develops a sense for when to call it quits. I did not have his experience but I did have gut instinct and I'd learned to trust it. I couldn't put my finger on it but something wasn't right. Detective Marsons smiled and pointed to my plate.

"Aren't you going to eat?"

"You're wrong, you know. I can feel it in my gut."

Detective Marsons smiled again and without another word, turned and walked out the front door. He said something to Leti as he left, and she came over to the table, collected his empty plate and mug, and then sat in his chair. She leaned forward on her elbows, dishware in her hands, and smiled. I caught a feint aroma of decomposing leaves.

"I'm not sure about you, yet," she said.

At close distance, there was more age in her face than I'd seen last night. Fine, shallow lines between the brows, puffiness below her lower eyelids, a looseness to the skin along her jaw line. She may have dressed like an artsy, twenty-something bohemian, but really studying her now, without the pheromones and the howling jet engine distracting my perception, I could see her clearly and she looked to be approaching late 30s. I smiled before taking a bite of my patty melt.

"But I have a feeling," she said.

I took another bite and then drank from the goblet.

"You have good Chi," she said. "It's helping me decide."

Leti had a feeling, Detective Marsons had a feeling, I had a feeling: A good deal of decision making this evening was based on nothing more than feelings.

"Really. Like, you do."

She held the dishware at the edge of the table and swept some crumbs to the plate.

"You know I like you, right?"

I don't know if my silence were propelling her conversation or she was in one of those brutally honest moods that accompany an ill-timed lapse of judgment and leave you wishing you'd said less than you had. Something different was in the air, and it wasn't the absence of her flirty personality or the fecund funk of pheromones that had almost driven me to smash through the Four Café windows. She hesitated, a hint of insecurity at the corners of her half open mouth, and in that moment I knew what it was: it wasn't her, it was me. I'd just come from Tamara's bed with a post-coital funk of my own. Somehow, in the mystery that is women's intuition, she knew it. She knew that someone else wanted me, and even if she didn't, the fact that someone else did, was enough to make me desirable. Just like the group of women from the reunion who, until Marce befriended me and I was granted social clearance, were entirely disinterested.

In sixth grade, I had a crush on Christy Brasher but she ignored me. I told my mother, and during a rare moment equal parts sober and medication free, she offered some simple advice: Pay attention to someone else. So I did. I focused my interest on Annette Hammond, and it worked. Although a relationship with Christy never developed, at the end of the school year, on the night before my family moved to California, I had a long telephone conversation with her. She said that until I began paying attention to Annette, she never had any interest in me. But after Annette liked me, she liked me. Too little too late, but proof positive of one thing: whether toys, careers, or partners, people want what someone else has. We learn most of the lessons of human behavior before we leave elementary school.

"This isn't the place to talk, really. You're the last table and then I'm off. We can go somewhere else," she said. "Stick around?"

I finished the first half of my patty melt. Leti rose from the table, head nodding up and down as if confirming my unspoken consent, and walked off. She twisted her head around with a pleasant smile, a professional server to customer smile, stopped and smiled again before she disappeared into the kitchen. I hadn't said one word and yet it felt as if we'd had a conversation. Whatever she wanted to discuss was important to her, important enough to share it with a man she'd only met yesterday and, outside of a luke warm assessment from Detective Marsons, a man about whom she knew next to nothing. Grant's cell phone chimed in my pocket.

"Martin, two things: First, thank you for your service. All charges are being dropped. Second, a funeral is arranged for Saturday morning. I realize that it is short notice, but Carolyn has requested you attend. The public burial will be 11:00 AM, at Rose Hills."

"Grant, I can't take credit …."

"I'll see you then. Goodbye," he said and the call ended. The phone in my hand was not mine; it had not been in my possession all the time; and the person that gave it to me was the person most interested in Edward's whereabouts. The phone didn't look any different than before but it felt different. It felt like a violation of privacy and I felt like a conspirator to a felony.

Leti returned to the table with a pitcher and refilled my goblet with lemonade. She put the pitcher down and sat in the chair opposite me.

"You're like curious, aren't you? I can tell."

I continued eating and nodded my head. Leti leaned forward on her elbows and spoke softly: "Remember what I said last time?"

I swallowed and drank some lemonade. She watched my actions and put a hand on my forearm. I had no idea what she'd said last time.

"This isn't something that just came to mind, you know. I've been thinking about it for a long time, waiting, considering my options. I don't have a lot, really. Like I'm a waitress, right, and I'm not getting any younger, either."

I raised one eyebrow in confusion.

"What are you talking about?"

"We have good energy, don't you think?"

"I do," I said.

"You have good Chi, too".

I nodded.

"You're tall and healthy, right? You look pretty healthy. I can tell that you're smart, you eat like you're smart. Lots of hair, too."

Leti smiled, but there was nothing romantic in it, not a hint of sexual attraction, nothing libidinous in her tone of voice. More patronizing than salacious, and when she spoke it sounded like a pragmatic recital of a prepared punch list.

"I like you and you like me, right?" she said. "That's important, too."

I smiled as I swallowed, wiped my mouth with a napkin, and cupped her hand on my forearm.

"I am attracted to you and, to be frank, the other night I almost broke in here to get my hands on you."

"Oh, rad!" she said with a gleam in her eyes, and then the gleam faded. "Well, anyway, here's the deal…."

Something fell in the kitchen, crashing to the floor with a metallic rattle. The front door swung open and the head that I'd seen before poked inside. Someone yelled from the kitchen and the door closed. Leti leaned across the table to my right ear and I think she said *"My clock is ticking. I need your sperm."*

I took the last bite of my patty melt: "What?"

She sat back, the expression on her face rife with confusion, her arms crossed over her chest.

"Leti, I can't hear very well in that ear. An old accident. What did you say?"

The front door opened and the same man stepped inside. A gust of wind brushed my cheek and the hair rose on the back of my neck. The man stood with a blanket wrapped around his shoulders. His dark hair was a mess, one side windblown and the rest matted as if he'd been lying down. Someone yelled again from the kitchen: "Get outta here. Now! You know the rules!" The man looked around at the empty tables, at me and Leti, and exited. Another gust of wind crossed my cheek. I turned my good ear toward Leti.

"Say it again."

Leti stared at me and stood up. "This isn't the place. Wait for me, all right?"

The food was settling in my stomach and all at once, as I nodded my head to Leti, I was spent. Even after the catnap at Tamara's, the activity of the long day was catching up with me and I was exhausted. It seemed to take all my energy to lift the goblet and drink. And something other than the patty melt was churning in my gut.

"Leti, I'm beat. How about we talk another time?"

Leti stared. I couldn't tell if she were confused or angry. She pulled a scratch pad from her apron pocket and scribbled on it.

"Call me, tomorrow," she said. "But not too early."

The number had a local area code.

"I will."

"Promise?"

"Yes Maam."

Leti tilted her head to one side and looked at me as if she were appraising the years in my tired face. Then without a word she waltzed off, untying her apron as she went. There was no ticket on the table for me to pay and it didn't seem like she'd be returning. All I had was a $20 bill so I put it under my plate and got up to leave. The entire café was deserted. The cash register was vacant and the room was silent. No muffled voices from the back; Not a clanging pot or pan from the kitchen. I walked out the front door into the windy night. Just east of the Four Café, huddled on the sidewalk against the side of the building, was the man who had stepped inside. He was seated with a blanket around his shoulders and a piece of cardboard folded to his chest like a warrior's shield battling the ferocious Santa Anas. Another one of the homeless, like Edward or John, caught out in the weather on a windy night, waiting for the arrival of aliens and in the mean time just trying to survive. As I climbed into the MG, I looked back to see the chef in checkerboard pants, white coat and a ball cap backwards on his head, carrying two Styrofoam containers. The homeless man reached for the containers and then hunkered down behind the cardboard windbreak. The chef stood up, looking less like an alien and more like a guardian angel, nodded at me, and went back inside. It was going to be a long, windy night for that homeless man, but at least it wouldn't be on an empty stomach.

Chapter Thirty-two

Tom was in the office when I arrived. I parked in front of the empty bay and stepped through the shop door. He had the musket disassembled on his desk and was examining each piece with a jeweler's loop.

"This isn't authentic."

He held up a small, machined fitting and then put the jeweler's loop to one eye, squinted and screwed up his big, round face. His nostrils flared, his mouth gaped, and he held his breath as he squinted through the lens. The intense concentration forced a ropey vein to pulse at his temple.

"Yup, I am certain. This has been replaced," he said and sucked up a mouthful of spit. "Definitely."

I leaned against the doorframe.

"Parts here yet?"

"Just got here. Over there," Tom said and pointed toward the front door without removing the jeweler's loop.

"And the wheels?"

"Tires already mounted."

"All right. I'll change and get to work."

Tom was holding a small screw, his focus on that and not on me. I carried the parts to the garage, changed into my work clothes and began. It wasn't a complicated procedure; install the swivels, the control arms, attach the tie rods and sway bar, backing plates and Tom's precious brake assemblies. Installation moved forward with no surprises. The machinist had done a thorough job and everything was ready for assembly. I focused on the task and as is my nature, when directly engaged, tangential thoughts crept into my head. This time, it was a conclusion that seemed patently obvious after the fact. Marce had lived an important clue, and as I was tightening a bolt, the revelation dropped on my head like the Alfa falling off the lift. That time in high school, after Marce broke up with Edward and disappeared for a while, she returned for senior year a different person, changed in a way that I could understand only after my own experience with heartbreak, loss, and the inevitable disintegration of adolescent innocence. Now I knew what had happened. She told me so herself: *"God took the second one, punishment for the first."* The clues were there, just like Detective Marsons had said. Clear tracks in the snow that reveal the evidence of what has gone before. Marce aborted Edward's baby. The realization of Marce's pain reminded me that she had lost Edward as well. But that wasn't what was digging at my gut.

Tom hadn't moved from the office the entire morning. He sat with his face pressed close to the computer screen, typing away on the keyboard and talking to himself. The phone rang, he said a few words, put the receiver on the desk and leaned his big head into the garage.

"It's Bill," he said. "How's it coming?"

I was wiping my hands on a shop rag and putting tools back into the toolbox.

"Good," I said. "I need about two more hours and then it should be ready to go."

"You sure?"

"I'm sure. No problems with anything," I said. "Machine work was perfect."

"Always is," Tom said. He picked up the receiver, talked for a few seconds, hung up, and then came into the garage.

"He'll be here at 4:00," he said and clapped his hands together. "Then it's Showtime!"

"I guess so," I said. "What're you doing with the musket?"

Tom pursed his lips and stuck out his chin in a serious face.

"Verifying authenticity."

"You think it's a repop?"

He shook his head and raised his forearms from the elbows, rolled his hands over palms up and shrugged his shoulders. The serious face slipped into wry humor and he grinned.

"Trust but verify," he said with a wiggle of an index finger. "Trust but verify." He stepped over to the Alfa and looked at the front brakes, and then the remaining parts on the bench.

"You know what's missing?" he said with a wide grin.

I shook my head 'no.'

"Lunch!"

I laughed with him. He was a good-natured guy that never seemed to get down. I always admired his even-tempered attitude. The smallest things could bring Tom delight.

"I'll pick up some food. Burgers OK?"

"Make mine a Veggie burger," I said.

"Veggie burger…you changing your diet or something?"

"I'm changing a lot of things."

Tom shrugged his shoulders and waved one hand over his head as he walked off. "See you in a minute."

He passed through the office, out the front door and climbed into his Suburban. As he drove off, I washed up at the sink, gabbed my cell phone and stepped outside into the sunshine. The fall days are the clearest in the basin. After a night of Santa Anas, the sky is a brilliant blue that is different from the blue any other time of the year. I don't know what the airlight artists would call the color, but it is remarkable. I'd procrastinated long enough: Marce answered on the first ring.

"Hey, how are you?"

"Who is this?" she said.

"Martin."

"Martin…Martin? I knew a Martin, once, but he never answers his calls."

"Guilty," I said. "I owe you an apology."

The phone was silent but the signal was good. All the bars were visible in the upper corner of the display.

"So let's hear it."

"I'm sorry I didn't return your call. It's been coming at me in bucketfuls."

"Because you're the only one who has problems, huh?"

She wasn't going to let me off the hook. "I'm sorry. I am. Forgive me?"

"You'll have to make it up to me."

"Name it?"

"It's going to cost you…."

"Anything, just name it," I said.

"I'll let you know later."

"Fair enough. How are you?"

"Upset. That policeman came to my office. He wouldn't tell me anything. What's going on?"

It wasn't the question I wanted to answer. Talking in person to the ADD Chapstick girl would be better.

"I need to talk with you about that. Can we do it face to face?"

"Talk to me about what? What is it?"

"I'd rather do it face to face."

"Don't be an asshole. What's going on?"

I checked the time on my cell phone. It was just after noon, so Marce would be either out at lunch or eating at her desk in the office. I suppose there were worse places to receive bad news, but I didn't know of any.

"I have some sad news, Marce," I said. "Are you sure you want to hear it?"

"Tell me!"

"Edward is dead. That was why the Police arrested Carolyn."

Silence met me from the other side of the connection. I waited as long as I could for Marce to say something.

"Are you there?"

"I'm here."

"I'm sorry you have to learn about it like this. I'm really sorry, Marce."

Again the line was silent. This time I waited without speaking. Almost a minute passed before she spoke.

"I don't believe it."

"I wish it weren't true, Marce, but I just spoke to Grant."

"Are you sure it's, it's…."

"The Police are sure."

"I just can't believe it," she said. "I knew it would come to this. That asshole! I knew it! I wanted to help him, I did. You remember, I tried. I said I'd come again …."

"I'm sorry."

"Was it Carolyn? Was it? Did she '*Remove*' her brother?"

"The Police don't think so."

"It's probably Guy. She got him to, didn't she? That slut. She's evil…Evil! She gets whatever she wants!"

There was no talking sense to Marce. If she needed to vent, she might as well vent now. She wasn't alone in her disbelief and anger. She wasn't wrong in her assessment of Carolyn, either. But the record would show a different perpetrator and I didn't want to tell that to Marce. I didn't want to tell her that the man she had loved in high school, the man with whom she'd made a baby, the father of the child she aborted, had taken his own life. I didn't want to tell her that because I didn't believe it myself, so I took the coward's way out, neither confirming nor denying what she said. Soon enough we'd both know.

"Maybe. The Police will sort it out. I know the detective and he's good at his job. At least he's committed to learning the truth."

"It's that skinny one?"

"Detective Marsons. He is skinny."

"What do I do now, Martin? What?"

"Go to the funeral."

"I want to go home."

"All right. In case you're interested, the funeral's Saturday morning. 11:00 AM. That's the burial. I don't know anything about a memorial service."

The line was silent for a long time. I was about to hang up when Marce spoke.

"Pick me up."

"OK."

I heard a deep breath, clearing of a throat, and then a calm, measured tone of voice.

"We'll take my car. I'm not going to a funeral in your piece of shit."

I had tried to be considerate when I delivered the terrible news, but it didn't matter. The terrible news was now a fact, and the fact was, Marce was confronting a tragic reminder of her past. All the stages of coping with death were present. Denial had come and gone, anger, bargaining, and depression. Acceptance was next. That was the reason for the funeral, I suppose. For anyone who had known, loved or cared about Edward. That was where it began. But you had to get through all the stages. Marce wasn't lashing out at Carolyn, Guy or even me. It was her role in Edward's demise that needed rationalization. Like Tom said, no good deed goes unpunished.

"Carolyn was cleared of all charges, by the way," I said.

"I don't care about Carolyn."

"All right."

"I'll be ready at 10:30," she said in a calm, measured tone of voice. Before I could respond, the line went dead. I walked outside into the sunshine. A few cars passed in front of the garage. An elderly black man with a cane traversed the intersection and stopped at the coffee shop across the street. Another man, white and equally aged, joined him at the front door, shook his hand with a smile and clap on the back, and they went inside. Two friends celebrating another day, having lunch together as they marked the inexorable countdown to their final meal. All around me people were living their lives, finding ways to ignore the inevitable, managing their own set of joys and tragedies for as long as they had. Who knew what personal burdens each carried, what demons each faced day in and day out? This is the modern age in which all of us live complex lives interrupted by obligations that steal away what little time we have to share with those we love. Parents, his sister Carolyn, Marce and Tamara had loved Edward. Now he was gone and they would continue on, maybe a little sadder, maybe a lot sadder. Edward had been a schoolmate, part of my circle of acquaintances. I could remember him as he was in high school with his huge brain and entire life ahead of him, and then behind the Police station, where he was living a different life, a separate reality, anticipating alien visitation and some kind of interstellar resurrection. I'd been through the death of grandparents and a few older colleagues who had passed, but Edward was the first from my circle. When you reach a certain age, the world stops giving and starts taking. No one gets out alive.

The Suburban pulled into the lot and parked. Tom climbed from behind the wheel, lunch sacks in hand, and I met him inside the office. We sat, mostly in silence, chewing our burgers, thinking our thoughts. Tom kept putting down his burger and picking up that worrisome fitting from the musket. I finished my meal as he opened his next sack of food and got back to work. It wasn't long before I'd checked everything and installed the wheels. I lowered the lift and stood back to admire the car. Tom was right; it was worthy of those rare, Italian alloy wheels. It looked like a Best in Show winner. I climbed in and started the engine. Tom stood in the doorway and watched as I backed out.

"Going around the block," I said. "Check the brakes."

He nodded, held up his hands with his fingers crossed, and yelled something. It was probably 'Be Careful' as I was driving a hundred thousand dollar's worth of machinery that belonged to a customer.

The car did just what it was suppose to do. It cornered, accelerated and stopped the way it was designed. Driving a vintage car like this was probably a lot of fun if you didn't already make your daily commute in one. I gave Tom a thumb's up when I pulled into the garage bay. He smacked his hands together with enthusiasm and went into the office. I could imagine him smiling as he tallied the bill. He was a good businessman and always watched the bottom line, but his reward came when the customer paid. This would be one nice payday for him and for me. I hadn't forgotten about my bonus. I didn't think he'd forget about it, either.

We were sitting in the office, watching the local news on television, when a late model, white, convertible Mercedes pulled into the lot and stopped behind the Alfa. Bill stepped out of the driver's side, closed the door and went to the passenger side. He opened the door, held it, and stood there waiting. One dangerously tall, purple stiletto appeared beneath the door line. Then another, and then a striking, hourglass shaped blond stepped around the door as Bill swung it closed. She must have been in her late thirties, but dressed younger in that teasing, eye-candy mode that women know make men take notice. Definitely not American, most likely European or Russian, with all the unsmiling affected sex appeal of a wily professional for whom working a man's libido was just another career path.

She stood next to Bill, a few inches taller, in a sleeveless purple dress that clung to every curve of her body like wet paint and was so short there was minimal freeboard between hemline and crotch. One spaghetti thin dress strap drooped provocatively off a smooth, bronze shoulder. Her legs were equally smooth and bronze, and her breasts were perfect, spheroid mounds that almost looked natural. She had the facial features of classic statuary: broad forehead, wide set eyes, prominent cheekbones, tapering jaw with square chin, and she wore those high fashion, goggle-eye sunglasses that make women's faces look like bugs. Streaked blond tresses spilled from her head to the smooth bronze shoulders, a skin tone more likely the result of a tanning salon than Southern California top down motoring in October. She was a type, well-heeled and high maintenance, perpetuating the iconic image of beauty sold to millions around the world. Women were told that they should look like her. Men were told that they should desire her. And she knew just what that meant and just what it was worth. The clinging purple dress she wore was like a ticking time bomb awaiting detonation. Any man caught in the shrapnel would pay for the pleasure of taking part in the explosion. Bill stepped into the garage bay and stopped at his Alfa. He rubbed his chin and shook his head with a joyful smile cracking his small, hard mouth.

"Fantastic," he said. "Looks even better than I imagined."

"I told you it would," Tom said.

"Those wheels really make the car."

"They do," Tom said. "All these years I had 'em and this is where they belong."

Bill nodded his head, looked at Tom with a joyous twinkle in his eye, and then waved at the woman next to the Mercedes. She was standing perfectly still, with shoulders back and square chin held high and haughty, one leg slightly ahead of the other like every model poses in every glamour magazine at every newsstand.

"I'll see you at home," Bill called. She remained motionless by the passenger door with a stone cold expression on her face. Nothing about her changed; the haughty posture, blank stare, not even an ankle wiggle from the dangerously tall stilettos. Bill lifted an index finger as if he'd remembered something and went back to the Mercedes. He took her arm, led her around the car and held open the driver's door while she disappeared into the driver's seat. The Mercedes started and backed away. Bill came back to the garage looking a little less joyful. He reached out and shook Tom's hand.

"I have you to thank," he said, and then extended his hand toward me. "And you, too."

"You're welcome," Tom said.

Bill looked at his Alfa and the joyful smile cracked his small, hard mouth again and put some life back in his milky, blue eyes. "Really, really great," he said.

The Mercedes pulled forward and Bill waved his hand. The woman looked his direction as she crossed the lot but her stone cold expression never changed.

"Bye honey," Bill said in a singsong voice. He clenched his lips and one corner of his mouth lifted in a scornful sneer. All the joy had evaporated from his face. "In case you missed her, that was my wife."

Tom and I nodded in unison, neither one of us knowing what to say. How could anyone miss her? Wasn't that the point?

"You'll get to know her, soon enough," he said to me. "If you take the case."

I looked at Bill and he held my attention in a steady stare. There was no animosity in his face, just the detached resolve from a man who seemed to know what came next. We stared at each other until Tom broke the awkward silence.

"Well, it seems you're pleased with the transformation. Ready to drive her home?" Tom said.

"I can hardly wait."

"Good. Come into the office and I'll get the paperwork."

Bill followed Tom into the office and they sat down. I went to the bathroom to wash up and change my clothes. When I came out, Bill was behind the wheel and the engine was idling.

"Take it easy for a few miles," Tom said. "You need to bed in the brakes. Give yourself plenty of room to stop."

Bill nodded his head and backed out of the bay. He waved as he pulled out of the lot and into the street. I could hear the rise and fall of the engine's whine when he shifted gears before he disappeared up the block.

"That was easy," Tom said and rubbed his palms together. "Let's call it a day."

"Fine by me," I said.

Tom went into the office and shut off the computer while I pulled down the bay doors. When I joined him, three, one hundred-dollar bills were fanned out like a deck of cards on the office desk.

"A little bonus to get your weekend started right," he said.

"That's very generous, Tom. Thank you."

"You're welcome."

Tom chuckled under his breath and shook his head. Just like before, he pressed the fat fingers of his thick hands together, and drummed the tips against each other. He may have regretted selling his precious parts, but it wasn't going to get him down.

"Oh well. We made some money on that job," he said with half a smile. "When Big Magic has a good week, everybody wins."

Chapter Thirty-three

By 8:00 the next morning, I hadn't heard from Tamara. I'd called last night and left a message. I didn't know if she were avoiding me or not. I fed Stray and took him for a walk. He seemed his old self, tugging against the leash, investigating new odors, sniffing and lifting his leg on every bush we passed. Herrera Park was deserted but the Mercado was open, so I stopped for a breakfast burrito and some people watching. The man who sold me my field jacket was rolling his rack of discount clothing out to the sidewalk. I said *'Hola'* to him and he nodded. I don't know if he remembered me or not, but I was wearing the field jacket. I finished my burrito on the walk back to the apartment. My answering machine was blank so I called Tamara again. No answer. Last night my message had been clear: Day, time and place for the burial. The ball was in her court.

I changed into my only suit, white shirt and a paisley tie. My dress shoes were a little dull, so I tried to buff some shine on them with a tee shirt. The weather was indecisive, cool but not uncomfortable, gray rain clouds gathering to the west. I gave Stray a bone and closed the front door behind me. He began to follow me down the steps so I brought him back to the veranda and put him on a 'Stay' command. As I got into the MG, his eyes were glued on me. I let the MG roll, released the clutch to start the motor and sat idling at the bottom of the entry drive. When I looked back, Stray had descended the stairway, walked to the middle of the parking court and dropped his bone. He sat in place, staring at me, his bone on the concrete drive in front. His routine was disrupted and I was going somewhere without him. Sitting in the middle of the parking court and saving his bone as if it might be his last meal were evidence of worry. I opened the passenger door and Stray picked up his bone, raced down the entry drive and jumped inside. He took his sentry position with front legs planted on the center console, dropped his bone on the passenger seat and gave my bad ear a lick. He didn't know where we were going, or that the coming activity was not one that I looked forward to attending, but he knew I shouldn't be going anywhere without him.

Marce was wearing a black, sack dress, dark hose, black, kitten heel shoes, and she carried her black, wool jacket. She could have been in mourning in her widow weeds, and as someone sharing a significant history with Edward, probably felt as gloomy as she looked. I helped her into the passenger side of the SUV and put Stray in the back. He stepped onto the center console and I pushed him to the rear seat. Marce never smiled, commented on Stray's presence, or offered more than a single worded response to my conversation. Her thighs were still on the seat and her normally busy feet stayed planted on the floor. Twenty minutes later, when we exited the freeway near the cemetery, I heard her loudly exhale.

Rose Hills Memorial Park occupied more than one thousand acres of Puente Hills with scattered, mature oaks and mouth-watering views. When I was in high school, my Psychology class took a field trip there when we were studying death and dying. I couldn't remember much about the trip. That experience like many was still submerged deep beneath the murky surface of my previous life. It was the only time that I'd entered the park; I knew that much, and not withstanding the additional population, I doubted it had changed. A memorial park is supposed to provide serenity and comfort. With a sightline to the San Gabriel Mountains, the comical adage of 'a final resting place with a view' was apparent. Without doubt, a nice place to come and pay respects to those who have passed on. I understood that and, with time, probably could come to better appreciate the surroundings. Today, it was a final period on a life sentence written far too short for someone I knew. Someone with whom a brief history had been shared; someone with whom I had become inextricably entwined. The Edward I remembered had been an enigma. The Edward I was requested to locate, 30 years later, was a man living in a fractured world, navigating the razor thin edge between genius and insanity. Had he been an acclaimed scientist, award-winning scholar, or world champion chess master, his eccentricity would have been tolerated. That he lived the life of an indigent branded him a lunatic. When hired by Grant, I was mislead by the implication that help would come following on my heels, and then when it was too late for help, directed to prove that his death was not fratricide. One entry on a coroner's death certificate and the case was closed. No history left to deconstruct, no truth left to reconstruct. Those were the facts but my gut still churned and wouldn't let it rest. And I knew why.

Signage directed me up the hill and to the east. Along a sloping section, Tamara's Fiat, two black limousines, and a Honda were parked. A signboard, placed near the Honda, stated 'Cochran' in Old English font. Ten yards down the slope there was a dark green canopy and three rows of folding chairs. A priest and an elderly couple I assumed to be Mr. and Mrs. Cochran sat in the first row. Behind them, Grant and Carolyn occupied the middle row. In the last row, alone, sat Tamara. I parked, left Stray in the SUV, took Marce's arm and escorted her toward the canopy. As we approached, Carolyn met us mid way.

"Hello, Carolyn," I said.

She wore a black dress like Marce but where Marce was gloomy in mourning, Carolyn was mourning in elegance. Her dress was black velvet with a scoop neck, long sleeves and embroidered, white lace at the wrists. An onyx lavaliere hung from her neck. Gold earrings completed the picture of sophistication and her long hair was gathered with the gold barrette at the back of her head. She wore the high-heeled leather boots from when I picked her up at the airport, which made her at least half a foot taller than Marce, and a black Pashmina shawl over her shoulders. Behind a pair of dark glasses, I caught a view of tired, red eyes.

"Thank you both for coming."

"You're welcome," I said and Marce nodded.

"Carolyn never expected this."

Marce reached up one arm and pointed her index finger at Carolyn. "Yes you did," she said, walked to the folding chairs and sat in the last row. Carolyn dismissively shook her head and reached out her hand.

"Carolyn has something for you."

In her palm were a key ring and a business card. I looked at the keys, one rectangular and the other round, with Ford script on both. The business card had Mr. Everett Cochran's contact information.

"Call with your address and he'll send the papers."

"All right."

"Father gave it to Edward when he retired. Now it is yours. Carolyn doesn't know where it's parked, but for a man in your profession, finding it should not be a problem."

"Why?"

"To show you that Carolyn forgives you."

"Forgives me for what?"

She took my forearm and squeezed.

"Edward."

She let my arm go, turned around and returned to her chair. I joined Marce in the last row and Tamara glanced back at me. She wore a long, gray cape with an additional layer of material across the shoulders like folded wings, and the image of an angel came to mind. Although I wanted to sit with her, Marce was my date. I'd figure out how to make it up to Tamara at the first opportunity.

Marce and I sat staring at the simple, dark wood casket. Around it was a grass green skirt covering the mechanism that would lower it into the ground, and at each corner a subdued arrangement of funeral flowers offered some sense of reverence for the occasion. The sky was darkening with the rain clouds I'd seen earlier. The local forecast was for an afternoon rainstorm. It wasn't raining yet, but stormy weather was coming and it wouldn't be long before it arrived.

A priest in a black suit and white collar rose from a chair and stood clutching a bible. Carolyn's mother looked around the small group of people and then nodded. Until that moment, I had not realized the priest was female. The short hair and androgynous, black suit obliterated any sense of gender. What followed was the briefest, nondenominational graveside service imaginable. The priest recited the particulars: Edward's full name, date of birth, an assumed relationship with a higher power, and finally, the Psalm of David. Edward's mother rose with assistance from her husband, put her hand on the top of the casket and stood for half a minute. Then her husband escorted her to one of the limousines. Mrs. Cochran looked once toward Carolyn as she climbed the slope but Mr. Cochran never acknowledged his daughter's presence. The priest, her duty done, bowed her head, crossed herself, and climbed the slope to the Honda. That left the Parkers, Tamara, Marce and me seated in the folding chairs. For a few minutes we sat in silence. Then Tamara rose and walked to the casket. She stood alone, in that long, gray cape with the folded wings, looking like a death angel honoring its charge. Carolyn watched Tamara standing with hands folded in front of her, shoulders sunken, chin lowered. She stood and then Marce stood, and they joined Tamara on either side. The women, shoulder to shoulder with their backs to me, formed a chorus line of collective sorrow. Tamara reached her hand to Carolyn and she took it. Then she reached her hand to Marce and she took it. Three grieving women, banded together, with varying degrees of personal relationship to the deceased, holding hands like sisters in a protracted moment of memory and heartache, each burdened with a personal loss, each facing a finality that surely was not unexpected. Grant nodded toward me. I followed and met him where he stood a respectful distance from the gravesite.

"Thank you for coming, Martin," he said. "I know it means a lot to Carolyn."

Overhead, the dark sky lent gravitas to the ceremony, and the air tasted of rain. Grant smiled at me, almost with condescension, and looked up at the clouds. On the one hand, I only knew Grant as the result of a recently rekindled high school relationship. He was a professional acquaintance and not a friend, but his gregarious personality and western charm had colored my perception of our relationship. As a result, when I was hired as a private investigator, I forgot to eliminate friendship from the equation, to stand alone, as Detective Marsons would say, and see clearly the tracks in the snow. And now Grant was leveraging our relationship to his advantage.

"She's welcome," I said but I looked him hard in the eyes and accusations of homicide spun through my mind. He held my gaze, unmoved by the intensity of my stare, and then turned to look toward the women at the casket, side by side, holding hands beneath the dark green canopy. A raindrop struck my face.

"We'll be leaving in the morning," Grant said. "To happier surroundings. To our home."

He looked back at me and his face was almost white, his age clearly apparent, and in his dark suit he looked much older than the last time I saw him. I realized that each death in his life brought him closer to the day he would confront his own, to the sober realization that his wife would outlive him by many years, to the fact that the day when she would be standing over his casket was not so very far away.

"She'll be better, there. No more suffering over her brother," he said. "Everything is in place to provide for her for as long as necessary."

Grant's tone was soft but strong, no doubt the voicing of what he'd been rehearsing in his head for the short time that he'd been married.

"I can promise you that."

I stared at him and anger began to rise in my chest, seething at the hypocrisy in his voice, flushing my cheeks with heat and boiling my blood. I clenched and unclenched my fists, fighting the impulse to drive them into his body, to batter his face, punch and pummel and damage him in an effort to impose justice where it was required.

"I'd like it if you'd stay in touch," he said. "As a friend as well as a professional." Grant stuck out his hand. I stared at his hand, rigid between us, and looked him in the eye. All I could think of was the warring maxim *'Keep your friends close and your enemies closer,'* and the need to control my pugilistic impulse. Grant was not my friend. He was the husband of someone I knew a long time ago, and the suspect in a homicide. I'd almost lost my investigative perspective. Detective Marsons would think me an amateur and he'd be right.

"You still have my retainer," he said with a calculated smile, knowing good and well that with what was probably a nominal amount for him, he had contracted my services indefinitely. The contract was discharged in cash, but the debt was personal. It became clear that despite the age discrepancy, he and Carolyn were one of a kind, and now I was beholding to both of them.

"You can't buy immunity, Grant," I said.

"You might be surprised."

"They'll come for you," I said. "And if they don't, I will."

Carolyn had let lose of Tamara's hand. She turned away from the others without a word and climbed the slope to the limousine. Her cheeks were wet. She looked straight ahead as she passed and paused at the rear door of the limousine to be let inside by the driver.

"Don't be a fool, Martin," Grant said in that flat, officious monotone I'd heard his wife use on multiple occasions. "You wouldn't want to do anything that might result in close scrutiny of your past."

He started up the slope and stopped, taking a few deep breaths against the incline and his age. "Arson is a crime not taken lightly by the authorities."

He climbed to the limousine, got in, and the driver closed the rear door behind him. The cortege became to depart. First Cochran's limousine, followed by the Honda, and then Grant's limousine. Tamara and Marce had left the casket and were coming toward me. I reached out and took Tamara's hand.

"Tam, are you all right?"

She looked at our hands, mine holding hers, her fingers limp in my palm, and nodded.

"I need some time, Martin."

Marce walked toward her SUV. Her head was lowered and she clutched her stomach. She didn't look at me as she passed.

"If that's what you want."

Tamara nodded her head and then reached up and put one hand against my cheek. Her eyes were wet, color drained from her cheeks, a sadness on her face that made my voice catch when I spoke.

"I'll miss you," I said.

She offered a tired smile, turned and walked up the slope to her car. I watched as she got in and started the motor. A cloud of black smoke belched from the exhaust, lessened, and belched again when she drove away. It's not always bad valve seals that cause an engine to smoke; sometimes it happens when everything is worn out, when you've reached the point of diminishing returns and it is time to say good-bye and move on. I'd learned that lesson with

Susan, even though it took a personal breakdown to recognize it, and I was learning that lesson again. Time, as Tamara had said: Time.

Down the road, a utility vehicle approached. It parked behind Marce's SUV and two men climbed out. They descended the slope to the burial site and began disassembling the dark green canopy. It didn't seem as if they were affected in any way by the somber surroundings, the rows of burial markers around them, the proximity of mortality in their activity. This was a task for them, one of the many that were part of their job, no different from all the other times they'd done it before. You do anything often enough, the import wanes with repetition and routine. That's when mistakes can happen. That's when something gets missed.

I climbed the slope and stopped at the door of the SUV. Marce was inside, staring at the workmen, her face blank, one hand covering her mouth. Stray watched me as I opened the door and got in. He stepped onto the center console, gave my bad ear a lick, and took his sentry position. Marce didn't say a word.

Chapter Thirty-four

I met Detective Marsons at the impound lot on Monday, the day after Halloween. The ghouls and goblins had come and gone. My neighborhood street was a combination of smeared pumpkin from the local juvenile delinquents, and tattered remains of cheap, store bought costumes and paper decorations courtesy of the Santa Anas. Stray and I had spent Halloween prepared with a bowl of Funsize Snickers. Not a single trick or treater had ventured up the entry drive. The front gate was locked so I doubted anyone had been to the main house. I suppose that if I were committed to receiving trick or treaters, I could have sat at the bottom of the entry drive with a flashlight and my bowl of candy. But the idea never occurred to me.

Detective Marsons had cleared the way for the Crown Victoria to be released without incurring any fees. In my experience, whenever your car ends up in an impound lot, there is always some financial obligation. The Police had their own lot and I suppose that was the difference. Nonetheless, I was grateful to him.

On Saturday, rain had followed us home from the burial, leaving a greasy smear of moisture on the streets. Marce sat in the passenger seat with her arms tight to her chest and a hollow stare in her eyes. I made a few comments but she only nodded in return. When I parked the SUV behind the MG at her townhouse, I gave her the keys and she turned and went inside without saying a word. Everyone reacts differently to death. I can only imagine the anguish that Edward's parents must have felt. Even Carolyn, the sister who had come to *'Remove'* her brother, had tired, red eyes at the burial service. The event had taken its toll on many.

Today's morning sky was overcast. Tom waved from his Suburban as he drove away and I waited for the car to be brought around. I had the business card of Everett Cochran in my pocket hoping that would be enough to demonstrate ownership. It didn't seem anyone cared much as long as the car was going somewhere. The attendant hadn't asked for any proof of ownership beyond presenting him with the car keys. Detective Marsons showed him some paperwork and off he went. If possession is 99% of the law, the presence of an LAPD detective constitutes the 1% left over.

We leaned against the fender of Detective Marsons' Police Interceptor. He was wearing his usual attire; the silver running shoes, dark pants and blue windbreaker, and chewing the ever-present stir stick. The mood was subdued, part inclement weather, part lingering fallback from our last conversation.

"You're wrong, you know," I said.

Detective Marsons smoothed his pencil thin moustache and smiled.

"Huh?"

"Winter solstice. And needles."

"Solstice?"

"The hegira. He told me himself. Wrote his plan on the wall."

Detective Marsons' face was expressionless. His skinny wrists hung below the sleeves of the blue windbreaker.

"Winter solstice is December 21," I said.

"Needles?"

"Afraid of them."

Detective Marsons pressed two fingers against his pencil thin mustache. I knew his mind was processing new information, extrapolating every possible scenario. After a few seconds, he spoke.

"Maybe he got brave, changed his mind."

"He didn't," I said. "Ask Grant."

"Grant?"

"Grant Parker, CEO of Solate Pharmaceuticals."

"You sure about that?"

I shrugged my shoulders. "What do I know. I'm a nonprofessional, right?"

The Crown Victoria pulled through the chain link gate and stopped next to me. The attendant got out, left the engine running, and walked away.

"I missed it," Detective Marsons said. "Goddamn it, I missed it!"

"Like tracks in the snow."

Detective Marsons climbed into his Police Interceptor, slammed the car door and started it. He raced the engine and lowered the driver's window.

"Keep it up," he said.

"Keep what up?"

"Private investigation."

He dropped the gear lever and spit gravel in his wake as he sped down the road.

I climbed into Everett's, once Edward's, and now my Crown Victoria. Inside, it was spotless. No trash on the floor, no damage to the seats or carpets. It looked as if it had just come from the executive motor pool.

"I guess I saw something," I said to no one. "Tracks."

The Police Interceptor slowed, brake lights blinked twice, and then it turned right. In the cool morning air, the engine note whined under hard acceleration. Everything changes: nothing remains the same. People move into your life and move out of your life. If you're lucky, you get a chance to do what's right before they're gone. Someone missed their chance with Edward. Someone did Edward wrong. I had a feeling Detective Marsons would right the score.

I put the Crown Victoria in gear and leaned on the throttle. At the end of the road I stopped, looked right, left, and then right, again. You choose a direction and it begins. What happens next is not so much about planning as it is about luck. Life unfolds; a path beckons. Routine and obligation and occasional joy fill the empty places. With a little luck, even love. With a lot of luck, happiness. The pieces fall together and you find a fit; you are what you do. The tracks in the snow tell the story.

Made in the USA
Monee, IL
24 December 2021